The Apparent Heir

Betsey & Desmond

Lots of love

Jane

Other titles by the author

A Marriage of Mixed Motives

Fickle Friends

The Apparent Heir

JANEY WATSON

Bosworth Books Ltd

For Betsey and Desmond

First published in 2007 by Bosworth Books Ltd.

Cataloguing in Publication Data is available from the British Library.

ISBN 978 0 9553289 2 3

Bosworth Books Ltd, Whiteway Court,
Cirencester, Glos GL7 7BA

Design and typesetting by Liz Rudderham
Printed in Europe by the Alden Group, Oxfordshire

Thanks as ever goes to
Mary FitzGerald, my secretary, to Anne Rickard, my editor, and
Liz Rudderham for then turning it into a published novel.

And finally a huge thank you to all at Bosworth,
Richard and my boys.

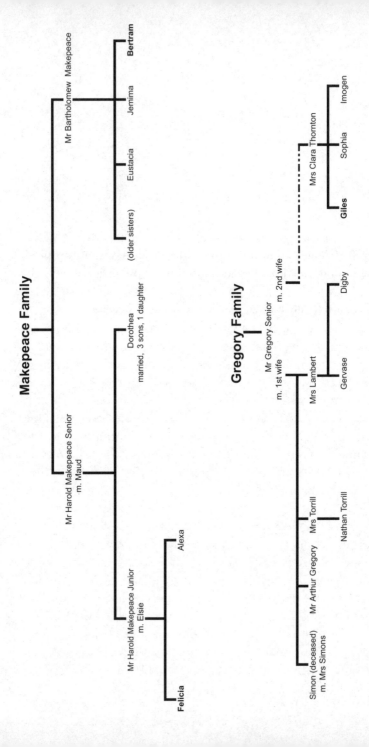

Makepeace Family

Mr Harold Makepeace Senior
m. Maud

Mr Harold Makepeace Junior
m. Elsie

Felicia

Alexa

Dorothea
married, 3 sons, 1 daughter

Mr Bartholomew Makepeace

(older sisters)

Eustacia

Jemima

Bertram

Gregory Family

Mr Gregory Senior
m. 1st wife

m. 2nd wife

Mrs Lambert

Mrs Clara Thornton

Giles

Sophia

Imogen

Gervase

Digby

Mr Arthur Gregory

Mrs Torrill

Nathan Torrill

Simon (deceased)
m. Mrs Simons

1

*C*astle Leck was a folly. Everyone acquainted with it knew that to be the case, but that made it no less enchanting to look at or endearing to live in.

The Castle had been built in the 1750s by one Harold Makepeace who had fashioned it on Château Chillon at Vevey in Switzerland. That ancient château, which had captured the imagination of many who had visited it, had worked its magic on Mr Makepeace while he was enjoying his grand tour. He had filled his sketchbook with drawings of its many turrets, balustraded walkways and vaulted rooms. He had viewed it from the land and from a pleasure boat on the great Lac Leman. He had longed for such an edifice himself and planned on his return to England to build himself a replica but, although his family owned a vast tract of North Yorkshire, he would find no site that offered him the vistas he had in his mind's eye.

It was not until he was in his early forties that Mr Makepeace came into his inheritance and only then did he settle into marriage. His young wife was a native of Gloucestershire and she introduced him to the pleasures of Cheltenham, an increasingly popular spa town. The town, however, held nothing but a passing interest for Mr Makepeace. It was the towering limestone escarpment to the south of it that held him spellbound. He toiled up its slopes and stood on the great wide shelf just below its brow. From there he could see the whole of Cheltenham with its burgeoning elegance, the medieval city of Gloucester and, in the distance, the ridge of the Malvern Hills. He coveted this spot. Here was where he planned to build his Castle. Château Chillon situated on the water's edge would have nothing to compare to his Castle Leck teetering on the top of this glorious hill. That he had allowed his memory to diminish the size of the great mounts surrounding the original, few of his associates had the knowledge to point out. His dutiful and adoring wife was happy to accept his word that nowhere was there a finer nor more extensive view. He was allowed to have his way for there was no one in authority over him to curb his expenditure. The Castle would have multiple turrets, six main stairways and a secondary stairway to each turret. Further, it would have external walkways, great archways leading from one courtyard to another and vast cellars burrowed into the hill. In this one item he was baulked. The rock thwarted his efforts to hollow it out and he had to be satisfied with smaller, more modest subterranean rooms than he had envisaged. It took some six years to build his Castle and during this time Mr Makepeace and his wife took up residence in one of the stately modern homes that were beginning to proliferate on the flatter areas beneath his eyrie. He plundered his Yorkshire estates and, had he not come to his senses before commissioning glorious frescoes and murals for his state rooms, would have endured a lean old age as much of their revenue was sunk in the glorious edifice.

Mrs Makepeace was a lady of gentle humour who continued to adore her flamboyant husband. She had no desire to make her own mark on the world and enjoyed a comfortable if restricted life in the suburbs of Cheltenham. In due course she dutifully presented her husband with a son and a daughter and endured with some reluctance the move from her pleasant town house to the new Castle. From then on she had tried her utmost to appear satisfied with the accommodation in the Castle, which she found was draughty and grandiose and thus in too much contrast to her understated nature. So when her lord, some fifteen years her senior, suffered a pernicious infection of the lungs and succumbed to its force one chilly winter's morning, she moved with almost unseemly haste to arrange a return to her old life. Her son, young Mr Harold, had expected her to make her home with him and his new wife, Elsie, but the widow would have none of it. She had heard from a gossiping friend that one of the very elegant houses set back from the main London Road was for sale and she requested her son to use her portion to acquire it.

The young Mr Harold, while a holder of some fairly well-formed views, had not anticipated so much responsibility so soon, as his father had always appeared to be in rude health. He was reluctant to start spending money before he knew how matters stood. His father, after all, had had to sell the first town house to meet some obligation or other, but his mother was adamant.

Finally, persuaded by his dainty redheaded wife, young Mr Harold had given in and settled his mother with all due care and attention into her sunny, south-facing house. This having been achieved, she proceeded to give him not a moment's care. She would visit occasionally to see her new granddaughter and she would expect her son to call if he had business in Cheltenham, but she speedily picked up the threads of her old life and returned to her previous contentment.

Young Mr Makepeace then turned his attention to his wife. Having become conscious that his mother had never loved Castle Leck as he did, he approached his wife with some trepidation.

'My dear,' he began cautiously as he visited her in the nursery to find her rocking their baby daughter. He had had to climb three separate flights of stairs to reach her from the library on the ground floor and therefore there was a touch of breathlessness in his voice.

'Yes, Mr Makepeace,' responded his wife, her eyes a merry twinkle at the seriousness of his tone. Her husband had a taste for portentous announcements.

'Would you prefer to live in the town? Either here in Cheltenham or in Harrogate near our estates?'

She was surprised out of her merriment. 'Why so, my love?' she asked.

Mr Makepeace shuffled his feet. 'I would be loath, my dear, to feel that you would suffer the years of discomfort my mother so obviously did rather than disclose to me your dislike of this abode.'

Mrs Makepeace laid the sated baby in its cot and walked towards her husband. She saw the earnestness in his square face and the anxiety in his grey eyes and she smiled.

'Oh come, come, dear Harold,' she laughed, 'surely you know that I wedded you for the Castle and very happy I am with my choice. It goes without saying that I would not have called our daughter Felicia if I had not been so content.'

He smiled a perfunctory smile in response and took her out-stretched hands involuntarily. 'From what I know of you, my love,' he grumbled, 'you are more likely suggest it in irony than in truth.'

'Oh come,' she cried in mock anger, 'you have let the cares of your father's passing weigh you down. I know they are heavy but you must not let your father's follies taint our young lives.'

This, for Harold Makepeace Junior, was a hard task to perform. At twenty-five he had embarked on marriage with a young lady of modest means, not quite appreciating the straitened circum-stances in which his father's activities had left the family.

He and Elsie had married for love and, with neither of them anticipating any great change in their circumstances, had com-menced on a family immediately. No sooner, however, had little Felicia made her entrance into the world, than her grandfather had left it. It took weeks of sifting through documents with his man of business and monthly visits to North Yorkshire to ascer-tain what the situation was. Castle Leck generated no income of its own; it had but five acres of hillside as its estate. All monies to support it came from the estates in Yorkshire and these had been drained almost dry over the years. Visiting the rolling hills, Harold found his tenants and his land in poor health. Tithe houses had not been repaired and the land had been over-grazed in a desperate attempt to replenish the coffers. Harold saw years of pinching and scraping ahead before their finances would be secure.

It was fortunate for him then that he had a wife who was easily pleased. She had no driving need to experience the London season, she demanded no string of hunters nor a posse of servants to be at her beck and call. She divided her time between her little daughter and the hillside beyond the Castle walls, which she was determined to tame into a garden. This pleasurable activity kept her well satisfied but, as the years rolled gently by, there came one blot upon the landscape of her future. Little Felicia, who was rapidly becoming a much bigger Felicia, had no siblings. A dozen years had gone by and there was no brother or sister to increase the family's numbers. Mr Makepeace felt it keenly. Without a son, the estates in Yorkshire would pass to his father's brother Bartholomew Makepeace and in due course to his son, Bertram, a callow youth some four years Felicia's senior. Seeing the perils that awaited his wife and daughter if anything was to befall him, Mr Harold Makepeace made overtures to his uncle suggesting that a union should be planned for young Bertram and Felicia. Uncle Bartholomew, as great a pragmatist as his elder brother had been a dreamer, agreed with the proviso that the young people should be told, long before they were likely to have formed an attachment of their own, that this was to be their fate.

Thus the day after her thirteenth birthday, her parents informed young Felicia that she must look to the future and prepare herself to be partnered with her cousin. Miss Felicia Makepeace was unimpressed. She was a pretty child who had taken her colouring from her mother. She had soft copper-coloured curls that fell naturally about her heart-shaped face. Her hazel eyes were bright and took in with interest everything about her, and her body, while giving a mysterious hint of frailty, was surprisingly robust. She had seen off all the childhood ailments from measles to whooping cough without any lasting or damaging effects. She, like her mother and her paternal grandmother, preferred the simple life and thoroughly enjoyed the benefit of the countryside. So, when her father made his announcement, she turned large innocent eyes upon him and asked him why.

'That should not concern you, my dear. Financial matters are not suitable conversation for young ladies.'

'So it is about money,' responded Felicia, who suffered from few illusions.

Her father, a gentleman who might have developed a tendency to portliness if he had not had to work so hard to keep the wolf from the door, stiffened and was about to admonish the girl when his wife broke into the conversation.

'It is not fair to command her obedience, dear Sir, if you are not prepared to justify it.' She turned to her daughter who was sitting rather primly on a settle in the vast, echoey room they were inclined to call the withdrawing room and smiled at her a trifle wanly.

Mr Makepeace, a just man, divided his tails at his back and sat down upon the chair opposite his daughter.

'When your grandfather built this place,' he said making a circle with his arms which encompassed everything from the towering ceilings to the narrow slit windows and the huge stone fireplace, 'he spent not only the revenues from the estates but he also borrowed money against the properties themselves. As a result of that borrowing, I have to find money from the revenues we receive today to pay off the interest and some of the loan. All our income comes from the farms in Yorkshire, Castle Leck contributes nothing.' He paused, took out a large linen handkerchief and mopped his brow. 'These farms, in fact all the land in Yorkshire, is entailed. It must follow the male line.' He saw the bewilderment in his daughter's face. 'This means,' he said more gently, 'that I cannot give it to you, I can only give it to a son.'

'But you have no son,' said Felicia, looking from one parent to the other, 'how can you give it to a son you do not have?'

Finding the explanation more difficult than he had perceived it would be or indeed as he felt it should be, Mr Makepeace cast an imploring look at his wife, but she was too much mortified by her own failure to produce an heir to be any help to him. Bravely he continued.

'If there is no son then we must step back a generation, the estate would go to my brother.'

'But you have no brother,' said the child, increasingly confused. 'There is only Aunt Dorothea.'

'Yes, yes,' blustered Mr Makepeace, becoming more and more uncomfortable. The handkerchief put in another appearance while he struggled for the words. Eventually he mastered himself.

'I have no brother,' he said painstakingly, 'so we must look back further to the brother of my father.'

Felicia blinked. Circumstances had meant that she had never met her grandfather and she did not recall any mention of a brother.

'Did he have a brother?' she asked curiously.

'Yes, indeed he did and my Uncle Bartholomew Makepeace is very much alive. He has a bevy of daughters who visited you when you were a babe in arms but his youngest child, a boy, is not much older than you. He, Bertram, is your first cousin once removed and both his father and yours believe it would be a suitable match for you.'

'But I am too young to marry, father,' said the unhappy daughter, 'I gained but thirteen years yesterday.'

Mrs Makepeace now overcame her own distress to come to her daughter's aid. 'It is not of now that your father speaks, my dear, but later when you are older.'

'I cannot marry a man I do not know,' the child cried. 'Why need I do so. I am happy here at Castle Leck, I have no need of the Yorkshire estates.'

'Have I not just explained,' bellowed her father, his exasperation taking expression in a leap to his feet. 'You would not be able to remain here as there would be no funds to support you.'

Felicia, shocked by her father's anger, began to weep. Her mother moved to take the place beside her. She put her arm around the girl's slender shoulders.

'Please do not distress yourself, my love,' she said. 'There is much time to become accustomed to the idea, God willing.'

2

*M*iss Felicia Makepeace did not allow the weight of her father's pronouncement to cast her down for long. She had a sunny disposition and spring was coming. After the long cold blast of winter, she was excited about being able to enjoy the pleasures of the outdoors. It had been her habit when not submitting to the gentle persuasions of her earnest governess to take to the hill and scramble amongst the rocks and the bushes. Her mother had permitted this from quite a young age because there were few inhabitants around them who might be disturbed by a noisy child. Mrs Makepeace would sometimes wish that her daughter had a companion, particularly on the occasions when Felicia did not immediately reappear at the sound of the dinner gong, but in the main, she embraced the idea of a tomboy daughter, it soothed her feelings of guilt at the absence of a real son.

The enticement of a mild spring day was too much for Felicia who, very soon after nuncheon, changed into her oldest but thickest cotton frock, some stout boots and a warm jacket. She hurried away from the Castle, stopping only once to look back at its fairytale turrets.

She passed her mother's now well-established rose garden, and then travelled on up the terrace to the infant knot garden. Beyond was the beginning of a weeping ash arbour. Even at thirteen, Felicia appreciated her mother's vision. One day the arbour would be a sanctuary from prying eyes. Today however there was only a hint of its future glory. The bare grey branches were decorated with great black buds swollen with the promise of warmer weather. Felicia put out a hand to touch them, then moved on. At the edge of this shelf, which would one day become another formal layer of Mrs Makepeace's terraced garden, was some woodland. Great beech trees mingled with the yews and hollies and specimen oaks. In autumn Felicia loved the crunch of her feet on the dead leaves but in the spring she was on the watch for the appearance of the wild flowers. First the snowdrops and aconites, then the white wood anemones, followed by the primroses in the glades or the cowslips on the open banks and then finally, before the full symphony of summer, the carpets of brilliant bluebells. Today she passed a clump of soft yellow primroses emerging into the dappled sunlight and smiled; spring was really here at last.

Felicia had a favourite tree, a giant oak with strong limbs reaching out in all directions. It was not difficult to climb and once up in the great branches there was a magnificent view rivalling even the one from the Castle that was now away on a promontory to the east. Felicia made haste to clamber up the tree; she was soon in her favourite spot some twelve feet off the ground. She leaned her back against the trunk and looking out up the line of the branch could see the hamlets below her nestled amongst such features as Robinswood and Chosen Hill. She sighed and reviewed her father's words. Without outside finances, Castle Leck would no longer be hers, this view would not longer be hers to command. This, she decided, she would not allow, something would have to be done. She had no plans to marry Bertram Makepeace; he sounded dull and dutiful if he was prepared so lamely to accede to his father's wishes. No, Felicia concluded, she would have to find her own source of funds.

The sound of footfalls breaking twigs below her brought her out of her abstraction. She peered around the riven trunk of the great tree and was startled to see a boy standing in the glade looking up at her. Unaccustomed to the company of other young people, Felicia could only guess his age. She thought that perhaps he was sixteen. He was dressed in tan breeches and a white shirt, open at the neck. Both items of clothing appeared to be of far too high quality for exploring the woods. His wavy golden locks shone in the sunlight, his face was open and his countenance pleasing. Felicia thought she might have liked him if he was not threatening her solitude. The boy moved and placed his right boot on the lowest limb of the tree; he was about to spring upwards when Felicia spoke.

'You cannot come up here,' she said from her hiding place behind the trunk.

The boy started and stepped back.

'Who's there?' he cried imperatively. Felicia smothered a giggle and decided to make a little mischief.

'I am the voice of the tree,' she cried, lowering her tone as best she could, 'I do not permit you to scale me.'

The boy, who, it appeared, did not embrace the fanciful, laughed and replaced his foot on the lower branch.

'Then you must stop me, fine tree,' he said and nimbly made his way up towards her.

'Stop,' cried Felicia, but he kept on coming. Felicia grabbed a higher branch and started to climb away from him up the trunk. The boy, catching a glimpse of the blue-grey dress, followed her for some little way, then let out a shout.

'I say do not fear me,' he cried. 'You should not ascend any further, the limbs may have been damaged by the winter snow, indeed they are much finer and might not take your weight.'

Felicia stopped and looked down at him. He was standing in a great bowl formed by several branches all leaving the trunk at the same level. He looked safely positioned there, while she felt vulnerable on the flimsy upper branches. She knew she should heed him.

'Turn your back, then,' she said 'and I will come down.'

It took her some minutes to make her way gingerly down to him and all the while he stood with his back to the noise of her efforts.

'You can turn now,' she said when she was standing safely beside him in the hollow. 'Who are you?'

The boy moved so that he was facing her. She found that her head reached only his shoulder, and she felt small and foolish.

'I might ask the same of you, oh voice of the tree!' The boy grinned; he put out his hand to shake hers in a mock formal gesture. 'How do you do. I am Giles Thornton.'

'Well, how do you do.' said Felicia after she had wiped her grubby hand on her skirt before shaking his, and bobbing a prim little curtsey, 'I am Miss Felicia Makepeace.'

'Ah, so you are Miss Makepeace. I am very pleased to make your acquaintance, I have heard much of your family.'

Felicia blinked at him. 'From whom? We are of no interest to anyone.'

'Well, there I beg to differ,' said Giles Thornton, finding a suitable branch on which to lean his lithe form. 'To me you are of great interest. Not many of my friends or acquaintances can boast a fairytale Castle.'

'Do you like Castle Leck?' she asked curiously.

'Do I like it?' repeated the boy, astonished by such a question. 'Who could not like it. It is a glorious edifice. It is the embodiment of enchantment. Why? Do you not like it?'

Felicia shifted her position so that through the boughs of the tree she could see the west wing of her home. 'Oh yes, I like it,' she breathed, 'I adore it.'

ප ප ප

'So tell me, Giles Thornton, how have we never met before?' Felicia had recovered her poise and was determined to learn more about her mystery guest. 'Has Mr Gregory kept you locked in some garret at The Chimneys for years and you have only just made your escape?' The Chimnies was the only other house of note in the area and Mr Gregory its bachelor owner. She looked him up and down quizzically and confirmed her original assessment of the quality of his clothes. 'You do not look to me like some escaped prisoner.'

Giles laughed and made a half-hearted attempt to rub off the green smudge that had appeared on his glistening white shirt. 'I suffer to disappoint you, Miss Makepeace, but I was not aware that Uncle Arthur had a garret.'

'So Mr Gregory is your uncle. You surprise me, you have not the look of him.'

'Not the look, no, but 'tis explained by the fact that he is my half-uncle, my mama and he had different mothers.'

'So you have come on a visit of ceremony to see your elderly uncle?'

'I have come to live with him.'

'Good heavens.' Felicia nearly lost her foothold in her surprise. Giles put out a hand to steady her.

'Is he making you his heir then?' Felicia gasped.

The boy's face clouded. 'You ask too many questions, Miss Felicia Makepeace.'

She was conscious that her inquisitive nature had betrayed her; she coloured and mumbled an apology.

There was silence between them. Giles appeared reluctant to accept her apology so she tried again.

'Forgive me, I should not have asked. It was wrong of me but if you but knew what a trial inheritance is being to me at this time you would understand why the question sprang so readily to my lips.'

Giles recovered at her words and reaching out took her hand. 'No, I should be begging your forgiveness. You are too young to be troubled by such things. I, on the other hand, have the responsibility of my family to attend to.' He would say no more and while she was insatiably curious she respected his reserve. They were, after all, but barely acquainted.

They made no arrangement to meet again, although neither was surprised to see the other the next day in the same spot. Giles had arrived before Felicia and this time he was attired in a flannel shirt and thicker breeches, more suitable for climbing trees. He was in the great hollow of the oak when Felicia arrived. She did not notice him until she was nearly on his level but it was almost as though she had been expecting to find him thus. She stretched out her hand for him to pull her up.

'Good afternoon,' she said primly as she straightened her skirt. 'I do not recall you mentioning that you would be here today.'

'That is because I did not,' he replied with a smile in his eyes, 'but I might make the same remark of you.'

''Tis my tree though, Mr Thornton. 'Tis my tree, you are a trespasser!'

'I think not, Miss Makepeace.' He was quick to refute the suggestion. He leaned along one of the thick branches and indicated a dilapidated wicket fence. 'You will see that the boundary runs up on the ground through the centre of the tree. This side is mine and that is yours.'

'So you are to be the heir.' Her words were out before she could stop them. She clamped her hands across her mouth, a look of deep chagrin in her eyes.

'No,' he said quietly, 'I am the heir to nothing but my father's meagre annuity. My uncle has taken my mother, my two sisters and I in on the death of my father. We are the poor relations.'

Felicia watched a shadow cross his face at the mention of his father. She saw that the grief was fresh and was mortified that she had added to his discomfiture.

'You do not look like the poor relation,' she said gently, trying to give comfort.

Giles shrugged. 'My uncle is very kind, he would not have me dress to disadvantage at school. He supplied the new uniform.'

'And are you to make your home at The Chimnies?'

'I believe so. At least my sisters and my mother are to reside here the year round. I have two more years of school but I will spend the holidays here.'

She was silenced, unable to find any suitable line of enquiry. Eventually she said, 'Well if you are to be my neighbour it behoves me to share my tree with you. I have, however, some rules.'

'Rules, what rules?' His face lightened and his eyes were smiling again. 'I will submit to no girl's rules.'

'These are not a girl's rules,' declared Felicia, trying not to laugh. 'These are rules of acquaintance.'

'I have never heard of such a thing,' he replied, shaking his head. 'What can you be about?'

'Oh do you not see?' cried Felicia. 'If you are to live at The Chimnies, I will see you much in company for my parents and Mr Gregory play whist quite regularly. We will be introduced to each other. There will be polite words, uncomfortable silences as we search for things to say. Let us have a little game with our elders, let us pretend we have not met.'

Giles shook his head, laughing as he did so. 'Surely it would be more entertaining to talk easily to each other because we are better acquainted?' he suggested.

Felicia considered this. 'No I think not,' she decided. 'While I am free to wander the hillside, I believe my mother would look askance at my meeting with you unattended.'

'Very well,' he said, showing that he understood the implication of what she was saying even more than she did. 'We will wait to be introduced, and you will be the dutiful hostess and make merry with my little sisters!'

'What age are they?' she interrupted him, hoping to find that they were not as old as she. Having acquired his friendship, she did not want it smothered by a gaggle of other girls. She was not to be disappointed.

'Sophia is ten and Imogen is seven. My mother keeps them very close and teaches them herself.'

'Good,' said Felicia unfelicitously, 'then I shall look forward to meeting them.'

Giles smiled at her want of tact, her motive completely transparent. 'So Miss Felicia Makepeace, now that you have me to yourself, what will you do with me?'

'I will show you your new home, of course,' she said with aplomb, 'because no-one knows it as well as I.'

3

*I*t rained for the next two days, so Felicia's intention to show her new friend the delights of the escarpment had to be postponed. When the following day dawned bright and clear, Felicia could hardly contain her excitement. She fidgeted through her French lesson, had to reset a whole sampler because she had misheard Miss Cuthbert's instruction and had to be called to attention three times by the sorely tried governess during her reading of their daily Bible passage.

'My dear, Miss Makepeace,' said the perplexed lady, 'this is so unlike you. You are normally a pleasure to teach. This morning, however, I do believe you have not heard a word I have said. I have a good mind to set you lines for this afternoon.'

'Oh no, please do not, Miss Cuthbert,' cried Felicia from her desk. She laid down her quill hastily and came up to her teacher. She knew she could cajole the poor lady into doing anything she wanted but she had a certain sympathy for her and did not like to add to her woes. Miss Cuthbert had neither youth nor beauty and from what Felicia could tell, she had little money or family. Occasionally she spoke of a cousin but she rarely left the Castle to visit them, she received few letters and no callers. Her life, Felicia realised, revolved around the inhabitants of the Castle and, as Felicia grew older and older and there were no little siblings following in her wake, Miss Cuthbert appeared to become more cowed and subdued. Despite her youth, Felicia appreciated that this was because the time would soon approach when she would not need a governess. What would happen to Miss Cuthbert then Felicia did not know.

'I do beg your pardon, Miss Cuthbert. I believe it is the sunshine. After all the dark days of winter it is a joyous thing to behold.'

The worn lady's sallow face broke into a bleak smile. 'Indeed I understand, my dear,' she said. 'You wish to be out in the fresh air. It is only to be expected. Now run along and try not to get too dirty.'

Felicia thanked her and made good her escape, clattering down the spiral stone staircase of the schoolroom turret. She passed the door to Miss Cuthbert's bedchamber and sitting room on the next floor and found herself thinking what a pity it was that the view was considered a distraction to children so the nursery area had been placed at the back of the Castle against the rock face. She remembered Nanny's room above the schoolroom and wondered what she thought of the arrangement now that she was pensioned off and only called upon when someone in the Castle was sick. Felicia ran her hand across the smooth sweep of the stairwell wall and peered through one of the slit windows that looked out over the central courtyard. She smiled. Whatever was the lot of those individuals inside the Castle, its fairyland features allowed the freedom to dream, to transport oneself into a fantasy world of romance and chivalry. Perhaps both Nanny and Miss Cuthbert found that some consolation.

There was a brisk wind, so after snatching a quick pastry from the meal that had been laid out in the breakfast parlour for her, Felicia donned a warm pelisse and headed for the oak tree.

She felt disappointment assail her as she attained the bowl in the tree, for Giles was not there. There had been some talk between her parents in the vast drawing room of the Castle about the new arrivals at The Chimneys and Felicia knew that her father had called on the family. They were expected to return the civility in a day or two. Felicia was certain they would not call at

Castle Leck today; it would smack of unseemly haste. She sat for some time watching a male chaffinch showing off his bright pink waistcoat as he flitted amongst the branches, and had just decided to leave the tree when she heard the sound of someone approaching. She flattened her body against one of the stems and waited to see who it might be. Soon there were the familiar sounds of Giles' boots on the tree. Felicia remained silent, a little embarrassed by the eagerness she felt to see him.

Giles made short work of the trunk and was soon up at her side.

'So,' he said in mock anger, 'a few raindrops and you stay away,' but his laughing eyes belied his tone.

'Did you brave the rain yesterday or the day before?' Felicia demanded.

'Of course,' replied her companion as he brushed off the floor of the great bowl so that he could sit down. 'You may be able to pick and choose your days, Miss Makepeace, but I have but a week before I return to school to take what enjoyment I can.'

She was touched and contrite. 'I am so very sorry. Did you wait for me in the rain? Miss Cuthbert would not allow me out. She fears April of all months for she says people weak from a long winter often succumb in April as its temperature is never as benign as we imagine and the showers are always cold.'

Giles had satisfied himself that the floor was now clean. He sat down and held up his hand to help Felicia to sit beside him. As she arranged her skirts he asked: 'And who, pray, is Miss Cuthbert?'

'My governess, surely I have spoken of her?'

Giles shook his head. He removed a penknife from his breeches' pocket and began to whittle away at a twig.

'Will I meet her when we visit you tomorrow?'

Felicia clapped her hands in delight. 'Oh, do you come tomorrow?'

'Yes, and my uncle gives us his escort. He shows my mother the most generous attention. I know not how to thank him.'

'I am sure you are everything that is appreciative.'

'I try to be,' said the boy simply.

Felicia pursed her lips. Giles, she felt, was taking his indebtedness to his uncle too deeply. Of course he should be thankful, even grateful, she decided, but surely what Mr Gregory was doing was no more than any brother would do for a sibling in such circumstances. After a few moment's silence while she sought for the words to lighten his thoughts, she said, 'I think it is very fortunate for Mr Gregory that he now has you as a family. He has resided in that vast house for too many years on his own with only occasional visits from his other sisters, Mrs Torrill and Mrs Lambert.'

Her words did not have the desired effect. Giles flung down his tool and his artwork and scrambled hastily to his feet.

'Do not speak to me of my Aunts Torrill and Lambert,' he said through gritted teeth as though uttering their names stuck in his throat. 'My mother turned to each of them for help before ever approaching her brother. Neither would grant us even a visit and both wrote to my uncle to dissuade him from taking pity on us.'

'Why such antipathy?' cried Felicia, still unable to curb her unruly tongue, 'why are they so agin your mama?'

Giles sighed. 'I believe they resented my grandfather marrying again after their mother died. They were never kind to Mama during her childhood and when she married a man of little substance they completely cast her off. They took no account of the fact that my mother and father enjoyed a harmonious partnership and lived most happily until ...' Here he broke off and struggled to master his emotions.

Felicia reached up and took his hand, giving it a sympathetic squeeze.

He pulled it away with a jerk and drew to the other side of the tree. 'Please,' he managed, 'give me no comforting words for it only makes this trial harder to bear.'

'Well,' said Felicia, determined as ever to help in some way, 'if it is of any solace neither Mrs Torrill nor Mrs Lambert are liked in these parts. It is said that they are awaiting the demise of Mr Gregory so that they can enjoy his great wealth. 'Tis why I was so keen to learn that you might be the heir. I have met their sons, Nathan Torrill and Gervase and Digby Lambert and I like none of them.'

'Miss Makepeace, Felicia, I beg you do not talk so. I ask nothing more from mine uncle than for him to keep faith with my mother.'

'But I must, Giles, I must put you on your guard, for when the young men visit, they are most unpleasant. The servants keep watch for fear of them doing your uncle some disservice. It is my belief that your aunts, having suffered the death of Mr Simon Gregory, think it is not unlikely that your Uncle Arthur will pre-decease them also.'

'Stop it, stop it, I will not believe there is anything in what you say. My uncle has been kind enough to offer me a place in one of his counting houses in London when I complete my education. By the time my sisters are of age, I hope to have earned enough to dowry them. For the rest I want nothing more.' He paused to draw a gusty breath. 'You are in the wrong to encourage me to do so.' He spoke with such sincerity that Felicia knew she must abandon the subject. This, however, did not stop the intrusion of private thoughts that any man as honourable and articulate as Mr Arthur Gregory need only compare the worth of young Giles Thornton against the dross of the alternatives to leap at the opportunity to make Giles the heir.

They did not stay in the tree for long; a bitter wind had got up and it was no longer comfortable to remain there. Giles helped her down, a quaint courtesy she was too youthful to appreciate. She was merely irritated that he appeared to think she needed the assistance.

'I have climbed this tree a hundredfold,' she snapped as she straightened out the sleeves of her pelisse.

'I do beg your pardon, Miss Makepeace,' he said frostily, 'but I am used to helping my mother and my sisters. It would be thought most remiss of me if I did not offer them any help.'

Felicia turned to look into his face. She was conscious of the kindness that went to the very core of his nature and felt ashamed of her churlishness.

'You spend too much time with thoughts of other people, Giles,' she said, 'with me you need think only of yourself. Make me a promise that when we are together here in the woods you will put aside these cares.'

He smiled at her earnestness. 'Thank you,' he said, 'I know you mean it kindly. I will not patronise you by saying your youth allows you to see life only in simple terms. It is the essence of Miss Felicia Makepeace to confront the world and its problems directly. I could well learn to benefit from this approach.'

She laughed at him. 'You could indeed,' she agreed. 'Although perhaps you would lose something of yourself if you did, for it is your kindness which makes you so well liked.'

'Do not say so, you know nothing of me,' he retorted as he averted his eyes to look through the budding trees to the faraway hills.

She came up to him eagerly and clasped his upper arm with both her small hands. 'Oh but I do. Mr Gregory already speaks of you with pride and affection and the servants I know have taken to you.'

'You cannot know that,' he countered.

'I can and I do. For Mr Gregory's servants pass comment to my father's people. I can assure you that you already feature in their thoughts as their future master.'

She thought for a moment that she had gone too far, that she had angered him beyond forgiveness. His reply, however, surprised her.

'Why this fixation with mine inheritance, Felicia?' he asked quietly. 'You said when we first met that this issue weighs much on your mind yet you have not told me why.' He had slid her hands from his arms and was now holding them both in his. He looked about him and spied a log. He dropped her left hand and drew her to the would-be seat. 'Come tell me what troubles you.'

Felicia sat down as she was bid and considered for a moment.

'I presume your uncle has mentioned that my father owns estates in Yorkshire?'

Giles, who had now taken off his coat and placed it around Felicia's shoulders to protect her from the force of the wind, nodded his assent. Felicia drew the coat tighter to her, realising with a flash of wisdom older than her years, that Giles could no more stop himself from considering her welfare than she could fly.

'He may also have given you details of our history.'

'A little; he has said that your grandfather built Castle Leck at great cost.'

'At too great a cost!' corrected Felicia. Then she shook her head in denial of her words. 'No, not too great a cost. Castle Leck is worth every penny.' She paused, then, and looked down into her lap, unable to meet his eyes. 'My grandfather used all his funds and more to build it and now my father toils to recover our fortunes. He works to restore the estates to order and profitability. The revenue from them supports us. However, these estates are entailed, they must follow the male line. I have no right to them should my father die. While I can inherit Castle Leck, I cannot afford to keep it.'

Giles, who was beginning to shiver but was working hard to conceal it, gave an exclamation of surprise.

'My uncle has not talked of this,' he said, standing up and digging his hands deep into his breeches' pockets.

'Why should he? It can be of little interest to him,' replied Felicia forlornly.

'Little financial interest but he has great affection for your parents.'

'Perhaps he feels it would be wrong to talk of inheritance to you at this time,' suggested Felicia.

Giles acknowledged this as a valid reason. 'So what brings it to the forefront of your mind now?' he asked, still bewildered. 'This state of affairs must always have existed.'

Felicia nodded. 'Twas my thirteenth birthday last week and my parents deemed me old enough to be told. It was the first I had heard of it. Their solution to secure my future is for me to marry my cousin who will inherit the Yorkshire estates. When I am sixteen I am to have a season to acquaint myself with him and then our engagement will be announced.'

Giles was thunderstruck, so much so that he forgot how cold he was. He stood before her, struggling to take in what she was saying.

'So you are already promised to your cousin?'

Felicia gave a minute nod; she could not look at him.

The boy who was so nearly a man spun on his heel and flung away from her. 'It is as well that you have told me of this now,' he said almost inaudibly.

Felicia leapt to her feet. 'I will not marry him, Giles,' she cried. 'They will not make me when they see that I am resolved against it.'

'And why should you be resolved against it?' he asked bitterly. 'You must wed someone with a fortune to keep you in your Castle. He seems an obvious candidate.'

'But I know him not, Giles,' she wailed, 'and he has assented to the scheme so tamely. I would rather marry you than someone I do not know.'

Giles' gentle face contorted with the effort he was making not to give himself away to someone who was yet too young to understand fully what she was saying.

'You cannot marry me,' he said at last, 'for I could not keep you in Castle Leck however much I might wish to.'

'Do you not see that that is why I wanted you to be the heir?' she blurted out.

Giles threw his hands up in exasperation, then, snatching his coat from her shoulders, set off running back in the direction of The Chimnies.

4

*F*elicia did not know what to make of Giles' desertion; she collapsed back on to the log and sat there for some time until the penetrating cold forced her to return to the Castle. She spent the evening wondering whether he would come to the tree the next day, then belatedly she recalled that the Thornton family would be calling upon them at that time. She foresaw no easy way to talk to him alone but at least he would be present; she would see him again.

The next morning dragged for Felicia. She struggled to maintain her concentration, conscious that Miss Cuthbert would suspect something irregular if she continued to neglect her studies; she had been such a conscientious student before.

The Thorntons arrived in the early afternoon; Mr Gregory, as had been foretold, arrived with them, he and Giles having ridden in escort to the carriage.

Felicia did not see the arrival but she heard the clatter of the horses' hooves as they were led away through the outer court-yard to the stables. She ran as swiftly as her skirts would allow to the base of the principal staircase. There she stood diffidently as Hayworth, the butler, took Mrs Thornton's wrap and the gentlemen's hats and canes.

'Ah, Miss Felicia!' exclaimed Mr Gregory jovially, 'have you come to do us the honour of escorting us to your mother?'

Felicia hesitated, seeing the look of significant disappointment on Hayworth's face. She knew he would wish to announce the guests, as Mr Gregory was renowned for tipping well for even the smallest service. Despite his roots in trade, Mr Gregory was welcome everywhere because of his gentlemanly conduct and generous disposition.

'Oh no,' she replied breathlessly, 'Mother would most surely scold me for not having you announced properly.'

Mr Gregory chuckled and flicked her cheek with his finger. He was a well-proportioned man, only slightly overweight, with a rubicund complexion and a receding hairline that he obscured with a wig. Felicia had always liked him as her father's friend but had not, until recently, been interested in the existence of his wealth. This was reputed to be enormous. His father had started out in the City and with one or two successful risky ventures had settled down to make money in earnest. Mr Arthur Gregory, succeeding to his father's room, had found himself in possession of two major banks and a string of lesser businesses. Mr Arthur, a cautious man, had husbanded the money carefully and rationalised the business interests. He had doubled his father's money and it continued to grow. It pained Mr Gregory that he had no child to succeed him and he had looked originally to his Torrill and Lambert relations to provide him with an heir. Early in their youth both Nathan Torrill and Gervaise Lambert had fallen foul of their uncle but it had only been relatively recently that Digby Lambert, succumbing to a predilection to gambling, had ruled himself out. Mr Gregory, who did not indulge in excesses and saw no reason for others to do so, had been deeply disappointed that he needed to look further afield. He reposed much faith in Mr Ponsonby, his manager at the bank, and when his nephews failed, had cut Mr Ponsonby into the business, but he still longed for an heir. Many might ask why he did not beget one himself. His answer to himself at least was that he had left it too late and would not now find a woman who would marry him for himself rather than his wealth. He wanted no child on those terms. The maxim, "clogs to clogs in three generations" had a tendency to sound in his head. Although Mrs Thornton was not to know it, her half-sisters' determination to divide her from their brother had worked in her favour.

Mr Gregory, fully aware of his full-sisters' greed, set out to reacquaint himself with his half-sister. He remembered her as a quiet, mousy child with a sweet and deferential disposition, many years his junior. The onset of some thirty years had done little to change her demeanour. Her colouring was still mousy, her voice still quiet and her disposition still deferential. He was disinclined to call a middle-aged woman sweet but she gave him no cause to think that her marriage had soured her. Mr Gregory's chivalry had been ignited when he found her dismal and grieving. He had been happy to take her under his wing for her own sake but when he had met the children he had been bowled over by the son. A fine and upstanding young man whose gratitude was quietly and emphatically expressed without being effusive or gauche, and this gave rise to the kernel of hope that he might have found a worthy successor. The caution for which he was famed prevented Mr Gregory from radically changing his will. He wanted to be sure that the boy was all that he promised. Mr Gregory did not forget that Digby Lambert had waited until he was four-and-twenty before his frailties betrayed him. Giles Thornton was but sixteen. Mr Gregory did however attach to his will a codicil that would result in each of the Thorntons enjoying an income of some £500 per year if he was to die before he had resolved the issue. A small sum in his eyes but a fortune to young Giles had he but known of it, struggling as he was to see a future for his family on the annuity of little over £300 his father had left.

Mr Gregory had begun to test his new nephew, landing gifts upon him such as the new clothes and a well-bred hack. The boy tried to refuse them, assuring his uncle that he could manage very well on the old gelding of his father's and the school uniform from the year before. Mr Gregory had had to insist and then had seen once more the deep and sincere gratitude in the boy's expression. The uncle then tried the nephew further, announcing without preamble that he expected Giles to start work as a lowly clerk in one of his businesses as soon as he had finished his schooling. Giles had not demurred; in fact he had expressed himself in some relief.

'I realised that I had to embrace a profession at the earliest opportunity but knew not for what I might be fit. If you are prepared to provide me with employment I will think it most generous of you.'

That evening Mr Gregory had grumbled to his valet, a slight, weaselly man whose demeanour belied his undying devotion for a master he had served for seven-and-twenty years, that the boy seemed too perfect.

The valet, who rejoiced in the name of Higginbottom, considered for a moment before replying. 'It is certainly true, Sir, that Master Giles exhibits many exceptional qualities but I believe he does have a frailty.'

'Humph,' had growled Mr Gregory, 'trust a gentleman's gentleman to notice a chink in a man's armour. Go on, man, tell me what you have found.'

'I fear, Sir,' Higginbottom had said, shaking out Mr Gregory's coat of rich burgundy before taking a clothes brush to it, 'that the young man cares too deeply and sets himself too high a standard. You will no doubt have noticed that he has maintained a constant grip on his grief for his father, a man we know he greatly admired, and he has gone out of his way to please and to be pleased by everyone.' Here the valet had coughed. 'Including Mrs Fiquot, Sir, who we all know to be a lazy good-for-nothing.'

The lifting of his master's hand had silenced the valet. 'Mrs Fiquot, Higginbottom, is a "cause célèbre." I cannot dispense with her culinary services, half my kitchen staff would leave, they are all related to her in some way.'

Higginbottom had hung up the jacket and taken out Mr Gregory's housecoat. Helping his master into it, he had sighed. 'I fear, Sir, that unless Master Giles has someone with whom he can share his thoughts, he will not shoulder the burden currently placed upon him.'

That someone was currently trying to make headway in a one-way conversation with Giles' two sisters. Both girls were dismally shy. The magnificence of the Castle had struck them dumb and they were in awe of everyone connected to it from the butler, dressed in severe black, to the pretty young lady only a few years their senior who was struggling to entertain them. Sophia Thornton, at ten, had all the mousiness and diffidence her mother exhibited and little Imogen, while favouring her brother's colouring, would have to enliven herself to be considered attractive. Felicia found herself looking involuntarily at Giles for help when neither girl had managed more than a monosyllabic answer to her polite questions. He would not meet her eye and was studiously listening to the Messrs Makepeace and Gregory's conversation. He was attired in a brown coat and simple cravat, which set him apart from Felicia. It exhibited the disparity between their ages and her heart sank. Was this the end to their brief friendship?

Mrs Makepeace, also labouring under the difficult task of conversing with Mrs Thornton, moved to pull the bell rope. She requested the answering servant to summon Miss Cuthbert; if neither she nor Felicia could strike the right note, perhaps the meek governess could communicate with their guests.

Miss Cuthbert arrived in haste to be of service and was a little surprised to be requested to join the tea party.

'Now, Mrs Thornton,' said Elsie Makepeace, placing her teacup carefully down upon a side table and leaning slightly forward, 'I understand from your brother that you instruct the girls yourself.'

'Oh yes,' said the poor lady in a hushed voice that was almost inaudible.

Miss Cuthbert's heart sank. She feared Mrs Makepeace was finding a not-too-subtle way of telling her that her employment was at an end.

'I would like to make you known to Felicia's governess,' pursued Elsie, indicating Miss Cuthbert with an airy wave of her hand. 'I am sure there would be some lessons when your daughters could join Felicia. I am conscious that Felicia sees very few young people and that this would be an excellent way for her to become acquainted with her neighbours.'

'Oh thank you,' stammered Mrs Thornton, 'really it is most kind but most unnecessary.' She looked wildly around for her brother. Mrs Makepeace was before her.

'Dear Mr Gregory,' she called, 'I have had the most charming of ideas to relieve your sister of what I am sure must at times be an irksome task.'

Mr Gregory excusing himself from his friend came over to the ladies.

'And what is that, pray?' he asked, his narrowing eyes, gauging perfectly his sister's feelings at that moment.

'That your lovely nieces should join in some lessons with Felicia – Italian for instance, Miss Cuthbert is about to start Felicia on that.'

Felicia had been listening with half an ear to what was being said and was not averse to sharing her governess with the girls. It would distract Miss Cuthbert's attention away from the increasing difficulties Felicia was having with her concentration. When Mr Gregory called the girls over to hear the change in their circumstances, Felicia saw an opportunity to speak to Giles. He was now standing alone by the table bearing the refreshments and was pouring some lemonade for his sisters.

Unable to put a hand on his arm in such a public arena, Felicia moved as close as she could to him before whispering: 'Forgive me, I should not have said what I did knowing how much you dislike the subject discussed.'

For the first time he looked at her and his face softened in response to the contrition in hers.

'No, it is I who should apologise. I should never have left you as I did. It was most unmannerly of me. No matter how angry I was, I should have seen you safely out of the cold.'

She smiled at that and her hazel eyes twinkled. 'Now you are touching on a subject about which we cannot agree. I need no mollycoddling!'

The Gregory party was beginning to make a move to be gone and the two young people had to draw apart leaving the lemonade untouched. Felicia moved to stand by the doorway and shook hands with each as they left. Giles was the last in the line.

'Meet me tomorrow,' he mouthed as he bowed over her hand. She nodded briefly to show she had understood.

The next day she waited in the tree in vain. Had she suggested the meeting she would have thought he had just decided not to come. The thought did occur only to be banished. She came the next afternoon and was rewarded with his appearance only minutes after her arrival.

Giles climbed the tree in haste, scrambling up it with none of his usual grace.

'Oh thank you,' he gushed, 'thank you for giving me a second chance. I feared that my failure yesterday would put you against me.'

'It would take more than that,' she assured him. 'What kept you?'

He sighed a heavy sigh. 'My aunt Lambert made an unexpected visit and she tarried all afternoon. My uncle was most put out because she poked and pried and bullied my mother.'

She saw the anger mounting in his face as he retold the event and knew not how to comfort him. 'She bullied my mother to such a tune,' he went on, 'that she was in tears when that woman finally left.' Giles' fists had clenched and he hit out at the tree trunk, grazing his knuckles. He did not seem to notice. 'If it had been my father's house I would have driven her out but I have no right to do so in my uncle's.'

'But surely your uncle ... ?'

'My uncle was not present all the time. He was called out to see his agent on a matter of some urgency. When he was absent her onslaught intensified.' He stopped, anxiety riven deep in his face. 'What am I to do?' he wailed. 'How am I going to protect my mother when I am at school?'

'You must not take on so,' cried Felicia, 'you must not think of it. Mrs Lambert has visited now, she is unlikely to come again and your uncle will be here. I know he will stand your mother's friend.'

He was little comforted. 'There is still Aunt Torrill,' he said bitterly, 'no doubt she will want to see for herself these ghastly relations who have designs on their inheritance.'

'Is that what your aunt said?' asked Felicia, shocked.

'In so many words.'

'Fie on her. I know your uncle will disregard that, he knows it to be untrue.'

Giles sighed. 'He may believe it now but they will repeat it often and often and he may begin to believe it.'

Felicia came to him now and, placing a hand on his shoulder, turned him to face her.

'No, Giles,' she said looking up into his troubled face, 'no-one who has come to know you as your uncle has would believe ill of you, I swear you need feel no anxiety about that.'

Giles gave a twisted grin. 'You speak the words I want to hear Felicia. I will try and find solace in what you say but your words are coloured by even more youthful optimism than mine own.'

'Is that so very bad a thing?' she questioned. 'If it makes life more tolerable is it so very bad to be optimistic?'

'No,' he said gently, 'Tis not so very bad.'

5

*G*iles had gone. He had left for school the day before accompanied only by his battered trunk and a manservant of his uncle's.

Felicia thought this very harsh and nothing Giles could say would convince her that he was being much spoiled by being driven to the door by his uncle's own carriage and horses.

There had been no real opportunity to say goodbye and Felicia felt the parting deeply; more deeply as each day passed for she had never had a friend before. She longed to write to him but he would not allow it. To the outside world their acquaintance had been too slight to warrant any correspondence. It was only when she remembered his little sisters that Felicia devised a route by which to pass messages to him.

Sophia and Imogen came twice weekly to the Castle to study Italian with Miss Cuthbert and Felicia. At first even the mild and kindly Miss Cuthbert had elicited no more than a hushed whisper from either girl but, gradually and unexpectedly, Sophia began to open up. She obviously greatly admired Felicia and looked up to her worshipfully. Soon she would complete a sentence and then one memorable day she even asked a question. Imogen was soon to follow her lead. It allowed Felicia to probe for news of Giles.

'How is your brother?' she asked one day amongst a plethora of questions about their mother's and their own welfare.

Sophia's eyes lit up. 'He is well,' she said; 'his letters speak of his achievements. He will be seventeen next month and mother says we may write to him ourselves.'

'Do you not already?' asked Felicia, surprised. 'I imagined he might expect a letter every week from such loving sisters.'

Sophia's luminous eyes widened with concern. 'Have we done something amiss?' she quavered. 'Should we be writing?'

Felicia felt a touch of remorse. She had not meant to upset her guests.

'No, no,' she assured her hastily, 'I'm sure he does not expect it but think how nice it would be. Indeed I could help you.'

The girls were honoured by the suggestion and too young to suspect an ulterior motive. Felicia appeased her niggling conscience with the thought that there would be no harm to the sisters and Giles might benefit from the knowledge that she was thinking of him.

The Thornton girls brought their quills and writing paper with them the very next lesson and so eager were they to write their letter that Miss Cuthbert allowed it before the lesson started. This was not part of Felicia's plan; she had no desire to have Miss Cuthbert stand over and correct each ill-formed word or badly devised sentence. The letter then was a poor relation to the one for which Felicia had hoped. She did take some comfort though in the fact that the girls wrote of their Italian lessons.

'You must remember me to him,' she said blithely as they spelled out her name. This they dutifully did which left Felicia desperate to know what he would say in his reply.

She was doomed to disappointment. Giles made no mention of her in his next epistle. Sophia and Imogen brought it eagerly to her the following Thursday and read the angular handwriting painstakingly. There was nothing for Felicia, no mention, and no return of regard. She stalked to the slit window and peered down upon the subordinate turrets. She could not fathom why he should still be punishing her. She thought they had made up their differences.

The letter was read and Miss Cuthbert called her class to order. Reluctantly Felicia moved from the window to her central desk in the circular room and sat down heavily. Her quill fell to the wooden floor and as she bent to retrieve it, she spied the discarded envelope close by. Surreptitiously she put out a slippered foot and drew it carefully to her. There was something just peeking out of it. Picking it up along with her quill, she placed it in her lap and lifted the desk's lid, ostensibly to get out her slate with her last lesson's vocabulary still written upon it. With sleight of hand she gathered the envelope into her desk. At last she could examine the contents. A dried oak leaf floated out on to her waiting palm. Felicia gave an audible gasp that was taken up by Miss Cuthbert.

'What is amiss, child?' she asked, concerned. 'Have you hurt yourself in some way?'

'Tis nothing but a paper cut,' replied Felicia, putting her finger to her mouth and sliding the oak leaf under her slate.

Miss Cuthbert rose from her lectern and came up to Felicia; she took the damp finger and examined it.

'It is nothing,' she said. 'It has not drawn blood. Try to be a little more careful next time.'

'Yes Miss Cuthbert,' Felicia answered meekly enough, but her heart was singing with joy. He had not shunned her, he had instead sent her a message only she could interpret. She wondered how she could let him know that she had received it.

Throughout the hour-long lesson, Felicia had ample opportunity to be grateful to little Imogen who was struggling with her verbs and requiring much of the governess's attention. Felicia's mind wandered constantly, searching for some means to communicate with Giles. Had Miss Cuthbert demanded her full attention in the lesson, she would have exposed herself to well-deserved censure. However, Miss Cuthbert, anxious that Imogen should not be deterred from learning Italian by the difficulties she was experiencing, concentrated much of her effort in that direction.

Eventually the lesson drew to a close.

'Would you like me to help you compose a reply to your brother?' Felicia asked as the girls began to put away their slates.

'Oh yes please,' was the chorus.

'Miss Cuthbert, do you mind if we remain in the school-room awhile,' she asked prettily.

Miss Cuthbert examined her timepiece, the only ornament Felicia had ever seen her wear with her drab clothes. 'It wants only twenty minutes to the hour when your mothers expect us to take tea with them. I will allow you to remain here for just that period.'

Without further ado the girls crowded around Felicia's desk and began to laboriously form the letter. Sophia had the writing of it but Felicia itched to grab the quill and hasten the process.

After lengthy thanks to him for his letter and responses to the few questions he had asked, the girls were stumped.

'We must finish the page,' announced Sophia emphatically. 'It would be too cruel to have him pay to receive only half a letter.'

'I know,' said Felicia, her face lighting up with the glory of her idea, 'you could write a sentence about me.' She paused for a moment as though forming something to say. 'I know,' she declared, 'tell him I was caught out in the rain yesterday and became really soaked!'

'He will think that a great jest,' agreed Sophia and began to write the long sentence in her large and loopy hand. Felicia could have screamed with impatience; the time was ticking by and the sentence might have to be put aside.

Fortunately Sophia was just adding the full stop as Miss Cuthbert returned to the room to collect them. Hurriedly Felicia, taking the letter from Sophia, scanned it; then, as the girls were readying themselves to depart the room, she scratched a line under the three pertinent letters in the word soaked. She smiled a secret smile, folded the letter and handed it back to her young friend.

'He will be pleased to receive this, I think,' she said.

Giles, enduring an arduous time at school, was indeed pleased to receive the epistle with its hidden message. He tried to think of other tiny items that he might send to see how she could weave the word into a sentence in his sisters' reply. The next time he sent an ash key and was rewarded with the information that there had been a summer storm with great flashes of lightning. Subsequently he filled the envelope with grains of sand, and his sisters' letter told of a new pair of sandals Felicia had bought in Cheltenham. All the while the Thornton sisters suspected nothing. They blossomed under Felicia's perceived interest in them and hung on her every word. They were beginning to enjoy a little fluency in Italian and would even exchange a few sentences with their mother and Mrs Makepeace once they were downstairs again in the glorious drawing room.

'You are most kind to my little ones,' Mrs Thornton gushed each time, still unable to relax in company. She continued to wear her widow's weeds that did nothing to enhance her mousy complexion and accentuated her cowed demeanour. Felicia had to pity her, yet she wished the good lady would trust to her luck a little more and believe Mr Gregory to be a consistent benefactor. Her anxiety and uncertainty seemed to centre on the fear that her half-brother would tire of her and remove his support. Felicia, not old enough to judge whether this would begin to irritate the kindly gentleman, had insight enough to know that it would not aid the poor lady's cause.

Felicia sat at these tea parties listening attentively, determined to catch any hint of when Giles would be home. The letters, coming as they did once a week, allowed her to keep a tally of how long he had been gone but did not give any clue as to how much longer she would have to wait for his return. Questioning the sisters was to no avail as they had little sense of time and had on one or two occasions given her false hope.

'So when do you expect your son's return?' Felicia almost gave herself away in her surprised reaction when her mother had finally asked the one question she wanted answered.

Mrs Thornton sighed sorrowfully before dabbing her mouth with a dainty lace handkerchief and putting down the pretty china plate from which she had been eating a tiny cake.

'You know how grateful I am to my brother, Mrs Makepeace,' she said, furtively looking behind her in case he was to be discovered amongst the heavy furniture lining the wall.

'Yes indeed, I know it well,' replied her companion, managing to keep her amusement at this behaviour under wraps.

'Well, you will remember that he has offered Giles employment in his London counting house.'

'Yes, I have not forgotten that.'

Felicia at this stage had to grip her hands tightly in her lap and cast down her eyes. She was terrified that her mother's love of a little gentle teasing would stem the timid lady's flow.

'It is most kind of him,' Mrs Thornton felt the need to say.

'That goes without saying,' countered Mrs Makepeace.

Mrs Thornton faltered. 'Perhaps it does,' she agreed nervously.

Mrs Makepeace saw that she had gone a little too far. 'We are all sensible of what a kind and generous man your brother is, Mrs Thornton,' she said, trying to retrieve the slip.

'Yes, yes of course.' Mrs Thornton was slightly breathless with nerves by this time. Silence fell and Felicia felt bitter tears prickle at the back of her eyes. She had been so close to discovering when Giles might return and now all she had was some tantalising snippet that implied that he might not be coming home at all.

'But do tell, Mrs Thornton, when will young Mr Giles be home to support you again?' Felicia's mother returned to the question.

'Oh dear, did I not say?' moaned Mrs Thornton, becoming more flustered.

'No, I believe you digressed to your brother's kindness.'

'Oh yes, so I did.' She took a deep breath. 'Giles' term finishes in less than a sennight but he has been invited by a friend to make a journey to London. My brother on hearing this news felt it would be an excellent opportunity for Giles to visit his bank. I believe he will stay in London for a fortnight after that. 'T'will therefore not be before the end of July that we see him here again.'

Felicia caught the sob that was rising in her throat and gulped it down. Another three weeks, the words reverberated in her head, another three weeks before she would have her friend with her again. Another three weeks before she could explore the woods and meadows with him. It seemed like forever and the cruellest part of it all was that the time in London would eat up the precious weeks which should have been theirs to roam free.

'Why did you agree to go?' she longed to ask him. 'Why did you agree to go to London?'

6

'hy did you agree to go to London?' They were the first
words she flung at him before he had even steadied
himself from the climb up the tree. 'Why?' The words burst out
of her because they had been trapped within her head for more
than three weeks and the pent up emotion came gushing out the
instant they were offered the opportunity.

For a moment he said nothing, his breath coming fast and
heavily. He had run the distance from The Chimneys to the tree,
so eager had he been to see her again. He bent forward and put
his hands on his knees, trying to recover himself. At last he stood
up straight and looked at the angry girl before him.

'What would you have me do, Felicia?' he asked pensively.
'Turn down an advantageous invitation when I can offer no reasonable explanation for why I am doing so? I do not have so
many friends that I can pick and choose. Guilliam is Lord
Mullinger's son. My uncle was very pleased to encourage the
connection.'

'That's horrid,' said Felicia, but the heat had gone out of her
tone. 'I never thought of you as a toadie.'

'I am not,' he cried indignantly, 'most certainly I am not.'

'No, no I know you are not,' she agreed hastily, 'or I should say
I believe that you are not but I was most distressed to find that
you had forfeited some of the summer weeks to serve your
uncle's ends.'

'What!' he cried, 'would you have me subordinate his concerns to ours? Surely not when you know how dependent on his good offices we are.'

She did not understand the word he used so she could not pursue the argument; she did not want him to think her ignorant.

'Oh never mind,' she said abruptly, 'let's explore, we have to make up for lost time.'

Giles grinned. 'I thought you would never come down off your high horse,' he said.

She laughed then and tossed her curly head. 'I think we should go towards Strawberry Wood,' she said.

Strawberry Wood was aptly named because in the summer months its glades were carpeted in the sweetest wild strawberries. Felicia guided Giles to the largest open area deep in the wood and the pair of them gorged themselves on the delicious red fruits.

'Tomorrow we should bring a basket and pick some for the kitchens,' said Felicia as she sat herself down on the ancient stump of a fallen tree. Her face and hands were punctuated with smudges of red from the berry juice. She looked more like an urchin than a demure young lady. Giles was still moving about the glade amongst the plants. Great shafts of sunlight illuminated his progress. At last he came back to the shady stump and stood before Felicia looking down at her.

'I thank you for this,' he said, stretching his arms out wide to encompass the whole clearing. 'Tis much the sort of afternoon I would spend with my father; he was a great naturalist. His interest was in all things living but particularly the flora and fauna of our countryside. He would take me about with him time and time again. I thought I would never enjoy another outing such as that without him.' It was the longest speech he had made thus far about his late father and he did it in a flat, calm voice that shielded her from his feelings. Felicia remained quiet, not wanting to stop him if he wished to continue. It seemed, however, that he did not. Suddenly he grabbed her hand and pulled her through the glade to the opposite side from which they had entered it.

The wood was thicker here, and there were fewer paths. It would appear that it was just too far from the good people of Cheltenham and its surrounds to be subjected to foraging for firewood or timber of a larger nature.

The two young people scrambled over the uneven ground, Felicia's dress catching frequently on the brambles. Some times she would squeak when a briar or a nettle assaulted her but in general she did not complain. Giles pushed aside or trod down what scrub he could and held back branches to prevent them from flicking in her face.

'Do we know our way back?' he enquired when they finally reached a wide path, which was unexpectedly well maintained.

Felicia screwed up her face and peered at the sun that was playing hide-and-seek behind the canopy of leaves above them.

'Home is that way,' she announced and pointed in the direction the path was climbing.

Giles drew out his timepiece. 'We have but half an hour before we should make our return. What think you? Should we follow the path a little way or use it to return for our supper?'

'Oh just a little way,' urged Felicia eagerly. 'I have never been this far into the wood before.'

They strolled down the track side by side, glad to have an easier route. Not far along it the ground flattened out and the path splayed to a rickety wooden gate. In front of them was a large open area devoid of the majestic woodland trees but studded with the occasional fruit tree. The ground was covered in herb bushes; lavender, rosemary, thyme and sage could all be seen and the air was full of their glorious smell. Amongst the plants, narrow paths wove their way towards a small cottage, which was barely visible, so shrouded was it in creeper and rambling roses.

'So who lives here, I wonder,' mused Giles, one hand placed firmly on the top of the slatted gate.

Felicia looked alarmed. 'I have heard talk of a white witch, a wise woman who lives in these woods but I did not believe it. I thought it only servants' gossip. Could this be her abode?'

Giles looked amused as he always did when Felicia came up with a fanciful idea.

'If you are so faint-hearted Miss Makepeace,' he said mockingly, 'you remain here and I will beard the lion in its den.'

'No surely not.' Felicia let out a muffled exclamation. 'Come away Giles. We have no business here.' She shrank back towards the trees. 'Come, take me home.'

'Not until I have found out more,' he asserted and nimbly vaulted the gate without opening it. Felicia did not follow him.

Giles strolled down the little paths examining the plants as he went. As he drew closer to the house he called out.

'Hello there. Is anyone at home? Hello there.' At first there was no response, nothing to indicate that anyone might be within earshot. Giles called again more forcefully. An ominous hush descended around him, and Felicia shrank back further into the wood.

'Come away Giles, come away please,' she mouthed ineffectively to his back. 'We have no business here.'

Suddenly there was a flurry from behind the cottage and a middle-aged woman erupted into their sight brandishing a long-handled yard broom.

'Get away,' she screeched. 'Get away from here.'

Giles stopped abruptly in his tracks. The woman looked almost demented, with her hair falling about her face in grey hanks. Her hands were covered in soil and her clothes were drab and stained.

'Good day to you,' said Giles bravely. 'We mean no harm.'

At his use of the plural the woman cast her eyes around wildly looking for his companions.

'Be gone,' she screeched again and wielded the broom in a great circle before him. 'Be gone the lot of you.'

Horrified at the scene before her, Felicia rushed to the gate, fumbled with the catch and entered the garden in haste. She grasped Giles' arm.

'Come away, Giles,' she begged, distress written all over her face. 'Please let us be away from here.'

Giles cast one more searching look at the woman and then, taking Felicia's hand, turned and went with her out of the garden. At the gate he replaced the catch and walked smartly with his agitated little friend up the path towards their homes.

For some time neither spoke. Felicia's breath was coming fast and in gasps; it took all her strength to keep walking away from the cottage. Giles had placed his hand under her elbow and supported her as best he could.

'I do beg your pardon,' he said at last. 'It was not mine intention to frighten you,' he paused, 'or even her, for I believe she was frightened more than angry.'

'Frightened of us?' demanded Felicia between little gasps. 'We are but children. Of what is there to be scared?'

Giles considered for a moment. 'We may be but children in the eyes of the law, Felicia,' he said thoughtfully, 'but you are becoming very womanly and you must remember I am seventeen. I stand nearly six feet tall. To a stranger we might appear a threat.'

Felicia, who knew only of the depth of Giles' kindness, could not imagine anyone fearing him. She slowed her pace and looked up into his face.

'You always see the other person's view,' she said, 'never your own. I await the day when you assert yourself and demand that your thoughts, your feelings are taken into account.'

'To what end?' he asked curiously, his blue eyes full of puzzlement. 'If I had asserted myself in this situation I would merely have frightened her more and the possible end result would have been an injury for both you and myself. She could have wielded a mighty blow with that heavy broom.'

She conceded the point and they spent the rest of the walk home trying to imagine what might have caused the woman's reaction.

Gentle probing during supper both at The Chimnies and at Castle Leck produced no information about the unknown woman. Independently and separately Felicia's and Giles' interest was aroused. Felicia even braved an almost explicit question at the meal table.

'I glimpsed a cottage in Strawberry Wood today,' she announced during a lull in the conversation. She sensed slight stiffening in her father's posture but it was so imperceptible that she could not be sure. She looked keenly at him for a comment.

'A cottage, you say?' he said when he had finished the morsel of duck and placed his fork upon his plate. 'There are quite a number dotted about the wood. I imagine it was one of Mr Gregory's farm cottages, for you know the wood forms part of his land.' Her father then indicated to a servant that he wished his wine glass to be refilled and Felicia knew she could not pursue her theme.

The next day she met Giles at the foot of the oak tree and they exchanged the little information they had gleaned from their respective families.

'Dare we go to the strawberry glade?' asked Felicia, looking forlornly at her empty basket. 'For I feel sure there is some mystery attached to that lady and I do not want to fall foul of her once again.'

'We shall not do that,' declared Giles emphatically. 'The fruit glade is some distance from the cottage, we need go nowhere near it.'

Manfully Felicia agreed. She was still a little apprehensive but she remembered that they had had to scramble some distance before they had stumbled on the cottage. As she trailed along a little behind Giles, she was reminded of the truth of his words when he had asserted that they appeared more adult than they were. He certainly had grown since Eastertide; although he had not yet filled out, he was lithe and strong. Someone who did not know him might be intimidated. For her part Felicia was glad that he was there to protect her.

The glade was full of warm sunshine and soon all Felicia's anxieties were dispelled. The birds were singing merrily and there was the constant drone of the bumblebees going about their work. Giles and Felicia toiled happily for nearly an hour filling their baskets with the wild berries. When at last the receptacles were full, they gathered a few of the fruits in their hands and sat on the stump to eat them. It was as they were standing up to leave that Felicia gave a little shriek. Standing across the glade, swathed in the shadows was the grey lady. Today her head was covered and she carried a basket herself but she was unnaturally still and that stillness frightened Felicia.

Giles, seeing the woman, gently detached himself from Felicia's clutch and walked towards her.

'Good day to you, Madam,' he said gravely. 'We are just about to leave, we will not disturb you.'

The woman's eyes flickered across his face and then back to Felicia who was now standing some way behind him.

'Who are you?' The woman's voice came out on a rasping note. She cleared her throat. 'What is your name?'

'I am Giles Thornton, at your service,' he said executing a bow, 'and my friend is Miss Felicia Makepeace.'

'Makepeace, yes I know that name.' The woman looked keenly at Felicia. 'So you are the sleeping beauty in the Castle.' She paused. 'Yes, you will be a beauty in not many years time but Thornton, I know not that name.'

'I am a nephew of Mr Gregory of The Chimnies.'

'No!' The woman seemed to shrink and hug her clothes tightly about her. She turned as if in flight, so profound an effect did his words have upon her.

'Please, do not go,' cried Giles, distressed by her reaction. 'I swear I mean you no harm.'

The woman was deaf to his appeal. She grabbed at her skirts, dropping her basket as she did so and ran as best she could away from the two young people. The inevitable happened, her foot caught in the loose hem of her skirt and she fell amongst the nettles at the edge of the clearing. In her fear and panic she seemed not to notice the discomfort of the stings, instead she rolled with a flurry on to her back and tried to push herself away from them with her feet. She gave a yelp of pain; her ankle had clearly been damaged in the fall and was of no use. She subsided into weak sobs of fear and lay rocking herself, her arms folded tightly across her body.

Seeing the extremity of the woman's distress, Felicia pushed passed Giles and made a signal to him to stay away. He withdrew to the stump and let Felicia do the ministering to her.

'Come Madam, please,' entreated Felicia, kneeling as best she could beside her with only a half-hearted attempt to avoid the nettles. A thought occurred to her but it seemed to have occurred to Giles at the same time. He had left the stump and was making for a large clump of dock plants. Felicia turned back to her patient. 'There is nothing to fear from us, dear Madam, I can assure you. I entreat you to believe me. We mean no harm; we were but picking berries.'

At first Felicia could perceive no alteration in the woman's demeanour, but gradually the sobs subsided and the woman made an attempt to struggle to her feet. Felicia was quick to act as a prop and she gently propelled the hobbling woman to the stump that Giles had vacated. He continued to stand apart clutching a sheaf of dark green leaves. Once Felicia had settled the woman on the stump, she took the leaves from Giles and began to scrunch them up so that they became moist with juice.

Mutely the woman stretched out her arms, then indicated on her face where the white bumps of the nettle stings were already clearly visible.

'Your poor arms too,' the woman surprised them by saying. She took the mangled leaves gently from Felicia's hand and began to scrape them up the girl's arm. She looked up briefly from her task and saw Giles watching them anxiously. She appeared to register that he was not in fact intending her any harm.

'Forgive me,' she quavered, 'I thought I knew with what quality of nephew Mr Gregory was provided. I see I have misjudged you. I should have known that a man as good and honourable as Mr Gregory would have some relations of whom he could be proud.'

'I gather you have met Mr Nathan Torrill and the Messrs Gervaise and Digby Lambert,' said Felicia conversationally, her youth protecting her from fully interpreting the woman's fears. 'I have tried to warn Giles against them for I believe they would do him a mischief if they could but he will not listen.'

The woman had shuddered at the mention of the cousins' names but she then recovered herself a little and, casting aside the dock leaves, she stood up.

'You do wisely to fear them,' she said emphatically, momentarily swaying on one foot. 'They are evil, evil men.' She staggered towards her empty basket but Felicia darted forward and picked it up for her.

'We must escort you home,' said Giles from afar. 'Would you permit me to help you?'

There was silence as she considered, then she smiled weakly. 'That would be most kind,' she said at last.

It soon became clear that she could not walk unaided and that her weight was too much for Felicia. Very quickly she had to use Giles as her support. At first she was rigid with some inner fear but gradually, as they made their slow progress back towards her cottage, her ramrod stance eased a little and she was even able to converse with them.

'Pray tell, Madam, what is your name? For you know who we are but we know nothing of you.' Felicia was ambling along in front carrying two full baskets and an empty one. She turned and walked backwards so that she could talk to her companions.

'My name,' the woman gave a mirthless laugh. 'My name will surprise you.'

'Well tell us do,' begged Felicia eagerly.

'My name, young lady, is for your ears only, my name is

Gregory. I am the widow of Mr Simon Gregory.'

Both young people were aghast. 'You are then another of my aunts,' said Giles, his face expressing his bewilderment. 'How can this be?'

7

*T*he trio had reached the cottage and Giles was purposefully cutting off Mrs Gregory's boot. He had not again asked for information for the woman was reluctant to divulge her secrets until she was back in the house.

The cottage was tiny with only two small rooms on the ground floor. The sitting room was crammed with stacks of drying flowers and herbs. There were seed heads in bunches hanging from the joist of the floor above and strings of shallots and onions across its corners. There was barely a place to sit down. Mrs Gregory had directed them to the kitchen that was cluttered with jars and pots and looked more like a pantry than a kitchen. In the midst of it was a small table with two wooden chairs and a stool around it. Giles had guided Mrs Gregory to a chair and had gently lifted her leg on to the stool so that he could administer to it. The woman seemed to have lost her fear of him but he was still cautious, afraid to startle her.

Felicia filled the kettle from a pitcher on the draining board and placed it over the smouldering kitchen fire. Drinking anything amongst all these herbs and potions did not appeal to her but good manners behoved her to follow her hostess' instructions. And anyway, she wanted to hear what Mrs Gregory had to say.

'Mr Simon Gregory was mine uncle's older brother, was he not?' asked Giles, meaning to distract her as he attempted to pull the boot off the swollen foot.

Mrs Gregory winced. 'Yes,' she acknowledged.

'But I never heard that he had wed. I thought him killed at quite a young age.'

'Yes, he was young as were so many who joined the army for the excitement it would bring them. But there is the nub of the matter. He was young, I was younger, but eighteen, determined to wed before he boarded his ship and was lost to me. We had no need to elope, my mother encouraged the match and Simon was of age.' She sighed as she cast her mind back to the stirring events some thirty years before.

'His family had no notion of what had occurred. He was away but ten weeks before he was killed and I feared I might be with child. I appealed to his parents to recognise me as his widow but they would not do so.' She shifted slightly on the hard seat while Giles made deeper cuts into the leather of the boot in order to free the foot. 'My mother with four more daughters to establish had little spare for me. I was left destitute and ruined.' She looked up into Giles' anxious face and was moved to smile a weak smile.

'You have the look of my husband, now that I see you close. He was a handsome man too,' she said.

Giles just shook his head, too overcome by the story which was unfolding before him. Felicia had abandoned the kettle that was taking ages to boil on the remnants of the fire and had squeezed herself down the other side of the table on to a chair against the wall. She remained silent, watchful, her mind struggling to grasp the implications of what they were being told.

'After some little while, it became clear that I was not with child, or maybe I lost it, I do not know and at the time I cared less. I had no prospects of redemption. Then one day a young man, younger even than my husband confronted me. It was Mr Arthur Gregory; he had learned of my plight and came to offer me what succour he could. He paid me money from his allowance and he found me board and lodging.'

Here she paused and gazed at Giles, who had a look of deep scepticism on his normally good-humoured face. She made no comment but pressed on with her recital.

'It was some years before Mr Arthur came into his inheritance but when that time came, he made haste to establish me here in a cottage of my own.'

'Why?' The question was almost a bark from Giles.

'Why?' She looked at him quizzically, a little surprised by the force of reaction. 'Because he saw himself as an interloper. The bulk of the inheritance should have been my husband's as the firstborn son. Then my circumstances would have been materially different, especially if I had provided an heir.'

'I have never heard tell of a widow Gregory,' said Felicia bravely, her voice a thin reed.

'No, and you will not,' agreed the woman, 'for I go under the name of Mrs Simons in deference to my widowed mother-in-law's feelings. It benefited no one for me to cause a stir.'

'So why are you telling us this now? If your identity has always been a closely guarded secret why suddenly divulge it all to a couple of unknown youths?' Giles' voice held a slightly acid note. He was struggling to believe these revelations.

'You think me a garrulous old fool, I accept that,' she said, 'but I cannot let this opportunity be passed up. If you are the remaining nephew, Clara's son, then you are the heir apparent. You must be brought to recognise the extent of your responsibilities.'

Giles backed away from her to lean against the sink. He put his hands to his head and tore at his golden hair.

'Why?' he groaned. 'Why when I have no aspiration nor expectation of such an honour must you all suppose I am the designated heir? My uncle scarce knows me. I know even less about his business. Why oh why must people persist in stigmatising me thus?'

Felicia had extracted herself from her corner and now that Mrs Gregory's foot was free of the boot had gone to collect up some rags from behind the sink. Gently she pushed Giles to one side and began to douse the cloths with water from the pitcher. She then began to wrap the cloths around the swollen limb. There was silence as the others watched.

'So what do you think, Miss Makepeace?' Mrs Gregory enquired of her nurse. 'Is he the heir?'

Felicia raised her coppery head from her task and considered a moment before answering.

'I think him worthy,' she said eventually, 'but I respect his feelings.'

'You are a cautious pair,' smiled Mrs Gregory. 'I like you for it and I would like you to visit me again. Is it too presumptuous of me to ask?'

Felicia's face softened and Giles straightened his back. He took his basket that had been full of strawberries and emptied it into a deep bowl on the table.

'We will most certainly visit you until your ankle mends. We can run errands for you if needs be, but now we must fly or questions will be asked of us.'

Taking Felicia's full basket and Giles' empty one they quitted the cottage and made haste homewards. They ran part of the way for time was against them but Felicia could not manage the whole distance. She wanted to discuss the events of the afternoon but Giles would not let her.

'Tomorrow,' he puffed as he made to set off for The Chimnies, 'tomorrow when we are more at our leisure.'

The next day set the pattern for the holidays. Each free afternoon – and these were often three or four in a week – Giles and Felicia would meet at the oak and then walk to the cottage to visit Mrs Gregory. As time passed their distrust of her lessened and they were happy to perform the small tasks she requested. These usually entailed picking fruit or, as the summer wore on, dandelion leaves, nettles, elderberries and eventually blackberries. With each fresh supply the lady would make jams or wine; sometimes she would bottle the fruit, and at other times she would purée it. The nettles she used either as food or to wrap the cheese she made from the milk of her single goat. Mrs Gregory clearly benefited from a close association with the young pair. As the summer wore on, she began to take more care with her appearance. She let Felicia trim her hair and dress it in an elegant knot at the nape of her neck. She mended her clothes and even added a touch of colour to some of the most drab of her outfits.

The change in her did not go unnoticed. Mr Gregory's trusted valet, Higginbottom, had long had the task of visiting her each week to ascertain if she was in any need. He would arrange for the carpenter to attend her if his services were required and he would purchase any of her produce that might conceivably be used by the kitchens at The Chimnies. Such was his devotion to this task that if the surrounding folk thought anything of Mrs Simons it was as Mr Higginbottom's fancy piece. More often however, they did not think of her at all unless they needed a herbal treatment for some disorder, which the local physician was unable to cure.

Dutifully Higginbottom reported back to his master and one evening, as he sat at his employer's side carefully manicuring the man's neat fingers, he set about describing the changes.

'Mrs Simon is much altered since your last visit, Sir,' he said. It was his custom not to add the 's' to the lady's pseudonym. He alone among the servants knew her true relationship to Mr Arthur Gregory for it had been to him that Mr Gregory had belatedly entrusted the task of tracking down the marriage certificate to prove the lady's story. Higginbottom misliked the subterfuge. He would have preferred to see her installed at The Chimnies as an acknowledged dependent, like Mrs Clara Thornton. To appease his conscience he always spoke of her as though using her husband's Christian name rather than a contrived surname.

'In what way has she altered?' asked Mr Gregory in quick concern.

'Oh in no adverse way, Sir,' said the valet hastily. 'Of that I can assure you.' He began to rasp the nails of his master's fingers.

'She seems well, although she did damage her ankle in a fall some little time ago. It is, however, her appearance in which there has been a change and her enthusiasm for work.'

'What can you mean, Higginbottom?' Mr Gregory looked at him keenly, his attention fairly caught. 'Mrs Simons has no need to work.'

'No, no, you misunderstand me,' the valet was quick to reassure him. 'I allude to her interests, Sir. Her penchant for the still room. She is surrounded by plenty and she is making jams and preserves by the score. Indeed, I was inclined to suggest that she took up a market stall and she said she was considering it.'

'Good heavens!' said Mr Gregory, greatly astonished, for the last time he had seen her had been on a dreary day in April when she had appeared to be weighed down by a great lassitude. He had been concerned for her attitude of mind and had wished he could have overborne her objections and moved her into his house to bear Mrs Thornton company. 'What do you think has wrought this change in so short a time, Higginbottom?' he demanded of his valet.

Higginbottom gave an artistic shrug as he transferred his attention to his master's left hand. 'I do not know,' he said, 'but she says she has met Mr Giles Thornton,' he went on in a speculative voice.

Mr Gregory jerked in surprise, so sharply that the nail file Higginbottom had been wielding with such care was knocked out of his hand. 'Does she know that he is my nephew?' he asked.

'She gave me to understand so, Sir.'

'And he has gained her trust?'

'It would appear so.'

'Well,' said Mr Gregory on a slow out-take of breath, 'we progress, Higginbottom, we progress.'

'I do not think that you should rush to take this as a sign, Sir.' Higginbottom was quick to try and prevent his master taking a step he might regret.

Mr Gregory chose to ignore the man's words and a gentle smile appeared on his lips. 'We progress,' he said again and this time on a note of deep satisfaction.

Higginbottom was alarmed at his master's obvious pleasure at the news and he could only blame himself for having broken it to him wrongly. If his master took it into his head to do something hasty and make the boy his heir now, they might all live to regret it. The memory of the betrayal of those other nephews was still too raw for Higginbottom. He knew he would be practising caution for many a day to come; it was incredible that Mrs Simon was prepared to trust again. It had surprised him as it had surprised his master. Such had been his concern, he had even alluded to past events to try and curb Mrs Simon's enthusiasm for her new acquaintance, but she had shunned his advice and had thrown back some advice of her own.

'Take the blinkers from your eyes, Mr Higginbottom,' she had told him. 'This boy does not have the Torrill or Lambert flaw that runs down their grandmother's line. His blood from his mother's side is pure Gregory and combined with the gentle Thornton blood leaves no room for the despicable behaviour of his half-cousins. Put aside your doubts and help him understand his responsibilities as I am doing. He will have enough to contend with when his cousins fully appreciate that they have been excluded forever and he has been set in their place. He will then need all the well wishers he can muster.'

It had been a harsh warning and as Higginbottom relived her words he realised it had not been a hollow one. For the time being, while he was still young, he thought Giles relatively safe from his cousins' machinations. However, as time went by and if he continued to please his uncle, they would indeed make attempts to discredit him. Higginbottom's spare frame shivered in his warm bed. Then all at The Chimnies would need their wits about them.

8

*H*igginbottom was being too sanguine if he thought that Giles' youth as yet protected him. Nathan Torrill had already learned that the boy had been welcomed at his uncle's bank and planned to make a career there. This he perceived as very dangerous indeed. Action had to be taken to prevent the boy taking up his place in the counting house after he had completed his education. To this end Nathan sought out his cousin Digby Lambert and bullied him into giving him information about which of his cronies had younger brothers at school with their cousin. Digby Lambert was still smarting from his own banishment from his uncle's good graces. As soon as he was sober enough to grasp what his most senior cousin wanted, he grappled with the problem with great gusto.

Digby Lambert was a dissolute young man for whom the excess of his recent past was already playing havoc with his complexion and his health. He suffered from a dry cough that plagued him constantly although he refused to consult a medical man. His clothes hung off him as he was losing weight and both his brown hair and eyes lacked lustre. Nathan Torrill, meeting him in a grimy tavern where neither of them was known, eyed him with disfavour.

'You are killing yourself with your debauchery,' he told his young cousin. 'What ails you man?'

Digby eyes his cousin with dislike. 'Nothing that a share of uncle's money wouldn't mend,' he said viciously.

'So you favour his early demise then?' sneered Nathan.

Digby's eyes dropped to his tankard. He stared into his drink, wishing his brain were not so sluggish. He used secretly to admire his cousin, whose general appearance was smart and well heeled. Nathan Torrill had possessed the entrée to many of the best houses. His Torrill connections were more refined than the Gregory ones but the Gregory connection smelt of money. The combination greased the hinges of many a door and Nathan had thought himself very well to do. Lately, however, there had been fewer invitations and not so many acknowledgements in the streets. Nathan had blamed his uncle but in fact that gentleman had not breathed a word about his nephew's dastardly conduct. It was more that Nathan had once too often taken too much money at cards from green and vulnerable young men, new on the town. The warnings were whispers but they did not fall on deaf ears. Nobody chose to be fleeced so they heeded the warning and parents of susceptible youths no longer encouraged him to haunt their houses. Nathan's sources of revenue were decreasing steadily and he was of a mind to do something about it.

Digby Lambert would not have been Torrill's chosen tool but the man was five years younger then himself and therefore so much more likely to have friends with siblings still at school. At first, as they supped a home brew, he feared his cousin was going to fail him, but then as they moved to the heavy red wine Digby's brain began to work and he recalled the name of a young man two years his junior who owed him a favour.

'I believe,' he said, after using a toothpick to free his teeth of some morsel of meat which had been troubling him since the previous night's supper, 'that he has a brother in his last year at the school. What would you have me tell him to do?'

It had been Torrill's plan to meet the young man who was to be his weapon himself but here was Lambert offering to do it for him. A gleam appeared in his eye. If the plan failed, if there was exposure, Digby would be in line for the discredit, not himself. He liked the thought. And, if the money began to flow in their direction, it would be a harness to constrain the fool's excesses. Nathan Torrill saw no reason to pour good money down this drunken sot's gullet. So, looking around the dimly lit room to check they were not being overheard, Torrill unfolded his plan to Digby.

Unaware of the dangers, Giles blithely returned to school for the Michaelmas term. He did not enjoy school but he knew it had to be endured. He had the memories of the glorious weeks of summer to resort to when times got bad and he had his secret code now well established with Felicia. It had become more important to be able to communicate with her now that they had the shared concern for Mrs Simons. They had devised the use of key words in his sisters' letters to refer to her well being and soon they had the exchange of news working to their satisfaction.

It was not long after the start of term that Torrill's plan began to affect him. The young man who had been chosen for the task came from malicious stock and, while he would not normally have chosen as his victim someone so near his own age, he was quite willing to undertake the commission such as it was.

A week after the commencement of term, Giles found that his tuck box, into which his mother and the housekeeper had tenderly placed all manner of culinary delights for him, had been raided. The lock had been broken and all the contents either taken or spoiled. Staring dumbly at the ruins of this lasting demonstration of maternal affection, he felt a wave of nausea assail him. He had never before been the subject of such abuse but he had seen its effect on others and his heart fluttered with fear that he would not be equal to the bullies. In the awful first moments of discovery, he accepted that it was all the more difficult because he did not know who the enemy was nor what he had done to awaken their wrath.

Giles tidied up the mess and said nothing to anyone. He knew that to draw attention to being the victim would cast him in that role more firmly. If there were occasions when he found himself gnawingly hungry then so be it, it was the price to be paid for the course he had chosen.

Unnervingly nothing happened for nearly two weeks and Giles was almost ready to believe that it had been an isolated incident. Perhaps it was someone in a fit of pique who was not even aware of whose tuck box it had been. Then, as term carried on towards November, other people began to lose items from their tuck boxes. Fewer people still had much left so it became more and more noticeable when items went missing. Some time during the course of the proceedings, the housemaster had been told. Nobody knew quite by whom and then almost with a seamless change Giles found the hint of suspicion heading in his direction. At first it was the less than enthusiastic welcome when he arrived in a classroom, followed by some telling looks when he walked past small knots of students in the corridor. Finally, when conversations paused as he walked into the room, he knew that he was now his classmates' principal suspect. He wished there was a prefect in whom he could confide but there was no one. Even his one-time friend Guilliam looked at him reproachfully if he tried to join him in a stroll around the grounds or out on to the shooting range.

The final straw was when Giles found a hunk of fruitcake in his locker that he knew he had not placed there. Hurriedly he secreted it under his coat and carried it out into the woodland beyond the school grounds where he crumbled it for the birds. After that he did a systematic search of the room he shared with Guilliam and a sickly lad called Johnson who spent most of his time in the sanatorium. Sickeningly, Giles found a bag full of walnuts under his pillow and a half-eaten sugar stick in his hairbrush case. He disposed of them rapidly and then sat at his desk to await the inevitable room search.

It struck Giles as he watched the faded housemaster performing this task that this was not something he was relishing. Giles wondered at this. Why should it matter to the man if a boy was caught stealing; the school had a waiting list, there would be no loss of finance to the school if he was expelled. Then he remembered some words between his uncle and the headmaster at the beginning of term. Mr Gregory had mentioned a possible endowment. He wished he felt reassured but he did not. Whoever was framing him was doing it determinedly and for a purpose. They clearly had no expectation of it being hushed up just because his wealthy uncle planned to give the school financial support. The little housemaster, who in his black robes and goatee beard, looked more like a fallen bat, heaved a huge sigh of relief when he failed to find anything incriminating in Giles' study. He moved on and, standing in the doorway, Giles watched him flit from one room to the next giving only cursory glances around each study. None of them were searched with the rigorousness of his. He wondered how, had they found anything, they would have determined that it had been him who was the culprit and not Guilliam. No wonder Guilliam was spurning his company.

Lying in his hard bed that night, Giles found himself breaking out in a cold sweat. He could not delude himself. He had escaped the trap on this occasion but his tormentors were unlikely to admit defeat. It was clear that they were systematically determined to discredit him and that they would repeat their actions. It was equally certain that he would not be able to outwit them every time. He had no alibi and no allies, no-one to take his part. He knew not how his uncle would react if he was expelled. Would he merely cast Giles off or would he cast the whole family adrift. The outcome was too ghastly to contemplate.

Tossing and turning, he knew he would not sleep until he had told someone, anyone the whole sorry tale. He threw back the heavy covers and began to fumble for his tinder box. He cared not if he woke Guilliam, if he was not awake already. Striking his flint and lighting his candle, he searched around for some paper and his quill. In the dim flickering light of the candle, he scribbled away, writing to Felicia, pouring out his misery and bewilderment to his little friend. What he thought she could or would do about it he knew not. The benefit was in expressing his fears. It was only when his toes, bare under his long night-shirt began to hurt with cold, that he signed off, blotted the text and hid it under his bolster. Within minutes of laying his head down again Giles was asleep.

Giles woke early the next morning even though he had been awake half the night. Guilliam studiously ignored him and showed no curiosity at Giles' behaviour during the night. Giles felt it was safe to assume the other boy had been asleep.

It was not until the afternoon that Giles was able to make his way to the receiving house and send his letter. He knew it would cause a stir at the other end but he no longer cared. Felicia would have to find a way to discover its contents.

For once Giles' luck was in. Miss Cuthbert had retired to bed with a thick head cold and Felicia was without any lessons when the mail arrived. Mr Makepeace paid for an early delivery and Felicia had just happened to be crossing the great hallway when it arrived.

Hayworth had always seen it as his duty to sort the mail. He would take the post bag and standing at the table by the library door would place the letters for Mr Makepeace, his wife and daughter and Miss Cuthbert, neatly in rows. Any letters for the servants he would then take through to the servant's hall and do the same on the side table there.

Felicia rarely received any missives, so it was with some surprise that she saw that there was a single letter lying between the clutch for her mother and the monthly periodical with which Miss Cuthbert indulged herself.

Felicia moved to the table quickly just as Hayworth shifted the bag from it.

'Your father will have had to pay to receive that,' he told her severely.

Felicia's eyes flickered to his face but she had already recognised the handwriting and had no intention of drawing more attention to the letter than was necessary.

'He will receive my apologies,' she said quietly and tried to steady her hand as she reached out for it.

Hayworth turned and left the great open space, his stiff straight back a study of disapproval.

The instant he had disappeared from view, Felicia was fleeing to her bedchamber. Entering breathlessly, for it was some way to travel along the arched corridors and spiral staircases of Castle Leck, she turned and locked the heavy wooden door. She had no plans to be disturbed.

Her hands shook vigorously as she fumbled with the ribbon with which the letter was bound. By the time she had released it from its bonds, it was crumpled and she had to spread it out on to the bed and smooth the creases. A coppery curl fell forward as she pored over the text. She flicked it back with a still shaking hand. Slowly and with some difficulty she began to decipher his words but the missive was crossed and re-crossed and it was not easy to make out what he was saying. However, it soon became clear that he was in much distress. Felicia gave an involuntary dry sob and struggled on with her task. The moment she had grasped the gist of what he was trying to impart, she was up and dragging on her pelisse and searching for her muff and bonnet. Once laced into her sturdy boots, she snatched up the letter and hurried down the coiling staircase.

It was not long before she was letting herself out of the side door and running as fast as her skirts would allow.

9

*M*rs Gregory was sitting at her small kitchen table dabbing the wart-covered hand of a swarthy teenage lad with a putrid brown liquid. Her thoughts were with the unprepossessing young man. His appearance was the antithesis of that of Giles Thornton and she could not help but make the comparison. Young Jethro Collins was of taciturn nature and made no conversation while Mrs Gregory administered to him. Mrs Gregory missed the lively chatter she was used to enjoy when Giles and Felicia visited her.

The door of the cottage burst open and Felicia stood gazing into the small living room.

'Mrs Greg...', she caught sight of the visitor in the kitchen and altered her cry, 'Mrs Simons, please Mrs Simons I have need of your help.' Standing up from the chair that had been across the door between the two tiny rooms, Mrs Gregory guided Felicia to a chair in the living room and bade her recover her breath. She then wrapped up her dealings with Master Collins in unseemly haste, admonishing him not to suck his fingers as wart wort was very poisonous, as she bundled him out of the back door.

Mrs Gregory returned to the living room drying her hands on the towelling cloth that hung at her waist. The girl's face was red from the bite of the November wind, her eyes were watering and her breathing was still laboured. It was, after all, some distance between the cottage and Castle Leck.

'My dear, what has occurred to cause you to come to me thus? Tell me, tell me, I beg.'

In response Felicia untied her bonnet and threw it aside, she then drew the letter out of her muff.

Mrs Gregory's eyes devoured its contents but she had even less success with it than Felicia.

'What does it say, girl? Quickly tell me!' Mrs Gregory took a seat beside her.

Felicia gulped and tried to control her breathing. Jerkily and punctuated by many pauses, Felicia took her through the words. As they came to the adieu, the woman and the girl's eyes met. There was silence as each digested the other's look. Eventually Felicia was the one to voice their thoughts.

'Forgive me,' she said as she began, taking the older woman's hand, 'but I believe this is the work of his cousins.' She saw the stricken look descend upon her companion's face, but bravely she pressed on. 'There can be no other explanation, no one else with a motive.'

Mrs Gregory swivelled in her chair and turned her back on Felicia, her hands now wringing in her lap. Felicia placed her hand on the woman's upper arm. 'We have to help him, Mrs Gregory. We cannot fail him when he needs us so badly. He has no one else to turn to.'

Mrs Gregory looked down at her working hands. She had thought this summer had healed the ancient wounds. The knowledge that the evil still persisted froze her to the marrow. She felt the crippling lassitude invade her and she believed herself powerless to resist it. Felicia, however, believed no such thing. Anger was now sounding in her voice.

'We must help him,' she yelled at the unresponsive back. 'Do you think I have run all this way to you only to have you spurn my request?' She stood up, her voice throbbing and, confronting Mrs Gregory placed her hands on the woman's shoulders and shook her vigorously. 'You cannot desert him, not when he has done so much for you.'

No one in all the time that she had been recovering from the encounter with Nathan Torrill and Gervase Lambert had demanded that she should put aside her own pain and act on someone else's behalf before. It was a measure of how much she had recovered that Felicia was able to reach her with her appeal.

Mrs Gregory bit her lip and then raised apologetic eyes to the girl's anxious face.

'Very well,' she said at last. She took up the letter. 'I will do my best.'

'Thank you,' sighed Felicia overwhelmingly relieved, 'but what can be done?'

This made Mrs Gregory smile. 'Will you let me take this letter to Mr Higginbottom, I believe he would know what is best to be done.'

Felicia looked appalled. 'Oh no!' she exclaimed, 'Mr Higginbottom is no friend of Giles. I cannot credit that he would do what is best for him.'

'You misrepresent him,' said Mrs Gregory quietly as she got up to gather up her large shawl and sheepskin muff. 'Mr Higginbottom's only concern is to serve Mr Gregory. If it benefits Mr Gregory he will do his utmost to succour Giles.'

Felicia's elfin face was a picture of conflicting emotions. Before she could speak Mrs Gregory continued: 'I think he would perceive how saddened Mr Gregory would be if he learned of these allegations.'

'Yes, yes, of course.' Felicia looked around for her discarded bonnet and, finding it on the floor, bent to retrieve it. Soon both ladies were ready to quit the cottage. They marched rather than ran to reach their destination, Mrs Gregory admonishing Felicia not to overtax herself. They parted at the point where the tracks to Castle Leck and The Chimnies diverged. Once the girl was out of sight Mrs Gregory paused to collect herself. Her heart was pounding. She had not admitted to Felicia that it had been more than two decades since she had physically called at her brother-in-law's house.

Mrs Gregory did not choose to call at the front door. She travelled to the back of the house and, passing a number of outhouses and sheds, she came into the kitchen courtyard and pulled the bell of the service entrance.

Penny, the scullery maid, came to the door and, not recognising her, looked enquiringly at the shrouded figure. The visitor's request to see Mr Higginbottom was met with some surprise. The little man was second only to the butler in the hierarchy below stairs and it seemed very unlikely to Penny that he would accept this drab visitor. She was reluctant to bother him so, closing the door in the visitor's face she went to consult with the housekeeper who was a much more approachable person.

Mrs Gregory, considerably incensed by this treatment, clanged the bell vigorously and pounded on the door. This time the comely figure of Mrs Ellis, the housekeeper, came to the door. Mrs Gregory gave her no opportunity to prevent her entering and barged passed into the cramped hallway.

'I wish to have speech with Mr Higginbottom,' she said with gritted teeth. 'Will you inform him of my presence or must I search for him myself?'

Mrs Ellis made an attempt to deny her but, fortunately for both ladies' dignity, Mr Higginbottom had heard the kerfuffle and had come to investigate.

'Mrs Simon, my dear lady, what a surprise. What brings you here?' The little man came hastily down the tiled passage.

'I must have private speech with you, Mr Higginbottom, it is most urgent.'

'You may use my parlour, Mr Higginbottom,' said Mrs Ellis, keen to recover ground now that she was aware of the visitor's identity.

Thanking her, Mr Higginbottom ushered Mrs Gregory into a small comfortable room off the passage that had a cheerful fire burning in the tiny grate.

Mrs Gregory was quick to show him the letter and to alert him to her and Felicia's suspicions.

When he was first acquainted with the contents of the epistle, he seemed unimpressed at the urgency or seriousness, but when Mrs Gregory made her claim, understanding the hardship this must have occasioned her, he took out his handkerchief and mopped his brow.

'Your faith in young Mr Thornton then is unshaken?' he asked probingly.

She nodded, still fighting the sensations that assailed her each time she had to think of Torrill or Lambert. 'If you knew, Mr Higginbottom, how often he would return to my cottage during the summer having seen Miss Makepeace home, to finish some chore or spare me a task, you would not question his integrity.'

'Such an accolade coming from you is of great worth,' he said, much moved. 'I will do everything I can to prevent harm befalling him.'

'Thank you, a thousand times thank you.'

Mr Higginbottom then insisted that she should be driven home and no amount of resistance would sway him, but as soon as the gig had swept out of the kitchen courtyard he turned on his heel and hurried to the butler's office. Here he dashed off a note, which he handed to the under-footman.

'To be sent express to Mr Sherbourne,' he said. 'Hurry man, I want it in London by tonight.'

The other servants were agog. All knew that Mr Alistair Sherbourne was Mr Gregory's man of business and it had to be very urgent indeed for Mr Higginbottom to take it upon himself to send the man an express without clearing it with his master.

Mr Higginbottom was on tenterhooks for the next three days, terrified that something might happen at the school before he could quash its damaging effects.

In London Mr Sherbourne received the express with a hurumph which camouflaged his deeper feelings. He had met Giles during his fortnight's sojourn in London and had had no difficulty in accepting him as the heir. He also found it easy to imagine that the cousins were at the root of his current difficulties.

Without delay, although he never appeared to hurry, Mr Sherbourne had despatched members of his considerable clerical staff to glean what information they could about the whereabouts of these disreputable young men.

Having waited impatiently for information from London, it was inevitable that Mr Higginbottom was away in Cheltenham when not one but two expresses arrived, the horsemen pounding up the drive to the imposing house not an hour apart.

Higginbottom had ordered a new pair of boots for his master some weeks ago and his master had been asking for them for the last two days. Higginbottom could no longer prevaricate; he had to leave his post and collect them from the cobblers. So, armed with the heavy wood moulds of his master's feet and legs he made his way, reluctantly, down to the town.

On completion of his errand, Mr Higginbottom went straight to his master's room to lay out the man's clothes for dinner. There was nothing in Mr Thornton's demeanour to suggest he had received bad news, as indeed he had as yet not done so. He too had come straight in from visiting a small bank in Gloucester into which he was thinking of buying. He shrugged himself into his fine burgundy jacket with only a little help from his valet, then with a cursory glance in the looking glass, he gave his cravat a final tweak and descended the stairs to await the dinner gong. Mr Gregory was handed the express as he stepped across the threshold into the Green Saloon. Normally he would look about him to check that his sister was not there before him but the express demanded his instant attention. He read it rapidly and was conscious of a leaden weight descending upon his shoulders as its contents revealed themselves to him.

Giles had failed him. Mr Gregory turned on his heel and shut himself in his study. He cast the headmaster's letter on his desk and went to stand in front of one of the large windows. There was little to see outside as it had been a grey rainy day and darkness had fallen very early. His view was as black as his mood. Once again his life had been blighted by the behaviour of a relative. He stood for some time feeding his anger, determined to make Giles and his family pay, but he could not sustain that anger; he found he was soon assailed by a creeping sadness. He tempered his feelings of revenge; Giles would suffer but he was neither ruthless nor heartless and he could not see himself venting his spleen on the hapless Thornton women.

The gong sounded. Mr Gregory jerked out of his abstraction; he would have to suffer dinner with his sister in silence. He could not tell her yet; he would not have grip enough on his own emotions to deal with hers. He made his way slowly to the dining room.

Mr Higginbottom was some time upstairs brushing out and hanging up his master's day wear so it was well over halfway through the meal before he descended down the back stairs. As he entered the passage leading to the servant's hall, Hayworth, holding the express from London, confronted him. Higginbottom almost snatched it from his hand, so eager was he to read it. It was only when he had come to the end of it did he look up and realise that the servants were huddled in anxious knots along the corridor.

'Good heavens,' he exclaimed, 'whatever is amiss?'

Hayworth cleared his throat. 'Mr Gregory received an express not half an hour after yours arrived Mr Higginbottom.' The servants not otherwise employed in taking the cheese board up to the dining room drew closer, listening intently. 'He did not read it until just before dinner was served,' Mr Hayworth continued, 'but it had a profound effect on him. He has eaten barely a morsel and before even the dessert was served he stood up and threw down his napkin begging Mrs Thornton to excuse him.'

Mrs Ellis pushed her rotund form through the maids and footmen surrounding the two senior men. 'We are affeared, Mr Higginbottom, that it is trouble for Mr Giles. Nancy went in to replenish the fire in Mr Gregory's grate and she saw a letter from the school lying on the desk. She knew it was so, though she cannot read a word, for the crest was there plain to see.'

Mr Higginbottom looked around at the circle of faces and read the anxiety in each expression. Every man and woman amongst them cared in some degree about the lad and that for him would have been testament enough had he not already received the epistle that would right Giles in the eyes of his uncle.

'Do not despair,' he said, holding the document above his head and waving it for all to see. 'I have the means to protect him, never fear.'

10

*G*ently pushing open the door of the study, Higginbottom found the room in darkness, lit only by the crackling fire.

'Go away,' snarled a voice from behind a winged chair near the hearth.

Ignoring the command, Higginbottom continued into the room until he was in the line of sight of the occupant in the chair.

'Oh it's you, is it?' acknowledged Mr Gregory, 'come to gloat have you?' he continued acidly. He was looking very dishevelled. The cravat that had last been seen by Higginbottom snowy white and neatly folded had been torn from his master's throat and now lay crumpled on his chest. The jacket was creased and the cuffs of his shirt loose and dangling. Even his hair that had sat in neat waves about his head was now in disarray. The valet's heart wept for his master.

'Gloat,' exclaimed Higginbottom startled. 'No indeed, most certainly I have not. I came ...'

'Well I don't want you here,' snapped the beleaguered Mr Gregory, 'let me enjoy my misery alone. What has brought about this blight on my family? Four nephews and all of them rotten to the core. I must have committed some heinous crime!' He waved his arm to indicate that Higginbottom should quit the room.

'I will not leave you Sir until you have heard me out,' the valet said boldly.

Mr Gregory was surprised out of his misery. He forced himself forward in his chair. 'What has got into you, Higginbottom? I have never heard you speak to me thus.'

'The case has never been so desperate, Sir,' the little man said vehemently, his wiry frame almost trembling in his determination to be heard.

'Then speak,' said his master, 'speak and I will listen.' So Higginbottom revealed the contents of the express sent by Mr Sherbourne from which he had learned about the schemes of the younger Lambert brother.

At first, thunderstruck by what he was hearing, Mr Gregory said nothing, but gradually as he saw the tendrils of the evil plot work their way towards his half-nephew, his brow cleared a measure and he interpolated the odd question. As Giles' role was revealed more and more as the victim he was almost smiling, for he had previously determined that he would never again allow himself to be shocked by the actions of the Torrills and Lamberts.

When the details had been outlined and the sworn affidavit by Digby Lambert's erstwhile friend had been read, Mr Gregory's mind cleared and he was able to ask some very pertinent questions.

'So how did you come by the information that the boy was in trouble? Did he write to you?' he asked Higginbottom, who was now lighting the candles in the wall brackets. The room was beginning to take on its habitual mellow appearance.

'No, Mrs Simon alerted me to the problem.'

'So he wrote to her?'

Pressed, Higginbottom returned to a guttering candle. 'Mrs Simon had it from a letter,' he said, hoping it sounded like agreement.

'I know you, Higginbottom,' Mr Gregory challenged him. 'You are concealing something from me. To whom did he reveal his troubles? Be plain with me!'

'Twas to Miss Makepeace, Sir,' Higginbottom capitulated, 'but I beg you not to reveal that you know. I gave my word of honour to Mrs Simon that I would conceal her part in this.'

Mr Gregory gave an exclamation and a pensive look possessed his face. He stood up.

'Tis a shame she is promised to her cousin. It is a match I could endorse.'

His master's utterance was so in accord with his own feelings that Higginbottom had to struggle to prevent himself from voicing his agreement.

Mr Gregory had not, however, finished his interrogation.

'It would appear to me, Higginbottom,' he said, watching his valet closely with grey eyes that rarely missed much, 'that you have suffered a full revolution of feelings towards my nephew. Can you explain your change of heart? But a week ago you were warning me to continue to practise caution where he was concerned. Now you are acting as his champion.'

Higginbottom put down his taper and squared up to his master. A good eight inches shorter than him, he had to look up to meet Mr Gregory's eye.

'It was difficult to maintain my position, Sir, when so many disinterested parties were expressing such care for his welfare. Before I entered this room I was met with a deputation of your servants in great alarm that something adverse had befallen him. Who could not be moved when it endorsed Mrs Simon's concern about him. Even Mr Sherbourne seemed disposed to give him his support. Who could continue to hold contrary views?'

'It is well for the boy that he has acquired so many friends. Tomorrow I will visit the school and have him righted in the eyes of the authorities.' He cocked an eye at his eager valet. 'And yes, you may accompany me.'

Had Giles any notion that his uncle was now in possession of nearly all the facts he would have been spared a desperate night. The trap had been sprung and he had not been quick enough to rid his study of the food that had been planted in ever more ingenious places. It was the deputy headmaster who had achieved this success. He was a man of severe moral code; he was also a stickler for the social structure. Although he was forced to welcome the nephew of a gentleman who embraced trade because of the financial rewards to the school it might bring, he was not prepared to allow such an individual to bring the school into disrepute by behaving in an immoral way. If the boy was poisoned then he must be cut out and the money should be forfeited. When he learned of the suspicions surrounding Giles Thornton, he had no hesitation in pursuing the matter; he did not even feel it behoved him to inform the headmaster until he held the culprit in his grasp.

Giles, when confronted with the evidence, held his ground and was dragged into one of the smaller classrooms for his pains. Three prefects and Mr Stokes, the deputy head, surrounded him and threw him to the ground. Norton, who was the instrument of the scheme, could not resist viciously kicking him whilst he was down. Mr Stokes looked down his long thin nose and appeared to condone the action. This allowed the punishment to continue unabated, with the others enthusiastically joining in, for some minutes. Then a shout from the corridor informed him that the headmaster was on his way. Giles was allowed to struggle to his feet.

'Fetch the boy's things,' commanded Mr Stokes. 'I want every last item contaminated by his possession brought in here.'

Then, turning on his heel, he went to meet the headmaster before the man could enter the room and see the bruises that were now appearing on Giles' body between the shreds of his torn shirt.

His belongings were thrown into the room and the door locked. Giles was left to await his fate. It had already begun to get dark when Giles had been forced into the room so there was no light except the flicker of the candles in the corridor from under the door. For some little while Giles stood grasping the desk in front of him. He had been winded and though his breath was gradually becoming easier, he felt sure he had a couple of broken ribs. Gradually his eyes grew accustomed to the dark and he could make out the heaps of his clothes. The room was becoming steadily colder so eventually he moved with an effort to find his greatcoat. Only when he was wrapped tightly into its rough folds did he allow himself to contemplate the full enormity of his plight.

He could not imagine how he was going to maintain his mother and sisters if his uncle visited his wrath on them as well. The tiny income from his father's estate might pay for his lodgings but what would they do for food and clothes. His chance of work would now be restricted, for who would employ someone who had been expelled from school? The scenario was too appalling. Giles had to push it aside or he would have been unable to contain his emotions. Instead he tried to think what he might do if it was only him cast out. He hoped that Mrs Simon might take him in. He could accept that for he would be of use to her. It was only as the deep coldness of the November night penetrated even the thickness of his coat that he realised that Mrs Simon would not choose him if housing him caused his Uncle Arthur displeasure. Giles wished he could be one of his little sisters and wail and sob out his misery but there was no release. He would have to endure this long night, the gnawing hunger and the humiliation and then try to re-establish himself when he knew how low he was to fall.

The darkness of the night stretched before him. After about eleven o'clock the candles in the corridor were snuffed out and there was not even a glimmer under the door on which to focus. The blackness engulfed him, leaving him woozy and disorientated. The damage inflicted on his body by the prefects had reduced to a dull ache but he could find no position to alleviate the discomfort. He longed to sleep but the narrow gap between the desks and the chairs bolted to them prevented him from leaning forward and resting his head on his arms. The rim of the desk stabbed at his damaged ribs hurting him further. In desperation he tried to sleep on the floor but there was little space and nothing to cushion him against its stone hardness. Eventually Giles fumbled into contact with a single wheel-backed chair. On this he placed himself and waited for dawn.

Dawn was later than the noise of the school rousing. November mornings were as late as the evenings were early as the year marched towards the shortest day. The candles in the corridor were lit and Giles could hear the scraping of the brush along the corridor as the juniors carried out their duties. There were distant noises as the pupils made their way to the dining room for breakfast. Giles thought he would even welcome the oily porridge that constituted school breakfast this morning. Slowly the gloom lifted and he was able to see enough to draw a fresh shirt from his clothes that had been strewn about by the prefects. Gingerly he took off the tattered remnants of yesterday's shirt and eased himself into a fresh one. He found his hairbrushes and a broken piece of mirror amongst his belongings. He tidied his hair and decided he was ready for his ordeal before the headmaster.

The morning wore on and no one came for him. Giles had folded his clothes and put them in his recently battered suitcase and dressed for travel; he was now totally ready for his dismissal and still no one came. His stomach without supper or breakfast was a tight knot of pain. He longed for someone, anyone to come if only to escape from the hell which was in his head.

The minutes dragged; the hours were interminable. He began to count the seconds to try and gauge what time it might be but it made no difference. He was adrift in an eternity of waiting and wondering. The day was grey so even peering out of the barred window gave him no clue to how close to noon it was. The school bell tolled for the various lesson changes but he lost track of that and could not calculate how close to lunchtime it was. Each time he heard footsteps come along the corridor, he prepared himself to face his accusers but each time they passed the door by. He began to think he had been forgotten. Gradually his resolve to stoically await his fate began to weaken; he found himself at the door prepared to batter it for an answer. He raised his arm to give the first thump but could not quite bring himself to do it. He turned and slid his back painfully down the door until he was sitting on the floor in a crumpled heap. It was as Giles sat there trying to contain his emotions that he caught the sound of more than one footfall. He scrambled to his feet faster than his hurts would allow and tottered forward. He grabbed the nearest desk and only just managed to straighten himself in time as the doorlock mechanism turned and Mr Stokes appeared in the aperture flanked by Norton and one other prefect.

Mr Stokes looked down his aquiline nose at Giles and sniffed a contemptuous sniff.

'Escort Mr Thornton to the headmaster's office,' he said before turning on his heel and leaving his two cohorts to grapple with Giles and attempt to drag him along the corridor.

Giles came unresistingly which destroyed some of his assailants' pleasure but it did not entirely save him from the pain. They poked and prodded him as they walked beside him, sometimes holding his arms cruelly, other times directing kicks at his shins and ankles. The headmaster's office seemed almost like a sanctuary when he reached it as the other boys could not administer their rough justice in his presence.

The headmaster was a head shorter than his deputy and was very short-sighted. He peered owl-like through a pair of plain pince-nez, dismissed Norton and Coates and let his eyes travel briefly to Giles' face. He had a rounded rubicund face and was only able to throw a thin veil over his obvious dislike for such a situation as presented itself to him now. He had always liked Giles Thornton, noting his patience with and care of younger boys, his lack of pretension and his great willingness to learn. Mr Falkirk could not imagine what could have brought about this behaviour which was so out of character. He stood behind his desk, clothed in his full academic robes and hat and awaited the arrival of Mr Gregory, his speech well prepared for he had been practising it all morning.

Mr Gregory was ushered into the office by one of the younger teachers. Mr Gregory was a big man, but clad in his many-caped driving cloak he filled the doorway. Giles tried to look in his direction but could not manage it. He himself stood rigidly beside the desk, dressed in his own brown cape, bravely ready for his dismissal both from the school and his uncle's esteem.

Mr Falkirk bowed his head briefly and stretched out his hand to Mr Gregory.

'Good of you to come yourself, Sir,' he said, 'a bad business, I'm sorry to say, a very bad business.'

'A bad business indeed Mr Falkirk,' agreed Mr Gregory, taking the man's hand momentarily and barely acknowledging the deputy headmaster's presence.

The headmaster cleared his throat but before he could embark on his prepared speech he found that Mr Gregory was speaking again.

'I have come,' he said rather deliberately, 'to hear my nephew's version of what has occurred. I assume that you have heard him out.'

Mr Falkirk looked enquiringly at Stokes. The man gave an infinitesimal shake of the head before answering the headmaster.

'The facts were self-evident Sir,' Stokes said snidely. 'There could be no satisfactory explanation other than the one at which we have arrived.'

'I disagree,' Mr Gregory said firmly. 'I think we should hear the tale.' Without giving the others a chance to reply he turned his bulk to Giles.

'Now, my boy,' he prompted, 'let us have this tale from its outset.'

Giles moistened his lips with his tongue, affeared to open his mouth unless it was truly what his uncle wanted. 'Come on, come on,' Mr Gregory urged him, 'start from the beginning, tell us it all.'

So, haltingly at first and then with more assurance as he realised that his uncle knew it all already, he told the three listening adults everything including the mauling he had received at the instigation of the deputy head.

'So you see, Mr Falkirk,' Mr Gregory said as he withdrew a

batch of papers from his breast pocket, 'there is always a different version of events to consider. And,' he said before pausing to eye the fuming Stokes, 'I have brought corroboration of my nephew's story.' He threw the papers down on the desk in front of the headmaster. 'You will find there a sworn affidavit by one Terence Norton, brother of Jessop Norton who currently adorns your sixth form. It seems that Mr Terence Norton's family loyalty stretches only as far as a fistful of guineas. He explains how he acted as a go-between for Digby Lambert to instruct his younger brother. Not content however with the testament of a Judas, my staff have statements also from frequenters of the dive in the city where these two met and devised their plot.' Suddenly he swung around and turned his attention to Stokes. 'I do not say,' he enunciated deliberately, 'that Mr Stokes was party to the plot but his enthusiasm to find my nephew guilty without trial speaks for itself.'

Mr Falkirk surprisingly appeared unperturbed by the accusations levelled at his deputy; in fact he seemed to relish them. He squared his shoulders and thanked Mr Gregory for the insight into the matter.

'I believe,' he said, 'that young Mr Thornton would be advised to take a few days rest with you, Sir,' he turned his head and directed his attention to Giles. 'And when you return next week the matter will have been dealt with.'

'That is what I came to hear,' said Mr Gregory, turning towards the door. 'Come Giles,' he commanded, 'come now with me.'

11

*G*iles' legs just managed to support him until he was outside the great oak main door and then they failed him. Fortunately Higginbottom had been hovering on the steps, unable to wait patiently in the carriage any longer. He caught Giles as he fell and prevented him from tumbling headlong down the steps.

'Quickly,' ordered Mr Gregory, rushing to support Giles too, 'he is dead with fatigue and hunger. Let us get him away from here to a posting house as soon as may be.'

They bundled him into the carriage, careless of his aches and pains and once they had him laid against the squabs, they loosened his neckerchief and undid the button of his shirt at the throat.

'He has not eaten since midday yesterday,' said Mr Gregory, thumping on the roof of the enclosed carriage with his cane. The vehicle moved off as Higginbottom bent Giles forward to try and make the boy recover from his faint.

'I have nothing with me, Sir, that I might give him,' he said anxiously, 'not even a flask.' Then he turned his attention to Giles as the boy groaned.

'You stay there, Master Giles,' Higginbottom beseeched him, preventing Giles from sitting up in his corner, 'do allow your head to clear please.'

Giles remained leaning forward and put his head in his hands, desperately trying to get a grasp on what had happened. The swaying of the carriage did nothing to aid him. His uncle patted his shoulder in an awkward manner, unused to any physical demonstration of emotion but feeling it was necessary on this occasion.

'There, there, my boy,' he said in his deep voice, 'it is done with now.' Yet each of the occupants knew that it was not. If Giles were to return to the school after the week was out, it would not be easy to walk back amongst his classmates as though nothing untoward had happened.

Only when Higginbottom and Mr Gregory were thoroughly convinced that Giles had recovered did they further their journey to Cheltenham. They had hastened to a private parlour at the first hostelry they came to and they had chivvied and pressured him into eating, adjuring him not to speak until he was sated. Unfortunately this was erroneous advice. Soon Giles' stomach hurt as much from the rush of too much food as it had done from the lack of it.

The journey home, therefore, was an uncomfortable one for him but he did not complain. He was too conscious of his own good fortune in being rescued to want to make any show of ingratitude. So it was not until he was readying himself for bed that either Higginbottom or Mr Gregory became aware of the full extent of his hurts.

Giles had greeted his mother cautiously and with reserve, knowing that his uncle did not wish to worry her unduly. Giles looked into his mother's pale anxious face and wondered whether perhaps she would have preferred the truth rather than a lukewarm and unconvincing account of the reason why he was temporarily at home before the conclusion of the Michaelmas term. Mr Gregory, knowing how tired Giles was, had banished him to his bedchamber with a promise of supper on a tray, which, privately, he thought Giles would not be awake to eat.

Giles had waited until his uncle had escorted his mother safely away to the Green Saloon before attempting the main stairs to his great square bedroom. His body had stiffened from the blows it had received and every movement brought fresh discomfort.

He took the stairs with great caution, leaning heavily on the solid oak banisters. Once he stumbled and had to pick himself up painfully, unaware that Higginbottom was crossing the hallway at the time. The little man made an involuntary movement to aid the boy, then thought better of it. He slipped quietly through the door to the servants' area, took the back stairs two at a time to be in Giles' room before the boy had even reached the top of the grand staircase.

Giles started when he discovered Higginbottom in his bedroom. He stood in the doorway, undecided as to what to say. It was a great honour to have his uncle's valet wait upon him and no little surprise considering Higginbottom's previous attitude towards him. Giles had gathered from what had been said during the interminable journey home that afternoon that Higginbottom had been principally responsible for his rescue but he did not know the details.

At the noise of the door catch clicking, Higginbottom turned from the bed where he had started to retrieve some of Giles' possessions from a roomy cloak bag. There was a moment's silence as man and boy looked at each other. Giles cleared his throat.

'I believe I have you to thank for my deliverance, Mr Higginbottom,' he said in a rather stilted voice, which masked the depth of his feelings. 'I am most grateful.'

Higginbottom was not deceived; he had seen how bravely the boy had borne the day and its indignities.

'Anything I can do for you, Master Giles, is a pleasure,' he said formally. 'I am your servant to command.' Then he saw the boy sag and he ran forward to grab his arm should he fall. The boy winced.

'Come, come quickly to the bed, Master Giles,' Higginbottom urged. He sat Giles gingerly on the edge of the four-poster and quickly removed the bag and its contents to the floor. He helped him sit back more securely. 'Let me see, let me see,' he said urgently as Giles' wooden fingers tried to prevent him from undressing him.

Giles covered the valet's fluttering hands with one of his own. 'You must swear you will not give Uncle an account of how badly I am hurt,' he said, his grey eyes searching the little man's wizened face.

'I can do no such thing, Master Giles,' Higginbottom replied roundly. 'My first duty is to serve him.' He paused and returned Giles' gaze intently. 'I do believe you would not want it any other way.'

Giles' eyes dropped. 'Of course you are right,' he said in a hoarse whisper. He released the man's hand and he let Higginbottom remove his outer garments. It was only when Higginbottom tried to remove his shirt that he resisted. Higginbottom suddenly saw why. One of the wounds had been weeping and the shirt had stuck to it. The little man left the bedside and went to tug on the bell-rope. When the knock came in response to his summons, he put himself bodily in the doorway so that the footman could not see past to the limp form on the bed.

'Hot water and some carbolic soap,' he commanded. 'Immediately man! No dawdling!' As this was the last thing any servant in the well-run Gregory household was inclined to do, the man knew it had to be a matter of some urgency. He attempted to see round Mr Higginbottom's small frame but the valet closed the door in his face.

For a moment Higginbottom was at a loss what to do next for his young charge. He moistened his lips before saying: 'I wonder should you return to this school, Master Giles? Methinks they will not easily treat you as a friend again.'

Giles raised his tired head and his eyes acknowledged the truth in what the valet said, but he voiced what they both knew to be of equal validity.

'I must return, Mr Higginbottom, I have no choice. Mine uncle has won me this reprieve, I must honour it.'

Higginbottom returned to the bed. 'But should you have any recurrence of trouble, Master Giles, I beg you to communicate it to me. We need not trouble Mrs Simon or Miss Makepeace.'

A look of chagrin crossed Giles' face. 'I know it was wrong of me to involve the ladies,' he said. 'And I cannot even say that had I known the consequences, my honour would have prevented me from doing so. For Miss Makepeace's intervention has prevented so much misery.' He looked earnestly into the valet's sympathetic face. 'My only defence is that I had no expectation of her coming to my rescue, no expectation at all. I was merely venting my misery and isolation to the one true friend I believed I had. I have found that I am more fortunate than I knew and that I had several friends who were prepared to come to my aid.'

'Oh please do not think I blame you, Master Giles!' said the valet hurriedly. 'Indeed I believe you had no alternative. All I am saying is that if it were to happen again it would be much more expedient if you sent word straight home.'

'You are very kind,' said Giles simply. Silence fell between them as they awaited the footman's return. Higginbottom stood for a moment looking at the boy, then some thought of action came to him and he began to move more candles near the bed so that he could see better how badly the boy was injured.

Despite the aid of the soap and water, it took a little time to ease the shirt off his back and Higginbottom had to stifle a gasp of dismay as he viewed the welts and weals on the slim frame before him. At last he had Giles in his nightshirt and propped up against the bolster.

'I will fetch you some supper, Master Giles,' he said quickly when he caught Giles' weary eyes looking at him.

'Not yet, I beg you,' Giles returned. 'I must know, I can wait no longer to find out. Will you tell me what Nathan Torrill and Gervase Lambert did to Mrs Simon Gregory and why?'

Higginbottom dithered, reluctant to divulge such a ghastly secret, but he knew Giles needed to know, as much to protect himself as Mrs Gregory. Higginbottom made his decision. He went to a side table and picked up its attendant raffia chair; he placed it in front of the bed and sat carefully down upon it.

'I do not know what prompted the late Mr Torrill,' he said

inexplicably but by way of prelude, 'the matter had rarely been discussed for some time. Mr Arthur Gregory, my master, had set Mrs Simon up in Strawberry Cottage some years before and had kept her quietly there because his mother refused to acknowledge her. His sisters took their lead from their mother. Mrs Simon Gregory remained out of sight and my master presumed out of mind.' Here Higginbottom stood up and took an agitated turn around the chair, then sat down again. 'Well it seems it had not been the case. When Mr Nathan Torrill came of age, his father made him party to the information that Mrs Simon Gregory had a claim on the Gregory family. Mr Nathan did not contain this information but shared it with his cousin, Mr Gervase Lambert.'

Again the little man paused but this time to look hard at Giles. 'Are you sure you want me to divulge to you the full enormity of what occurred?'

'Yes,' replied Giles emphatically, 'for if you do not, I will only presume worse.'

'It would be hard to do that,' mumbled Higginbottom.

'I beg your pardon?'

'Nothing. I continue.' Hastily he resumed his narrative. 'The conscious feeding of the fears of their mothers made them devise a plan to rid the Gregory family of what they saw as an unnecessary encumbrance and a drain on their inheritance. They visited Mrs Simon Gregory and threatened her; when she refused to leave, they returned later that night and ...', the valet took out a small linen handkerchief and mopped his brow, 'and....'

'Did they use her, Mr Higginbottom?' Giles' voice was quiet and controlled.

Higginbottom nodded jerkily.

'Both of them?'

'Both of them.'

'My God!'

For a moment both man and boy fell silent, then somehow Higginbottom found the words to continue.

'She would have suffered it alone and told no-one had I not discovered her early the next day huddled in the corner of that small parlour, her dress ripped, her reason absent. She was a pitiful sight, defiled and terrified, a victim of their manifest evil. It took many a day for her to recover. Mr Arthur had the doctor to her but all his composers could not eradicate from her mind what they had done. She would not leave the cottage, not even to be cared for here. She feared it would bring further terrible retribution.'

Higginbottom stopped to catch his breath for he had rushed his fences and had allowed the words to tumble out.

'How long ago was this, Higginbottom?'

Higginbottom marvelled at the boy's control; he was taking the news better than he himself was delivering it.

'Mr Nathan wants but a year until his thirtieth birthday.'

'Eight years.'

'Eight years.' Higginbottom confirmed the boy's calculation. 'Eight years since Mr Nathan and Mr Gervase have been banned from this house and lands. Mr Arthur struck them out of his will on that very day. There never will be any forgiveness in that quarter.'

'As indeed there should not,' agreed Giles. The boy slipped down into the bed.

'Thank you, I needed to know,' he said.

Higginbottom nodded and stood up from the chair. 'I will get you your supper now, Master Giles.' He turned to go.

'Yes, thank you.' Giles jerked up, suddenly. 'No wait, one more thing.'

Higginbottom turned again to the bed. 'What more do you need to know,' he asked bitterly, his nerves on edge, his conscience stinging.

'My uncle, why has he never married?'

'That is not for me to say.'

'I know, I am sorry.' The boy was instantly contrite; he did not want to alienate his new-found friend.

Higginbottom relented. 'It is only conjecture on my part,' he said with a hint of a smile. 'But I believe he has always had a fondness for Mrs Simon Gregory, but the complications, the distress it would have caused had he pursued it would have made it an impossibility and after the attack unthinkable. She would not, could not, ever entertain a liaison with a man again. And a man cannot marry his brother's wife afterall.'

Giles nodded, accepting Higginbottom's interpretation of history. It made sense; there could be no other reasons for his uncle's abstinence.

Higginbottom hurried away to fetch the tray which Mrs Ellis and the butler, Mr Daniels, had been trying to decide whether they should have sent up.

'You have done enough, Mr Higginbottom,' said the stately butler, who tended to take a paternalistic attitude to all his underlings. 'Let me send Patrick up with it. Mr Gregory will be asking for you soon.'

The bell on the wall jangled, indicating that Mr Gregory was now in his bedchamber. Higginbottom smiled. 'I will take it on my way,' he said. 'Perhaps you would be good enough to ask Patrick to remove it for me in half an hour?'

Mr Higginbottom climbed the stairs again carrying a carefully prepared tray, every item on it designed to tempt an ailing boy. There was a fruit jelly, sweetmeats, tiny macaroons and some lightly boiled chicken. The glass was full of fresh lemonade.

On entering the bedchamber, Higginbottom was momentarily disconcerted to discover that Giles was fast asleep. He looked at the tray and thought of the consternation below stairs if nothing was touched. So, with alacrity and a certain amount of relish, the sorely tried little man stuffed his mouth full of food, swigged the lemonade, blew out the candles and then placed the disarranged tray quietly on the floor outside the door. Brushing his mouth with the back of his hand, he straightened his waistcoat and headed for his master's room.

12

Giles awoke late the next morning. The curtains around his bed had been drawn back and light was sneaking through the gaps between the heavy drapes at the window. He was warm and relatively comfortable; he wished it were possible to stay where he was. He imagined it had to be quite late if there was already strong light from outside but a great lethargy had overtaken him and he felt no inclination to move. It was not however many minutes before there was a discreet knock on the door and Patrick, the footman, entered the room cautiously. He was carrying a pitcher full of steaming water.

'Good morning, Master Giles,' he said as his eyes accustomed themselves to the gloom and he could divine that Giles was awake.

'Good morning, Patrick,' Giles replied courteously. 'What hour is it, pray? Have I slept very late?'

The stolid man's face lightened. 'I'm afraid it is beyond a quarter past eleven, Sir and Mr Gregory wishes to make a morning call to Castle Leck. He asked me to establish whether you were inclined to accompany him.'

Realising this was the one opportunity he might have to see Felicia and thank her before he had to return to school, Giles scrambled out of bed, ignoring his protesting body.

'Yes, yes please Patrick, tell my uncle, I indeed wish to go with him.'

It did not take Giles long to make himself presentable but he was glad that no-one was there to see him gasp and wince as he dressed himself. No sooner had he dressed than he ran helter-skelter down to the breakfast parlour where he found some cold bacon and kidneys. The butler, much put out at the thought of him eating these, attempted to order more from the kitchens but Giles would not allow it. So, it was not long after noon that he presented himself to his uncle, ready for departure.

Mr Gregory had decided to grace the expedition with a ride in his high perch phaeton. It was a bright but brittle day and he adjured Giles to wrap up before setting out in an open vehicle.

'Are Mama and my sisters not accompanying us?' asked Giles, a little nonplussed.

'No,' replied his uncle as he gathered up the reins. 'Your sisters are already there studying with Miss Cuthbert.' He lowered his voice so that the groom hanging on the back would not hear his words. 'Your poor mama, I banished her to her room with a composer and Mrs Ellis in attendance. I was forced to give her a fuller account of your trials than I would have liked. She was determined to know all but as I feared it took its toll.'

Giles turned his head away in chagrin to look up the steepness of the hill. Misjudging the boy's reaction Mr Gregory was quick to justify himself.

'I had no choice, young man,' he said sternly, 'she is your mother, she is entitled to know.'

Hastily Giles turned to assure him that he had implied no criticism of his uncle or his actions. It was his own predicament he regretted if it had caused his mother a moment's distress.

The older man accepted the boy's apology and he turned to more comfortable subjects. It was not a long drive so they were soon sweeping up the drive of Castle Leck. Their way was circuitous as the drive formed a great arc around the building, shielded from it by a dramatic ha-ha on three sides. Beyond the great gateway Mr Gregory drew his horses to a halt on the cobbles and alighted, handing the reins over to the groom.

They were soon ushered in by Hayworth and found the family in the vaulted drawing room.

Felicia looked up from her embroidery as they entered and her eyes flashed angrily at Giles. She remained seated in her chair and made no attempt to appear welcoming. Fortunately her parents were too busy making much of Mr Gregory and Giles to notice her odd reaction.

Eventually, as refreshments were served, Giles manoeuvred himself into her orbit.

'What ails you, my felicity?' he asked, a smile flickering across his face as he laughed inwardly at the irony of his saviour now glowering at him.

'I have heard nothing from you,' she hissed angrily. 'Nothing, no word that you were safe. I have been so worried but it is of no matter to you. I hate you, Giles Thornton.'

Giles saw her lips tremble and guessed she was close to tears. He was not to know that those were tears of relief that he could still walk into their drawing room with his head held high.

'I have had no opportunity, believe me,' he said quietly, trying to encourage her to put down her stitchery and walk a little apart from the others so that they would not be overheard.

'Why should I believe you, you ungrateful rat,' she said, her tone if not her words reaching her mother's ears.

'What's amiss Felicia?' that lady asked.

The girl had to pull herself up short. 'Nothing Mama,' she managed, 'I just set a stitch wrongly.'

'Well put it aside, child. We have guests, please put it aside.'

Doing as she was bid, Felicia rose abruptly and followed Giles to the window embrasure.

'So,' she demanded rather imperiously when they were well away from the adult group, 'what are your excuses?'

So, in a hushed voice, he told her of his ordeal, sparing her nothing and expressing his gratitude in such a heartfelt way that she could not help being mollified.

'I am on Mr Higginbottom's instruction not to bother you with my troubles in future,' he said quietly. 'I do not, however, believe that I am man enough to withhold my anxieties from you. You were the first true friend I have ever had and I find I cannot compromise that friendship.'

'And nor should you have to,' said Felicia boldly. 'You can always call on me, as I hope I can you.'

There was someone else on whom Giles wished to call. He knew that Higginbottom had sent a reassuring message to Mrs Gregory as soon as they had reached The Chimneys safely but he still wanted to see her and thank her personally.

It was not until the day before he was due to return to school that Giles was able to make his way to Strawberry Cottage. Mrs Gregory was so pleased to see him that she almost embraced him. In his usual courteous and sincere manner he made it all too apparent how grateful he was. Again Giles was required to tell the tale and although he tried to expunge the more lurid details, Mrs Gregory would have none of it, and while the colour of her normally pale face fluctuated wildly, she did not succumb to tears or vapours.

'I wish I could believe the matter is now resolved for good,' she said at the end of Giles' recital.

'Do you think Digby Lambert will try again?' asked Giles fearfully.

Mrs Gregory wrapped her heavy woollen shawl more tightly around her and shivered. 'I think the scheme was too clever for Digby Lambert,' she said in a hollow voice. 'It is my belief that Nathan Torrill is behind it all and he will not desist because of one setback, mark my words!'

Miles away in one of London's seediest taverns the aforementioned Nathan Torrill was currently berating his younger cousin.

'You are a fool,' he yelled at him, banging his tankard hard down on the table so that the liquid inside sloshed over the table. 'Could you not have picked a more reliable tool than Norton?'

'I'm most heartily sorry, Torrill, but how was I to know the bounder would sell his own brother down the river when it came to it?'

Nathan Torrill grabbed his cousin's cravat across the table and forced the man's head close to his. There was a vicious twist to his mouth.

'I would sell you, in such circumstance, you misbegotten cur, if you do not come up with other ways to ruin the Thornton boy.'

'Let me go,' demanded Lambert, trying to retain his dignity. 'If you are so clever you do the business. You don't need me.' He wrenched himself free and stood up from the table.

Torrill, seeing that he had pushed his cousin too far, attempted to appease him but in his anger and frustration he had failed to get the measure of his younger cousin. It had occurred to Digby Lambert as he looked into the livid face of his cousin, that Torrill felt no loyalty to him. If plans went wrong he, Lambert, would be the one at whom fingers of blame would be pointed. Digby realised in a moment of blinding clarity that he had no desire to fall further in his uncle's esteem. He planned to put a greater distance between himself and Nathan and if he were to go to perdition, he would do so on his own terms and not those of Nathan Torrill.

Giles returned to school to find that he now enjoyed a study of his own; even the sickly Johnson had been removed elsewhere. Giles tried not to grieve for the loss of Guilliam's friendship. He held his head high and walked amongst his fellow students as though nothing had happened but it was easy to see that he was still the topic of many a corridor conversation or some hushed sniggering in the dining hall. Few it seemed were prepared to forgive his part, however unwitting, in the expulsion of Norton. Some days Giles struggled to overcome the intensity of the rejection by his fellows; then he would catch sight of one of the letters written to him by either Mrs Gregory or Felicia, who now used Mrs Gregory as a conduit, and would stiffen his resolve to see the term through.

When the end of term came though, he could not put aside his melancholy, for this was to be the first Christmas without his father who had always made the festive season a delight in so many little ways. He was used to wrap a myriad of tiny packages for his children and adoring wife and hide them around their compact house. Once returned from church they would spend a merry morning hunting out their goodies until it was time to eat the sumptuous meal cook had prepared.

Giles was not to know that Mr Gregory, prompted by Higginbottom, had secured an invitation to spend Christmas Day at Castle Leck. The celebrations at this fairy-tale building were so wildly different from anything he had previously experienced that it was easy to put aside past Christmases.

Giles and Felicia were not allowed much private time together but they spent hours playing silly party games with Sophia and Imogen and on some occasions with Miss Cuthbert and Mrs Makepeace who had a laughing soul and could make any game seem jolly and amusing. Mrs Thornton was not quite able to put aside her mourning and would smile wistfully at the jollifications. Her brother, whose first concern appeared to be her comfort, would honour her with every attention and even she had to admit that she had enjoyed the day more than she would previously have imagined possible.

Boxing Day saw Giles and Felicia out watching the meet. Mr Gregory had invited them both to accompany him there and had them sampling some of the steaming mulled wine. The baying of the dogs and the stamping of the many horse's feet combined with the mist of warm breath in the cold air was a scene Giles committed to memory for the long hours when he would be alone at school.

Before he knew it, and with only a fleeting visit to Mrs Gregory, it was time to return to school and the term, from its beginning, seemed to him to stretch out interminably before him. Stoically he battled through it, only talking when spoken to by masters or servants. The loneliness cut him to the quick; without Felicia's chirpy missives and Mrs Gregory's sound words of support, he thought he would have packed his bags and made his own way home long before the term had passed its midway point.

When Easter came it was a great relief, but the weather was unkind and Giles and Felicia were only able to snatch two days to visit Mrs Gregory and to explore the surrounding area. Felicia was almost in tears when she said her goodbyes to him before he returned for the summer term. His face was bleak and closed and she knew he was steeling himself to face yet another ordeal of loneliness, the outcast in an unforgiving regime.

Giles had endured some three weeks of the term when, sitting at his desk in his lonely, austere study, he looked up and was surprised to see Guilliam standing in the doorway. That young man had put on some inches since the summer before and had thickened out. He had begun to take on the appearance of a man. There was a heavy moment of silence while their eyes met and held. Giles laid down his pen and waited.

'There is nothing I can say to ameliorate the damage I have done,' said Guilliam in a strangled voice.

Giles remained silent, watching, waiting, the throbbing of a pulse in his neck the only indication that he was, in any way, thrown by this unexpected visit.

'Oh God, Thornton, I'm sorry for what I have done, for failing you at a time when you needed a friend, but I entreat you to forgive me and I will do my utmost to make your life tolerable again.'

Giles blinked. 'Why now?' he asked. 'Has my uncle some deal in the offing that would be advantageous to your father?' he added cynically.

Guilliam showed an appalled face.

'Is that how low I have sunk in your esteem?' he groaned. 'I should have expected it. After all there is no reason for you to trust me after what I have done. I am, however, determined to win back your friendship.'

'As I have already said, it begs the question, why? Why now? Why at all?' Giles was riding his erstwhile friend hard. He could not believe that Guilliam was simply there to make amends.

'Tis a home question' agreed Guilliam. 'I cannot tell you except to explain that my mama was asking after you during the

Easter break. She reminded me what times we had enjoyed during your stay with me and the promises you made to show me your home and I knew I had made a profound mistake.' Bravely he stretched out his hand, a forlorn and tentative gesture to which there was little certainty Giles would respond. 'Forgive me, Thornton, Giles, I beg.'

As Giles looked at the outstretched hand, he was conscious of an overwhelming desire to slap it away for it ignited all the bitterness and resentment he had stifled over the months. He raised his eyes to meet, fleetingly, the beseeching gaze of his companion and found he could not reject him. With a hasty scrape of the legs of the chair on the floor, he stood up and grasped Guilliam's palm.

Guilliam moved to embrace him but Giles was not ready for such a breach of his defences; he withdrew and stood a bit away from him.

'What now?' he asked abruptly. 'Do you acknowledge me in front of others or is this thaw to be our secret?' He could not quite keep the hint of sarcasm from his voice.

'Now I have to prove my mettle, as you have proved yours over the last few months,' came the determined reply.

13

*T*here was an audible ripple of surprise that evening as Giles and Guilliam entered the dining room together chatting informally. It had escaped few pupils' attention that Giles Thornton was a pariah and should not be included in any social activity. To see one of the most respected seniors in the school behaving to him as though they were intimates was a wonder to behold. For a few days the school buzzed with uncertainty. The headmaster appeared to smile benignly at the new turn of events but Mr Stokes, the deputy head, seemed determined not to allow the new friendship to prosper. Guilliam found himself heaped with extra duties and punishments for the most trivial of misdemeanours. Smilingly, Guilliam took it in his stride and never wavered from his intent to prove to Giles that he was once again his friend.

Soon, however, as with all such events, the school became accustomed to the sound of Giles' voice which had been silent for so long and other sixth-formers, interested in the discussions between Guilliam and Giles, began to chip in and contribute their bit. It became clear to Mr Stokes that Thornton had to be allowed into the fold and he dropped his overt hostility. He would have done mischief if he could but even he saw that to be discovered penalising the dependants of two of the school's most generous sponsors would jeopardise his own position.

For Giles the rest of the term progressed speedily. He wrote light-hearted letters to Mrs Gregory and to Felicia and thanked

God that whatever Guilliam's motives he had made one of the few remaining terms bearable. If he could not quite quench the nagging voice in the back of his mind that told him the term he had spent in isolation would not be dissimilar to the years he would spend at the bank, he did at least muffle it so that he only heard it when he had woken unexpectedly in the middle of the night or when the dawn chorus was at its height at four thirty in the morning.

Giles, conscious of the promise made long ago, wrote to his uncle asking if Guilliam might spend a fortnight of the summer with them at The Chimnies. Mr Gregory wrote back an effusive and enthusiastic reply that did nothing to mask his relief in finding Giles still had a friend.

The only person who did not receive the news well was Felicia. She wrote him an angry letter explaining in detail her disappointment that he had once again made her wait to enjoy his company to herself.

Giles could not help but smile when he read the letter. His felicity, as he thought of her, was a girl of clear emotions; now that she was fourteen she was becoming more woman than child and he wished that her anger could be interpreted as a deepening of feelings between them, however impossible any future there could be for them. He had not forgotten that she was promised to her cousin and that he was destined for the dark and gloomy offices of his uncle's business. But a man could dream and it had been these dreams that had kept him stoically bearing the miseries of isolation at school. The reawakening of Guilliam's friendship had put aside the more fanciful of his aspirations, although a kernel of longing remained to be ignited by the flames of Felicia's intemperate letter. Giles wondered whether he should warn Guilliam that he might meet with hostility from this quarter. Then it occurred to him that it would be a breach of confidence to expose his friendship with that young lady, so he kept quiet and hoped that Felicia would contain her feelings in the presence of his guest.

The journey to The Chimnies at the end of the summer term was a light-hearted jaunt. Mr Gregory had sent an open-topped carriage and the coachman allowed the boys time to tool the equipage. Guilliam, much more experienced than Giles, had the horses well up to their bits and had them trotting smartly up the leafy lanes. Giles, on the other hand, needed constant instruction and good-naturedly took all the advice his friend and the old retainer offered him. When he finally mastered a corner without snagging the verge and avoided a ruinous pothole, Guilliam was moved to slap him on the back and compliment him.

'Well done, indeed, Thornton,' he laughed, 'we will make you a first-rate horseman.'

'Oh the young master is a fair enough horseman,' Costley, the coachman expostulated. 'Tis just that he had not experienced driving a team before.'

'I see you have a champion, Thornton,' laughed Guilliam. 'I must watch my step at this Chimnies of yours.'

'It is not my Chimnies,' said Giles uncomfortably. 'It is my uncle's. He is good enough to allow us to make it our home.'

Guilliam, conscious that he had offended his friend in some way, fell silent and allowed the coachman to continue to instruct Giles on his driving technique. It was clear to Guilliam that whatever Giles might think, the servants saw him as the heir and treated him with respect and not a little affection. For him that spoke volumes.

Sooner than either had expected, the great square house was reached. Guilliam, used as he was to grand seats, was a little taken aback by the imposing nature of the house, nestled as it was amongst the tall hardwood trees on the escarpment.

'Good heavens, Thornton, you never said the house was half as fine. It is magnificent.'

Giles laughed at the good-natured compliment as he sprang lightly from the carriage. 'Ah you may say so,' he agreed, 'but you have yet to view Castle Leck, our neighbour's house. There you will find a matchless grandeur and magnificence with which we cannot compete!'

Guilliam, still sitting above him, looked keenly at him. 'A Castle!' he exclaimed. 'And is there a princess imprisoned in some tower?'

'There is Miss Felicia Makepeace,' conceded Giles, thinking it best to have her name mentioned as a result of some casual enquiry rather than at some forced introduction. 'But Miss Makepeace is a resourceful girl and I believe would be inclined to rescue herself rather than await forlornly aloft.'

'Very interesting,' said Guilliam, trying to find in Giles' face any hint of what he might think of this young lady. Giles met his keen gaze with a bland expression. Guilliam was forced to look away and find some other topic. He gave the house another look and found a safer course of questioning.

'This house I understood to be called The Chimnies,' he said, alighting at last so that Costley could take his tired horses away to the stable. 'Forgive me if I err, for while I see a number of fine Chimneys, they are neither so grand nor in such great numbers as to be worthy of the honour as the name of the house.'

Giles laughed. 'It is not the chimneys of the house,' he said before dropping his voice to a hoarse whisper, 'but the Devil's chimney after which it is named.'

'You jest! What can you mean?' Guilliam was a touch alarmed. Again Giles laughed.

'Down the hill a little way there is a spectacular stone stack that rejoices in the name of the Devil's Chimney,' he said. 'I will take you there one of these fine days.'

By now they had reached the main entrance and the door was flung open by Mr Daniels before they even had the chance to sound the great iron bell.

Again Guilliam witnessed the enthusiasm and affection with which Giles was received and he had to admire the young man's kindness and interest in each of the servants as they came to offer him some slight service. Guilliam acknowledged that while he had always been trained to be polite to the army of staff his father employed, he had never suffered himself to learn more than their names and occupations. Giles it seemed knew of their families and their health. It struck Guilliam that Giles would make a fine successor to his uncle who had the reputation of being a philanthropist. He wondered if the uncle saw it as clearly as all his servants did. As this thought scudded across his mind, Mr Gregory came forth from his study to greet the new arrivals.

'Welcome, welcome,' he cried jovially, rubbing his hands with delight before putting out his great paw to engulf Guilliam's. 'I cannot tell you how delighted we are to welcome you to The Chimnies.' He released his hand only to place it on the young man's shoulder and guide him to the Green Saloon. 'Let me introduce you to m'sister Mrs Thornton and Giles' sisters Sophia and Imogen.'

Guilliam was surprised to find Giles' mother so quiet and frail in comparison to her gregarious brother. He was also disappointed to find that Sophia and Imogen were so young. There was, however still Miss Makepeace with whom he hoped to strike up an acquaintance in the next few days. Mr Gregory had promised a visit to Castle Leck.

The projected visit took place the very next day. Entering the impressive portals of Castle Leck, Guilliam was struck again by the finery to be found so far from the hub of London.

'You have a fine Castle, Mr Makepeace,' he was moved to say when introduced to his host. He would have liked to have discovered that Mr Makepeace had a fine daughter as well but though he had found her to be pretty enough, she had an angry sullen look to her face. He had not been granted more than a mumbled greeting and the faintest of curtseys.

The only aspect of the situation that offered any promise was that Giles was clearly amused by Miss Makepeace's expression. It made Guilliam watch her more closely than he had intended. As he was paying lip service to Mrs Makepeace's chitter-chatter, he kept a surreptitious eye on Giles and Miss Felicia Makepeace. He wished he could hear what passed between them.

'You should not scowl so, my felicity,' Giles had said as he passed her a glass of lemonade.

'Do not call me that,' she retorted angrily. 'I do not feel very felicitous now. You have not given me cause to do so.'

'Ah, but you continue to give me cause to be happy,' he countered. 'You are my friend.'

'I was your friend, I see you now have another.'

'Am I not allowed to enjoy friendship with you both?'

Felicia looked under her lashes across at Guilliam.

'I do not think so,' she said. Then after a moment's pause. 'I do not trust him or his motives,' she added darkly.

'While I detract nothing from your constant care and vigilance for me, Felicia, I must beg you not to see enemies where I have none,' said Giles, and considering he had spent as much time with her as he dared, he moved away to take his mother's cup and saucer from her.

The visit was soon over and Giles and Guilliam spent the next few days exploring the area. Costley had looked them out a gig and let Guilliam take charge of it although he knew Giles was perfectly capable of handling the ribbons of a single-horsed vehicle.

The young men scrambled to the base of the Devil's Chimney and Guilliam was tempted to climb it. Giles, however, dissuaded him.

'You are a cautious soul, Thornton,' Guilliam chided him after he had reluctantly withdrawn from the stack.

'Is it so unreasonable not to want to have you carried home on a pallet?' countered Giles. 'My uncle would be most displeased.'

Guilliam gave him a playful punch on the shoulder. 'And it is your constant resolve to be worthy of your uncle's good opinion.'

'It is indeed, he enjoys my undying gratitude.'

Guilliam looked into his friend's earnest young face and for a moment caught a glimpse of the burden the boy was carrying.

'You cannot be grateful for ever,' he said.

Giles' face darkened. 'Why must everyone be constantly

telling me that my gratitude is unnecessary, overindulged. If it is not you, tis Mrs Gr... Simon, Miss Makepeace, Higginbottom ...!'

'Ah Miss Makepeace,' Guilliam interrupted him. 'What is your interest there?'

'Interest?' asked Giles weakly, realising too late that he had given away too much in his irritation.

'Yes your interest,' Guilliam challenged him. 'She may not be the sunniest tempered but she is well enough to look at.'

'She is fourteen, Guilliam, a mere child!

Guilliam was surprised, for Miss Makepeace's charms were certainly more womanly than childlike.'

'And she is promised to her cousin,' Giles added, unwittingly giving an insight into his long-term hopes.

This conversation had Guilliam more keenly interested in Miss Makepeace. He knew himself to be well able to charm the ladies and he turned this to good account. He stayed close to Mrs Makepeace with a hope to be more readily available to strike up a conversation with her daughter. Miss Makepeace, however, kept him at arm's length and for the duration of the fortnight, he found he had not uttered more than six words together to her at any one time.

On the penultimate day of his visit, Giles took him to Strawberry Cottage to take his leave of Mrs Gregory. There had been a number of occasions when they had called there for refreshments during their rides and walks about the countryside. To Guilliam's intense surprise, they found Miss Makepeace leaving just as they appeared.

'If you will tarry a moment,' Giles said to her, 'we will walk you home and Guilliam can bid your parents goodbye.'

'There can be no need,' said Felicia ungraciously. 'I know my way and have no fear.'

Giving a quick glance around to see that Mrs Gregory had Guilliam's full attention Giles pressed home his case. 'Do this for me, Felicia,' he said. 'I mislike you walking these woods unattended.'

She looked up into his caring face and capitulated. She had allowed her irritation about the visit from his friend to wound him and she had not meant it to run so deep.

'Very well,' she agreed. 'I will wait at the gate.'

Guilliam had soon made his farewells and they were on the point of departure when Mrs Gregory called out to Giles. She had meant to ask him to carry down an ancient log-basket from her tiny loft and had only just recalled it.

Giles hurried in to favour her with his help, leaving Guilliam and Felicia standing uncomfortably together. After a moment's struggle Felicia thought of something to say.

'I do hope you have enjoyed your visit, Lord Guilliam,' she said coolly.

'Very much indeed, Miss Makepeace,' he responded quickly, grateful that she had broken the ice. 'This escarpment is very fine. I can readily see why your grandfather chose it for his Castle.'

'Is it not beautiful?' she agreed. 'I know of nothing better than to watch the changing seasons from its ramparts.'

'Giles had spoken of the view often and often, I was most desirous of seeing it.'

'It is hardly a sufficient reason though to be making up to him now.' The barb, uttered as it was in a light cold voice, momentarily left him bereft of speech. The girl was looking out at him from eyes veiled by long lashes. The curly hair that framed her face made her look so sweet and vulnerable. Guilliam wondered if he had heard her aright.

'What can you mean?' he blustered.

'Surely it is patently clear,' she replied, swift as an arrow. 'I mistrust your friendship with Giles. I wish you to know that Giles has true friends, who will act in his hour of need.'

Guilliam pushed back a lock of his dark brown hair that had fallen forward; dismay showed on his face. 'You know what happened then?' he asked.

'Chapter and verse and you were not part of the story line, my lord. You, knowing him better than most. You, who called yourself his friend, coolly turned your back on him. Giles does not need friends like you.'

Guilliam had to remind himself that he was talking to a young girl. It steadied him. 'In this world, Miss Makepeace, a man needs all the friends he can get.'

'And Giles more than most,' she said with feeling, 'but he needs reliable, honourable friends.' She began to move through the gate and walk slowly up the path when suddenly a thought assailed her. She turned on her heel to confront her companion.

'Do you know men going by the name of Torrill or Lambert?' she demanded.

Guilliam considered for a moment. 'I have heard the names,' he said slowly, confounded by the girl's strange behaviour. He thought Giles well out of any match with her, she was so unpredictable.

'But do you know Nathan Torrill or Gervase and Digby Lambert?'

'In connection with Thornton?'

'In connection with anything,' she cried, exasperated.

Guilliam shook his head. 'I can recall I have heard the name Torrill for it is unusual but I do not know the man.'

'Then if you truly are Giles' friend and want to prove your mettle, you will protect him from these men.' Felicia turned again and set off up the track. Luckily, however, Giles had finished his task and he came running up the garden to join his friends. Soon they were all walking towards Castle Leck.

14

'Who is Nathan Torrill?' Guilliam had waited until they were back at school the next term and alone together in the study they now shared.

Giles' golden head jerked up from his work in surprise. 'Why do you ask? From whom have you heard his name?'

'From your friend Miss Makepeace. She says I can only prove myself as your friend if I protect you from this man: I ask again, who is Nathan Torrill?'

'Fie on Felicia and her fears.' Giles dropped his head into his hands and ran his fingers through his thick locks. 'She will not let it rest.'

'Stop talking in riddles man and tell me all,' commanded Guilliam. So Giles explained in part about how Norton had only been a stooge. How it had been confirmed that Giles' cousin Digby Lambert had organised the thefts through Norton to discredit him but how both Mrs Simons and Felicia believed that Nathan Torrill had been the mastermind and that he would not halt just because he had been thwarted once.

'So Miss Makepeace would have me act as your bodyguard!' laughed Guilliam, not sure how deeply Giles believed these fears.

Giles grimaced. 'I don't know what to think,' he sighed. 'If my cousins believe that I am not yet my uncle's heir and that I must be discredited so that I do not become so, then perhaps I am at risk. However,' he drew a long breath, 'it is my understanding that my cousins have been completely ruled out so I do not see how they can expect to gain from ruining me.'

'A conundrum indeed,' agreed Guilliam, thinking, however, that a few gentle enquiries to his father would not go amiss. Miss Makepeace's words had driven needles into his conscience and he would have gladly proved to her that he deserved Giles' forgiveness.

Neither Giles nor Guilliam mentioned the matter again although neither could put it aside completely. For Giles the time at the school was passing too quickly, dragging him irresistibly towards the dreary, lonely life of drudgery. Sometimes he could feel a gnawing envy of Guilliam, who would have three carefree years at Oxford before he needs takeup any responsibilities. The days of freedom out in the countryside with Felicia seemed distant and took on a dreamlike quality. He dared not ask his uncle for one last summer, Mr Gregory had already shown him and his family so much kindness.

As the school year drew to a close and Giles was packing his bags for the final time, he could hardly bring himself to part formally with Guilliam. It seemed too final, too ghastly a wrench. Their ways would part forever, Guilliam to the round of events in the social calendar and possibly eventually politics and the House of Lords, Giles to the world of business and finance. His only comfort was that they would part with the sound of each other's good wishes in their ears.

Mr Gregory, only dimly aware of his nephew's fears for his own future, allowed Giles four weeks of summer break in Gloucestershire, but, as soon as the boy's nineteenth birthday was passed, his belongings, such as they were, were loaded on a carrier's cart and he followed on the stage to take up his new post. No amount of kindness from the staff nor wrapped offerings from the kitchen could make the journey feel anything but a banishment, a banishment from comfort and the care of his family. Giles sat numbly as the stage swayed and rattled him to his destination.

He arrived in London hungry, as none of the stops along the way had been sufficient to enable him to gulp more than a mouthful of a steaming drink or a morsel of food.

Despite it being August it was dark by the time he had arrived and he struggled to find his way to his lodgings in Little Wiggold Street, just north of the City. The premises when he found them, did nothing to lift his spirits; the house was narrow and crammed between two larger buildings. The doorstep was grimy and the road along which he had walked was filthy. He forbore to imagine what he might have stepped in on the way.

It took a few moments for the door to be opened in answer to his knock and he found himself looking up into the face of a huge and burly man with grizzled hair and a bulbous nose.

'Good evening, Sir,' said Giles diffidently, 'my name is Thornton and I believe lodgings have been arranged for me by Mr Alistair Sherbourne.' This, then, he decided was the seal on his misery. He had been advised by Higginbottom to write to Mr Sherbourne, Mr Gregory's man of business, and ask him to find lodgings for him. Giles had duly done as directed, requesting a plain and simple abode, which would not stretch his meagre purse. He had not expected luxury but he had not anticipated a hovel. He wanted to take to his heels and run and run until he reached Gloucestershire again. Before, however, the man could answer him, a busy little woman, wrapped in what looked like layers and layers of brightly patterned cloth, bustled passed the man.

'Well, so here you are dearie. Mr Sherbourne said you would be along tonight.' She turned to the big man. 'Take 'is bag then Mr B and we'll soon have him settled in.'

Then, much to Giles' surprise, she stepped out into the darkened street and indicated to him to follow her.

'No need to stand on the doorstep,' she admonished him as she drew her many shawls tighter around her shoulders. 'There's a nip in the air now the nights are drawing in.'

She led the way to the next-door house where there were candles burning in each of the big bow-fronted windows.

'I've made up a fire for you and there's a warming pan in the bed.' She continued to bubble. 'Mr Sherbourne suggested you might be 'ungry so there's an 'otpot on the range and some bread on the board.'

Soon Giles found himself upstairs and in a large front room that looked out over the street. The furniture was plain and heavy but there was enough candlelight to see that it was clean and tidy. There was a small but efficient fireplace in one corner and a desk in front of the window to catch the last of the day's light.

'Thank you,' breathed Giles in much relief, his worst fears not after all being realised.

'Me and Mr B, we live next door,' said the little lady as she made to leave. 'There's a bell in the 'allway which rings in with us if you need anything.' She put her hand on the knob when she thought of something else. 'We 'ave three other gentlemen 'ere staying at the moment. There's Mr Ribble, 'e keeps 'imself to 'imself, clerk to a local solicitor, Mr Dornoch, a nice man but a writer, then there's Mr Littlejohn, 'e's been working at the bank where you is for a couple of months now. 'E's a bit nosey but no 'arm in 'im. Now you get a good night's sleep as you've an early start in the morning.'

Giles took her advice. Once he'd sated himself on the hotpot, he rinsed his dishes in the great earthenware sink in the scullery and reclimbed the stairs to his bed, glad that he did not encounter any of the other paying guests on his way.

The first day at work held few surprises for Giles. He had already become acquainted with the workings of the bank on his previous visits and he was welcomed wholeheartedly both by Mr Sherbourne who was there to greet him and Mr Gregory's manager, Mr Ponsonby. However, there was no escaping the loneliness of the post he was to take up and he was soon installed with all the other clerks, who kept the cogs of Mr

Gregory's vast empire whirring. The other peaky young men, who were to be his companions for the foreseeable future, were polite enough but wary. They all knew who he was and thought they knew what he was destined to become. They watched and waited to see how Giles Thornton would comport himself before they would approach him with any semblance of friendship. And so the days were set for Giles, each the same except for Sunday when the bank and the counting house did not trade. Giles saw little daylight and less and less as winter approached. He prayed that he had the fortitude to withstand the privations of this life long enough to reach a position of authority and trust when he would have control over his own time again. His life stretched out before him, dauntingly restricted to the inside of the great buildings. There was no longer the wind and rain or flora and fauna to catch his interest and lift his spirits. All of this he could only enjoy second hand from the letters from Gloucestershire and they did not fail him; Mrs Gregory, becoming more articulate and lucid by the week, wrote every third day. Felicia wrote every day while his mother and sisters wrote weekly.

Again and again Giles could not think of a more aptly named person than his felicity. She took time to describe to him the changing patterns of the seasons and as autumn took hold she drew a picture with her words of the magnificence of the escarpment clad in its reds and golds. She would explain her feelings as her feet crunched on the first frost-covered ground and she found words to describe the smells and fragrances of her surroundings until his senses thought they were indeed assailed by the real thing. Felicia brought the countryside to him daily and he could return only his gratitude; there was little pleasure to be gained in harping on the shortcomings of his own surroundings. Felicia would have none of that, she wanted to know about the people with whom he worked, all their little idiosyncrasies and Giles' feelings about them. Soon she had him filling his evenings with the descriptions she was determined to receive. It whiled away the time and dragged his thoughts away from his drudgery.

Christmas was a difficult time for the family for Giles had to remain in London. Staff was only allowed the afternoon of Christmas Eve, Christmas Day itself and Boxing Day, so there was no opportunity to make his way home. He was not to know how much his mother longed for him and had even overcome her own timidity to ask Mr Gregory if Giles might not be allowed to come home. Mr Gregory itched to write the summons that would give his nephew a fortnight's holiday but he could not allow himself not do it. He knew the folly in setting the boy above his colleagues so he would not do it. Thus Giles remained in London and ate his Christmas lunch with Mr Sherbourne and his family, who would gladly have invited the boy without the request from his employer.

With the festive season over, another year arrived and quickly took up the baton of marching time. Before the families knew it, summer had passed and it was Christmas again. Mr and Mrs Makepeace began to look forward to bringing their daughter out. She was sixteen that April and they considered making the trip to London that year instead of the next but Felicia would have none of it and eventually wiser counsel prevailed in the person of her grandmother.

Mrs Makepeace senior rarely made the journey up the hill to Castle Leck. She had, however, acquired an interest in the business of the town. The whist parties she enjoyed so much frequently involved the businessmen of Cheltenham. Often parties were used to sound out financial backers for some venture or other. Mrs Makepeace, knowing that the men talked freely assuming the women had no interest, found increasingly that she understood their reasoning and unerringly found that ventures where she would have staked her money, had she had any, would prosper and those she mistrusted failed. Such had been her success that she felt it behoved her to point her son in the right direction. She had been moved to get into her carriage and make the journey to Castle Leck. She had arrived to find her granddaughter mulish and at odds with her mother.

'Good heavens, you cannot surely expect the girl to take on a season at barely sixteen,' she exclaimed when the situation was explained to her, 'why must you be in such haste to be rid of her?'

Here the normally cheerful Mrs Elsie Makepeace burst into tears. 'Harold continues to fear for the future,' she said once she had sent Felicia from the room. 'He heard a whisper on his last visit to Yorkshire that young Bertram is fixing his interest with a local girl. It seems he may well renege on the agreement to marry Felicia.'

'My dear Elsie,' said her mother-in-law with more authority than she was wont to use, 'how can you imagine that trying to jockey him into an engagement with Felicia will turn his attention away from this other girl. It is more likely to harden his resolve and turn something that was just a youthful dalliance into a more serious liaison. He is still very young, is he not? Not more than twenty if my memory serves me correctly.'

Luckily for Felicia her grandmother's words had enough wisdom in them to persuade the Makepeaces to abandon the project. Less fortunately, Harold Makepeace, unable to credit his mother with any business acumen, was not prepared to advance her the money to allow her to invest in some land that she believed would become very valuable.

'I'm sorry Mama,' he said stiffly, 'but I can ill afford to speculate at this time. There are many calls upon my income. Mills are setting up throughout Yorkshire and I must be seen to be supporting them.'

'This is all very fine, Harold,' replied his exasperated mother, 'but any investment you make up there will go with the land and the land is entailed away. Further you cannot keep a weather eye on what goes on. I know you visit every month,' she said quickly as he was moved to protest, 'but much can be hidden from an absent landlord. Now if you were to buy land here, you would be in sight of it. No one would be able to cheat you.'

Mr Makepeace, his usual cocksureness reduced by his mother's words, looked sadly at her. 'I perceive the benefits of what you say, Mama,' he said, 'but I cannot throw away money on a hunch, a speculation.'

'It is hardly that, Harold!' cried Mrs Makepeace. 'When such notables as Mr Wheatfield and Mr Emery think that much building will need to be done to accommodate the visitors to the spa! Year after year we see more people coming to take the waters. All I ask you to do is buy some land close to the town so that as the town grows we can prosper.

Nothing she could say would shift him. He was determined that he must not speculate, so he turned his back on her advice and did not even follow its fortunes. Much to his mother's grim satisfaction, the land she had tried to persuade him to buy was sold the following January for three times its original price. By the time the younger Makepeaces were preparing for their visit to London to grace the season, men were clearing the land to start the building work.

15

*A*cceptance had finally crept up on Felicia. She must have a season now that she was seventeen. Her acceptance, though welcomed by her parents, would have flustered them had they known that she intended to find a way to visit Giles. She had never faltered with her letter writing but she had found that she could no longer visualise his face. When she thought of him, she could recall only the vivid blue of his eyes and the thick golden hair; she could not remember the line of his nose or the curve of his mouth. More than two and a half years had passed and she longed to see him. If this meant she had to subject herself to meetings with her cousin, then it was a price she was prepared to pay.

Despite this she had repeatedly informed her parents that she would not submit to a betrothal with her cousin, so when she discovered her mother dissolved in tears in one of the back parlours, she presumed that this reluctance was the cause.

'Oh Mama,' she cried aghast as she perceived Mrs Makepeace slumped in a small padded chair with a handkerchief held to her face. 'Please do not take it so. I would not have you distressed by my recalcitrance for anything but I am sure you cannot want me to enter into a marriage which would only cause me unhappiness.'

In answer, her mother simply gave out a muffled sob. Felicia came further into the room and sank to her knees by her mother. She grasped the free hand that was now clutching the handkerchief.

'I have to tell you it is impossible for me to marry my cousin Bertram. I cannot marry a man I do not know.'

'But you must, my dear,' said her mother in deep anguish. 'There can no longer be any doubt. Circumstances leave us no choice.'

The desperate edge to her voice was new. It occurred to Felicia that something further had happened to produce this new depth of feeling in her mother.

'I do not understand, Mama,' she said forlornly. 'There are other men, who might have fortune enough to keep me at the Castle. And I could accept no man to husband, who would cast you out of your home should anything happen to my father. Why this need for it to be my cousin?'

Mrs Makepeace drew herself up to a forward sitting position in the chair and looked searchingly into her daughter's face. What she saw there must have profoundly affected her because she began to weep gently and earnestly.

Bewildered, Felicia put her arms around her mother's slight form and began to rock her as though she was a sick child.

Eventually, Mrs Makepeace mastered her distress and began to dab her eyes with the now very moist handkerchief.

'I do not say no man will take you with only the Castle as dowry, my dear,' she said haltingly. 'Indeed I am sure, many would enjoy owning such a folly but it is no longer that simple.' She broke out into a fresh wave of weeping.

'Oh Mama, Mama tell me what has befallen us. Please tell me,' Felicia beseeched the crying woman.

Mrs Makepeace shook her head. 'I cannot,' she gulped.

'Please try.'

The simple appeal reached Mrs Makepeace and she raised her head to look at her daughter.

'You are no longer a child, are you, my dear?' she said unanswerably.

Felicia waited expectantly.

'I am with child.'

'I beg your pardon.' Felicia hardly believed she had heard the words.

'I am with child,' repeated her mother and started to cry. 'All these years we waited for more children. Longing for the brothers and sisters you deserved but there was nothing, not even a failed pregnancy. Then the years when we accepted we had only you and we tried to make provision. Now this. What am I going to tell your father?' She blew her nose. 'I cannot tell your father.'

'Father does not know?'

'No, nor shall he yet,' snapped her mother. 'Do you hear. He must not know yet.'

'But why not?' Felicia was floundering.

'Oh sweetheart, do you not see?' wailed her mother. 'Imagine it. He will be so sure it is a boy, he will be filled with hope that the Yorkshire estates will be saved. Then think of the disappointment and the difficulties if it is a girl, not one daughter to dower but two. Two to share the Castle with no additional income to finance it.'

Felicia saw instantly her mother's reasoning although she did not feel that a second daughter would be the terrible burden her mother obviously perceived it to be. The Castle would still require the same amount of money to maintain it whether there was one daughter or two.

'So what do we do now?' she asked her mother.

Mrs Makepeace seemed to give herself a mental shake.

'We say nothing, we go to London and we meet your cousin Bertram,' she said with decision.

Felicia opened her mouth to protest, then thought better of it; perhaps when her mother had become more used to the idea of another child, she would see matters as Felicia did.

The Makepeaces made the journey to London at the end of April. Mrs Makepeace had so far kept her pregnancy from her husband. In this, she was aided by the fact that she was not much sick. Only her personal maid was aware of the change in her and she was wedded to her lady's interests so wild horses would not have dragged the information from her.

The journey took them two days and they stayed overnight in Reading. As they drew closer to the metropolis, Felicia put aside her reluctance and allowed a bubble of excitement to rise inside her. Even if she was unable to see Giles frequently, at least she would be nearer him; that thought alone gave her comfort.

The house Harold Makepeace had hired was commodious rather than large but it was very well situated in Endsleigh Gardens, close to the most fashionable areas where the grand houses of the very wealthy stood. Felicia was enchanted with it. Its pale stone reminded her of the new buildings in Cheltenham and neither she nor the servants, used as they were to the many staircases at Castle Leck, thought anything of the fact that it had five storeys.

The Makepeaces had hardly been there a day before they received a visit from Mr Harold's Uncle, Bartholomew Makepeace. He was a larger version of his nephew and he carried more weight. This had a tendency to accentuate the slightly pompous and portentous inclination of the family. Felicia did not take to him well and thought that if his son, Bertram, to whom she was promised, was in a similar mould then she would do well to refuse to marry him.

'My wife holds a select soirée two nights hence,' pronounced Mr Bartholomew Makepeace. 'We do not intend to hold a vast ball for our daughter Jemima's come out, for her elder sister, Eustacia, has not yet found a husband and we do not wish to draw attention to it. Mrs Makepeace feels that we can delay Jemima's come out no longer, she is already two and twenty.'

Felicia was moved to feel sympathy for the unknown Jemima. She could not imagine staying at home for six years waiting for an elder sister to find a husband, nor having parents who would insist upon it.

Both Felicia's parents made what sounded to her ears like slightly spurious indications of sympathy and then accepted the invitation with alacrity. It was as well to make an entrée as early in the season as possible so that other invitations could be gleaned upon the way.

'Will we be holding a party?' Felicia asked once he had left.

Mrs Makepeace showed a wan face. 'Indeed I hope so,' she said but did not sound as though she would have the energy to do so. Felicia noticed for the first time that her mother's vibrant hair now had streaks of grey in it. She longed to comfort her but her father's presence forestalled her.

'Of course we will be having a party,' asserted Mr Makepeace. 'You said yourself Elsie that it was of paramount importance that we should, why else have we brought Miss Cuthbert along but to help you with arrangements.'

The women's eyes met. Both knew that Miss Cuthbert had been chivvied into coming because Mrs Makepeace had foreseen a time when she would not feel up to the endless circle of parties and events. Miss Cuthbert, little did she know it, had come in the role of chaperone.

The soirée at Mr Bartholomew Makepeace's house was smarter than his nephew's family had been given to understand. There were many notable figures of the day in attendance and Felicia had to wonder how her great uncle, living as he did on the edges of their estate in Yorkshire, had managed to become a member of the ton.

'Oh the Makepeaces have always been well connected,' her mother told her wearily as they returned from the very successful evening. Jemima it appeared was quite a beauty with dusky curls and fine grey eyes. Her sister, Eustacia, whatever her similarities of looks to her younger sister, was shrewish and had a pinched expression to her face. Neither Felicia nor her mother spent time speculating as to why she had not obtained a husband nor why it looked as though Jemima would find one very quickly.

As a result of various introductions at the Bartholomew Makepeaces' house, two days forward found the Harold Makepeace family attending the come-out ball of a Miss Celeste

Ingelby, the daughter of one Sir Anthony Ingelby. To a girl brought up in a Castle, the size of room did not have the power to impress Miss Makepeace; however, the decor, which owed much to the Indian subcontinent, held her spellbound for some moments when she entered the ballroom. There were great golden and wooden statues of elephants, rich red and gold hangings and figures of multi-limbed goddesses that greeted her. Sir Anthony had made his fortune in India and wished to announce it to the polite world.

When Felicia had finally feasted her eyes on these marvels, she looked down at her dance card that was woefully empty. Only one name appeared on it and that had been placed there reluctantly by her cousin Bertram. The much-heralded meeting between the young couple had been tamely effected. He had been in the line-up at his sister's party and unable to look into his face, Felicia had received the impression of a stolid young man of medium height. In mutual embarrassment, they had bowed and curtseyed respectively and had moved on. Felicia from then on had only seen him when he moved to make introductions or to ensure that she was being cared for. His manners were well enough but he had little natural charm and Felicia had found herself comparing him unfavourably with Giles. Giles would have carried out the duties of host with a delightful willingness, leaving behind the impression that he was well pleased to serve the guest in any way he could.

Felicia had warmed slightly to her cousin the next day when he had arrived at their home for a visit of ceremony. He had attempted conversation and seemed at least prepared to become acquainted with her. Felicia, however, could sense in him a clear reluctance to embark on any behaviour that might hint of his willingness to wed her. Felicia could have laughed out loud when it dawned upon her that her cousin no more wanted to marry her than she did him. She considered discussing the matter with him but discarded the notion until she should know him better. There was as yet no insight into why a young man so nearly of age should be constrained into considering a marriage he so obviously did not want. Felicia decided to drop her own recalcitrance and give the man some small encouragement. This he needed in abundance and it was with muted exasperation that his mother had had to prompt him to mark Felicia's card for the next evening's entertainment.

So, standing there beside a carved wooden elephant as tall as herself, Felicia looked ruefully at her card and foresaw little pleasure to come during the evening. What dances she had been to in Cheltenham had always been well choreographed with local mothers ensuring that young ladies had a constant stream of partners. It was not possible here when there were an abundance of young ladies making their come out and the young men were much more independent and free willed.

Mrs Makepeace, who knew the dangers of her daughter commencing the season as a wallflower, looked around for any acquaintances from Gloucestershire. She had just spotted a couple from Painswick, who had the most unprepossessing son in tow but a son nonetheless, when she turned and saw a tall young man she vaguely recognised, move effortlessly through the squeeze to reach her daughter.

'I do believe it is Miss Makepeace, is it not?' said Lord Guilliam as he reached his target and bowed to Felicia.

Felicia, startled out of her abstraction, blushed rosily when she realised who the man who had accosted her was. She curtseyed stiffly.

'Lord Guilliam,' she managed.

'Indeed it is,' he said smiling, at her discomfort. He had not intended to single any young lady out that evening. He was too eligible, too sought after a party not to tread carefully, but he had seen Miss Makepeace standing irresolutely by the wall and his compassion had been stirred. It was only as she blushed that he remembered they had parted on less than amicable terms. He wondered if she knew he could make or break her reputation here. Already heads were turned in their direction. It seemed she did.

'It is good of you to know me, my lord,' she said humbly. Without the scowl and more than two years on she was a very pretty girl. Lord Guilliam felt a stirring of attraction.

'Well, we have a mutual friend to bind us together,' he said.

Her expressive eyes flew to his face. 'Yes, yes I know. I must thank you for maintaining the friendship. He tells me in his letters that you visit him. I am very grateful.'

'You need not be on Giles' account,' he said, wondering how she would respond, 'he is sufficiently grateful all on his own.'

This made her smile. Lord Guilliam was captivated.

'Come,' he said, 'will you not dance with me?'

'I would be delighted, my lord,' said Felicia, curtseying again.

16

*L*ord Guilliam was careful not to single out Felicia for too much attention. Having danced with one young lady it behoved him to dance with others, which he did. In conse-quence of his interest, Felicia soon found herself inundated with partners and was glad that Lord Guilliam had marked her card for a dance much later on in the evening. She had not had the opportunity to talk to him about Giles.

The two dances with Bertram were laborious and trying. Felicia attempted conversation about Yorkshire and the family where possible but Bertram's responses were rather stilted. His face was rigid with concentration and beads of perspiration clung to his large pale forehead. Felicia realised that the dance steps were claiming all of his attention and she subsided into silence. If she wished to know him better, the dance floor was not the place.

Lord Guilliam, in contrast, was a flawless dancer and was able to continue an endless flow of small talk as the dance pro-gressed.

'For how long do you make your stay in London, Miss Makepeace?' he asked as the dance came to an end and he helped her to return to her mother who was now sitting at the far end of the ballroom from them.

'For the season, my lord.'

'So I may have the felicity of seeing you at other such events?'

'Indeed you may,' she said, laughing at his choice of words.

'You mock me because you are so aptly named,' he said feigning hurt.

'No, of course not but Giles calls me his felicity and if I recall I have been far from yours!'

'That is all behind us now,' said Lord Guilliam quickly. 'I would have you forget anything to my detriment. Consider it a youthful folly and discard it. I am here to serve you.'

'Serve me? Why should you want to, my lord?'

'Why because you have grown into a charming young lady, with whom I would like to become better acquainted.'

'You are very kind,' she said gratefully.

'Would you come for a drive with me one afternoon?' he asked tentatively.

'Oh yes,' she breathed enthusiastically, her eyes shining. 'Would you drive me to meet Giles? Would you take me to him?'

It was at this point that a lesser man would have withdrawn in high dudgeon. Lord Guilliam had so much to offer a lady, his attributes both in form and wealth were incontrovertible. Every mother in the room would have been glad to have him make up to their daughter in the way he had to Felicia. He was very conscious of this and felt a moment of chagrin when he realised that Felicia thought of no one but Giles. That, however, was his undoing. She had never thought of anyone but Giles, she had never wavered, she saw him now as a link to Giles and she had encouraged him because of that. He could not blame her, he could not reject her appeal. He realised that he had just begun to pay the real price for his youthful abandonment of his friend. He could not fail again.

'Of course I will, Miss Makepeace,' he said, raising her hand to his lips. 'I would be delighted to escort you.'

The only day possible for such a visit was a Sunday, so Guilliam had time to arrange it with Giles. It was a grey day with a smattering of rain, so there were not many people on the streets as he tooled through them to pick up his fair passenger. Felicia was ready for him when he arrived and clad for the rain. She wore a fetching bonnet that made her curls frame her face more closely. Guilliam thought she would make a very pretty picture to gladden Giles' heart.

'So how goes the week, Miss Makepeace?' he asked once she had settled on to the perch of his phaeton and arranged her skirts.

'Well enough, thank you, my lord,' she said. 'I have met so many people my head is in a whirl. I shall never recall all their names.'

'Already your come out is a fair way to being a success, Miss Makepeace. All you need now do is capture the heart of some wealthy and titled gentleman and it will be a triumph.'

Felicia giggled. 'If only it were so easy, my lord.'

'Oh come, come, it is no difficult task, you have captured my heart already and I am thought to be most eligible!'

'You say so, of course, my lord, because you are a gentleman but you know too that I am promised to my cousin while looking elsewhere for my husband. I am afraid you must stand in line.'

He saw that she thought him merely teasing and realised it would be better for all concerned if that remained the case. He laughed in response and drove her on to Green Park where he had arranged to meet Giles at the entrance.

'A word of warning, Miss Makepeace,' he said as they neared their destination. 'It is well in London for me to be driving you in an open carriage but if you are seen walking alone with a gentleman in the park, it might damage your reputation. I urge you to be careful.' In answer to his concern she pulled out from under her light pelisse a veil attached to a small pill-box hat. Untying the strings of her jaunty bonnet, she replaced it with the hat and veil.

'I defy anyone to know me now,' she said.

Guilliam smiled but it marked a sinking feeling in his stomach. He wondered if he would now be expected to facilitate many such meetings. He hoped not.

They reached the entrance to the park, Guilliam helped Felicia to alight and then waited as she walked towards a figure standing a little apart from the few brave souls who were walking out in the intensifying rain.

Giles too was dressed for the rain; he had a huge coat with an extra cape across the shoulders. On his head was a wide-brimmed hat; the whole ensemble made him appear almost swashbuckling. He turned and moved towards the veiled figure, knowing instantly by her walk that it was Felicia.

As they came together, he grasped both her hands and brought them to his lips in wordless delight at seeing her there. One look at the intensity of feeling between these two young people was too much for Guilliam; he jerked his horses round and with a salute neither saw, he trotted them smartly down the street and away.

'I cannot believe that I have you before me,' said Giles at last as he established mastery over the feelings that had welled up inside of him. He threw his head back to look skywards before looking down into the veiled face.

'If you knew how I have longed to see you,' he went on in a husky voice. He was glad the veil was in position, he dared not move it for he knew the urge to kiss the sweet mouth beneath it would be too much.

'And I you,' she said, shaken by the strength of emotion between them. To steady herself she said: 'Come, let us walk under the trees.'

He dropped her hands and drew one through his arm. They headed towards a walk of lime trees that afforded them some protection from the rain.

'Lord Guilliam has promised us an hour,' said Felicia as she heard the local church strike the half-hour. 'We must not be later.'

For some few moments, it seemed there was nothing to say, after all. They had described the minutiae of their lives in their daily letters. They walked in silence listening to the sound of the raindrops on the new leaves, then a squirrel dashed across their path and they were transported back to their summers when there had been fewer cares and much more fun.

Eventually the conversation veered round to more immediate matters. Giles drew Felicia's little hand even tighter through his arm and was moved to ask about her cousin.

'You do not speak very highly of him,' he said tentatively, not wanting to encourage her negative view of Bertram Makepeace but needing the reassurance that she still could not accept him as a husband.

'Poor man, that he is,' agreed Felicia. 'I believe he no more wants to wed me than I him but I struggle to draw him out. He guards his words but he is unable to mask his feelings.'

'So you are still betrothed to him?'

'Oh no, nothing so formal,' said Felicia quickly. 'It has not been announced, no notice in the paper. It is merely the will of both sets of parents.'

Giles felt the cold hand of certainty slap him in the face. He had known he could never aspire to be her husband. He had come to London aware that she was promised to her cousin, yet to make his toils more bearable, he had dreamed that there might be a time when she could be his. Now he had to accept the truth, that Felicia, though she walked with him arm in arm, was as far away from him as she had ever been. It was time to call a halt to his hopes and let her travel down her own inevitable path without him.

'We must not meet again thus, Felicia,' he said, his voice unsteady with emotion. 'It was wrong of me to agree to it.'

Her head came up at the abrupt words her eyes searching his face, oblivious to the raindrops that were streaming off the brim of his hat.

'Do not say that,' she cried, 'of course we can meet. The only reason I have agreed to this London season is so that I can be with you.' She caught her breath up on a sob. 'Two and a half years I have been parted from you, longing to be with you and now you tell me you do not want to see me.'

'Oh Felicia, my darling, I do want to see you but I cannot. Not while you are promised to another man. Can you not see how base, how wrong it would be to continue a clandestine arrangement while you are still engaged to your cousin.'

She saw it then, the sackcloth and ashes of Giles' conscience and she felt more defeated by it than if he had said he no longer cared for her. The strictures of his own code would separate them as nothing else could. She did not argue for she knew it would be fruitless. The tears began to flow down her cheeks and a little sob escaped her.

'May we still write?' she asked forlornly. 'Or do you forbid me even that?'

Giles, smitten by the pain he was causing her, could no longer resist the temptation to lift the veil. The rain mingled with her tears.

'I wish I had the power, the strength to say that we should not write,' he said, fighting hard the surge of longing within him, 'but I cannot. I cannot live without your sweet words ringing in my head each day. And I shall hear them more clearly in your voice now we have had this meeting. We must, however, write as friends not lovers. You know that to be true at least.'

She nodded pitifully, unable to sustain meeting his eyes that held so much unspoken misery. She turned from him, unwittingly helping him to overcome the temptation to sweep her into his arms. She began to walk back towards the entrance, her distress evident in the hunch of her shoulders and the slowness of her gait.

Giles followed a little distance behind until he had seen her reach Lord Guilliam's phaeton waiting obediently for her. She did not look back and he did not call out to her. He turned and melted away into the park.

17

*A*lthough Felicia had replaced the veil so it obscured her face from scrutiny, it did not take Lord Guilliam many minutes to discover she was in deep distress.

'Come, can you not tell me what saddens you so?' he probed gently.

''Tis Giles,' she said, her words muffled by the handkerchief she had rushed to her lips. 'He will not see me again until I am free of this promise to my cousin.'

Lord Guilliam's first reaction was relief for himself that he had been drawn back from the brink of aiding action he knew might lead to her ruin but he could not hear the hurt and unhappiness in her voice without pain to himself.

Knowing his friend, he tried to reassure her. 'It is so very much in Giles' nature to behave in this way, Miss Makepeace,' he said earnestly. 'He can no more take the dishonourable course than you or I could breathe.'

'Do I not know it!' she responded vehemently. 'Why do you think I do not fight his decree? It would only bring more misery to us both if I did.'

'Is there no way you can bring the matter of your cousin to an early conclusion?' he asked, not fully aware of the foundations for this proposed marriage.

Felicia fell silent, the rhythm of the horses clip-clopping sedately down the roadway, lulling her into a more settled frame of mind. She considered what he had said but remained silent.

'To be frank with you, Miss Makepeace, from my observation, I see no great enthusiasm on Mr Makepeace's part to hasten a formal engagement. Would it not be fairer to both parties if you were to draw back?' He had been prompted to speak by her failure to do so; his words, however, elicited no response. He felt suitably chastened until suddenly she spoke.

'It is a conundrum, my lord, and I believe you speak the truth when you say he is unwilling to marry me. I have observed it also. You must know, however, how the inheritance is fixed.' Here she explained the family dilemma.

'And you will wed him rather than lose the family Castle?' demanded Lord Guilliam, shaken by the disclosures.

'Oh no, certainly not,' replied Felicia instantly and with sufficient conviction that her companion knew it to be true, 'but there are other complications into which I cannot take you that prevent me from making a stand at this time.'

She fell silent again. It had stopped raining and although they were both soaked to the skin the air was warm so neither was cold. Lord Guilliam delayed returning her to her home by taking a rather circuitous route while Felicia busied herself changing back to her bonnet. Lord Guilliam sensed that he would get nothing further from her on this topic so he searched around for something that would divert her mind.

'I believe you will be well pleased with me when you learn that I have been keeping a weather eye out for Torrill and the Lamberts,' he said, startling her out of her abstraction.

'And what is their situation?' she asked eagerly. 'Have you discovered whether they have further plans to Giles' detriment?'

'No, none, other than I can tell you that you need no longer fear Digby Lambert,' he said, glad that her interest had been so keenly aroused.

'How so?'

'He is confined to his bed in some seedy hovel. It is understood that his liver is failing. The on dit is that he is not long for this world.'

'He is dying?' Her expressive hazel eyes showed how appalled she was at such news. 'I never imagined,' she stumbled on the words, 'never imagined that it should come to such a pass. Poor soul.'

Lord Guilliam gave a crack of mirthless laughter. 'Now you have compassion for him? What am I going to make of this? How am I to proceed?'

'You wonder at my concern?' she queried, surprised. 'I would be saddened by anyone's death but this is tragedy indeed, that a young man who had all to live for has brought himself to this.' There was a moment's pause as she further digested the news.

'Is he reconciled with his parents, his uncle?'

'No I believe not. The lodgings he inhabits are sordid and the care he is getting is limited to the little he can afford.'

'Poor soul,' she said again, genuinely sympathetic to Digby Lambert's plight. She turned agitatedly to Lord Guilliam and placed a small hand imploringly on his arm. 'Will you arrange for me to visit him; I must discover what he knows about Nathan Torrill's plans and perhaps we can take him a little comfort at the same time.'

'I do not think so, Miss Makepeace. It would not be possible for you to visit a gentleman's lodgings.'

'Surely that cannot be the case if the man is dying? I must see him, my lord. I must.'

There was nothing Lord Guilliam could do to turn her from her purpose and she petitioned him on two subsequent occasions to submit to her request. It made him glad to be able to tell her that his sabbatical in London studying antiquities in the British Museum was soon to be coming to an end and that he must return to finish his third year at his college in Oxford. She would have none of it and determined that he must take her to see Digby Lambert before he went back up.

'If you will not, my lord, I shall go alone,' she declared, looking defiantly up into his face.

He was appalled and wished he could seek counsel from his parents on the subject. He took a step towards this and visited his father in his club one evening.

Lord Mullinger was sitting alone in one of the panelled reading rooms. He looked up at the noise of the door and could not suppress a moment's pride in the appearance of his eldest son. The young man held himself upright and tall. He was all that a man in the public eye, like Lord Mullinger, could demand. Guilliam had never given him a moment's concern when it came to the errant behaviour of youth, and apart from sporting a rather more flamboyant dress then he himself would wear, he could not fault him.

The older man stood up stiffly, feeling an old hunting injury.

'Well Alexander, this is a nice surprise,' he said, extending his hand to his son.

'Thank you, Sir, I am pleased to have it so for I have come to seek you out. I have not seen you but in passing for some days and I must return to Oxford for my finals.'

'It is a shame to have to go part way through such a promising season,' remarked Lord Mullinger, helping himself and his son to a glass of brandy. He wrinkled his lined brow and fired a shot across Guilliam's bows. 'Your mother dreams of bridals. She has taken a fancy to Miss Makepeace.'

'Oh come, Sir,' cried Guilliam, aghast, 'I am but one and twenty, far too young to contemplate matrimony.'

'But you have,' said his perspicacious father, handing over the drink.

Guilliam took the glass but grasped the back of a chair with his free hand and looked unhappily at his father standing across the room from him. Lord Mullinger had the bearing of a military man as he had commenced his career in the army. His face was lean and angular and his nose was a smidgen too long but in his youth he had been considered a handsome man. Guilliam had always admired and respected him; he wondered now whether he could trust him with his confidences.

'I considered it, Sir, but Miss Makepeace is not for me, she has other suitors whom she favours.'

'Oh come, come my boy, no sane parent would allow a girl to ignore your suit.'

'I have not pressed it.'

'For goodness sake why not? If you have a fancy for the girl, why hold back. She is a lady with good parentage and heiress to a Castle.'

'Ah the Castle.' At last Guilliam smiled. 'That is the nub of the matter. It is a millstone, Papa,' he said emphatically. 'You will not advise me to take it when you know the whole. No land goes with it, no revenue. Any husband would have to take on the cost of its maintenance after Miss Makepeace's father's death.'

'And you have let this stand in your way?' demanded his father. 'Clearly you are not as taken with the girl as I thought.'

The knuckles of Lord Guilliam's hand went white as he gripped the back of the chair even more tightly. He knocked back the drink he was holding in his other hand and drew in a deep breath. 'I am in every way smitten, Sir. There is nothing I would not do for her but she is promised to her cousin, who does not want her and she promises herself to Giles Thornton!'

There was an arrested look on Lord Mullinger's face. 'Thornton, you say. Well that puts a different complexion on it.' He clasped his hands behind his back before saying: 'She may well have to wait a while but methinks he will be worth the wait.'

'You think Gregory will make him the heir?' Eagerly Guilliam looked for confirmation.

'Ha! You ask me?' cried the older man. 'I do not know. Had he been my nephew, I would have had him named such and begun to groom him already. I know not what the man is waiting for.'

'It is about that which I came to speak to you, Papa,' said Guilliam, convinced by his father's support of Giles. 'I must know if you have any information about his half-cousins, Nathan Torrill and Gervase Lambert.'

'Nothing save that they used to be seen in almost every drawing room but with the passage of time their welcome has diminished. I believe they have fallen foul of lady luck on many occasions and have reached a point where they cannot pay their debts. Do not have any dealings with them my boy, I entreat you.'

So there surely was his father's answer if Guilliam proposed the visit to Digby Lambert. Guilliam did not ask the direct question and he left his father resigned to having to inform his mother that there would be no early marriages in the Guilliam family.

Felicia, however, would not rest until she had visited Digby Lambert, so, much against his better judgement, Lord Guilliam found himself escorting her there the day before he was to return to Oxford.

Heavily veiled and clad in fabrics more suitable to a country scramble, Felicia was ready long before the knock came on the door to tell her that her carriage awaited.

'I beg you to reconsider, Miss Makepeace.' Guilliam could not leave the environs of the rich and cultured without assuring himself that he had made every effort to prevent this visit.

Felicia merely pursed her lips and shook her head.

'Then in all earnestness, I advise you not to reveal your name to him. He may guess because of your association with me but it must only be a guess.' He looked down at her rough skirt and a lopsided smile reached his lips. 'At least in that you have heeded me,' he said. 'You are dressed more suitably for the cow yard rather than the sick room.'

They reached the squalid streets of the poor and destitute and Felicia was forced to put a handkerchief to her mouth and nose, the smell was so noisome. The open drains were blocked by rotting vegetables and horse dung, and ragged dogs and other animals ferreted amongst the rubbish for food.

'How can someone born outside this allow themselves to end their days here?' Felicia's voice was a thread of its normal self.

Guilliam, concentrating hard on manoeuvring his horses between the open watercourses and the many grimy people who lingered in the streets, made no move to answer.

Eventually they came to an ancient row of houses and Guilliam drew his horses to a halt. On this occasion he had brought his groom, a taciturn individual, who had exuded disapproval from every pore of his body since the commencement of this outing.

Handing his reins to the man, Guilliam helped Felicia to alight, then he rapped his hand upon the door. The door was opened in a moment, as though the occupants of the house were already aware that a smart equipage had drawn up. The woman within the aperture was dressed in a greying mob cap and sombre clothes. Her face was comely enough but the teeth were blackened and her cheeks were smudged with grime.

'We have come to attend Mr Digby Lambert,' said Guilliam. 'May we enter?'

The landlady peered myopically at Guilliam and, judging him not to be the bailiffs or other such debt collector, stood back and let them enter. Guilliam had to stoop to cross the threshold.

For a moment Felicia thought she would retch at the smell. She grasped Guilliam's arm and he placed a reassuring hand over hers.

'Tis this way if you please, Sir, Madam.' The woman led them up a steep wooden staircase and ushered them into the one room that was under the roof. Guilliam could only stand erect in the central part of the space as the roof sloped almost to the floor. The room was lit by two filthy, cobwebbed casement windows and it took the visitors a few moments to accustom their eyes to the gloom.

At last they were able to perceive that the bed at the far end of the room was occupied.

'Mr Lambert, Mr Digby Lambert?' Guilliam walked towards the bed leaving Felicia standing stock still near the doorway.

'Who the devil are you?' cried their host. 'I told you no visitors woman.' He picked up a slipper from the floor by the bed and attempted to hurl it at his landlady. It fell well short as his strength was feeble. She cackled a laugh and watched him fall back against the pillows before she left the room.

'I am Lord Guilliam, a friend of Giles Thornton and this is my sister.' He waved an airy hand in the direction of Felicia, doubting very much that Digby Lambert knew whether he had a sister or no.

'What do you want to bring a woman here for? 'Tis no place for a woman.'

Guilliam could not but agree and this put him in better charity with his host for it showed he was not lost to all sense of right and wrong.

'Why are you here?' Digby demanded testily. His hair had grown and was plastered to his forehead with the sweat of fever. His eyes were clouded and Guilliam suspected he would not recognise them should he see them again.

'We are here to divine whether there is a further plot to discredit Giles Thornton.'

'Giles Thornton, who on earth is he?'

Guilliam cast a look in Felicia's direction, trying to make the point that their visit was futile. He could not see the response on her face through the veil but her whole stance was defiant.

'You must recall Giles Thornton, you set the Norton boy to do his worst against him.' Her voice was a thin thread but it carried to the man on the bed. He struggled to prop himself up on to an elbow and peered at her through the blur of his vision.

'What's it to you? The boy is stealing our inheritance, we have a right to defend it.' It seemed he did know about whom they were talking after all.

'I understood that you had already waived it,' she said mercilessly. 'It cannot be Giles' fault that he is next in line.'

Digby sank back against the dirty pillows. 'I have nothing to say to you, leave me.'

Guilliam made a move to the door but Felicia edged closer to the bed, stifling a gag with the handkerchief she had now doused liberally with scent.

'You cannot wish to end your life this way,' she said distinctly as though talking to a child, 'out of charity with half your relations and at odds with the rest. Would you not extend the olive branch before it is too late?'

Her words appeared to reach him, for there was an arrested look upon his face. 'How could you know?' he said thickly. 'How could you know that I regret my folly, that there is much in my life I would undo?'

Guilliam saw that Felicia had reached beyond the unprepossessing exterior that repulsed others involuntarily and had found a repenting core. He moved to get her a seat and, cleansing it with his handkerchief, he placed it as close to the bed as he dared.

Felicia seated herself and resolutely put away the handkerchief.

'We can help you make amends,' she said, 'and I know we can make you more comfortable. Now tell me what we need to know.'

18

They stayed for a little over an hour and it could be seen as they took their departure that Digby Lambert was more comfortable in mind if not in body. He had no direct information from Nathan Torrill about his plans as that gentleman had lost patience with his cousin and had little use for him now that he was so ill. Gervase Lambert, however, was party to Torrill's schemes and had discussed them with his brother on the two occasions he had been moved to visit Digby on his sickbed. It would appear that Torrill was confident that he could discredit Giles at the bank and was a fair way towards implementing this threat.

Felicia felt a cold hand clutch her heart when she heard this and was impatient to leave and warn Giles; she could not leave though without making arrangements for Digby Lambert to receive better food and regular clean linen. The landlady, taking her measure, agreed to the extra work for an additional payment, conscious as she did so that the young lady would very likely send someone round to check that all was being done, if she did not come herself. Although the landlady had made a show of reluctance, secretly she was delighted by the extra financial reward.

On their way home Guilliam and Felicia failed to agree on the best course of action. Felicia was adamant that Giles should be warned while Guilliam wanted the information to go to his uncle.

'Be reasonable, Miss Makepeace, I beg,' cried Guilliam as they turned into her street, 'what good can come of warning Giles? He has little hope of protecting himself. If I speak with Mr Gregory, then at least the evil and lasting consequences can be averted.'

Tears pricked under Felicia's eyelids. She knew he was right but she had wanted the excuse to see Giles legitimately without flouting his decree. 'Very well,' she said at last, her voice muffled once more by the handkerchief, 'have it your way.'

'Thank you.' Relief vied with nervous anticipation. Guilliam did not look forward to discussing the matter with Mr Gregory but he went immediately to do so.

He called at the grand London house, financed by the Gregory business empire. Entering the great marbled hall, he could not suppress the thought that it was so wrong that Giles was in exile in a comparative hovel. It made it hard for him to be polite to his host when he was ushered into his study.

'Guilliam, a pleasure to see you. How do you do, my boy?' Mr Gregory shook him forcefully by the hand. 'I thought you would be up at Oxford at this time.'

'I go tomorrow, Sir, but I had to see you first.' He cleared his throat, determined not to falter. 'I have come with some information about Giles.'

Mr Gregory started and eyed him keenly, Guilliam was surprised to see the man's hand shake slightly as he fiddled with a button on his waistcoat.

'Giles! What of him?' It was almost a bark.

'There is a plan afoot to discredit him at the bank.'

'I beg your pardon?'

'It would appear that Nathan Torrill has in his employ someone who currently enjoys your patronage at the bank.' Guilliam pushed back a lock of his wavy brown hair and stared fixedly into the eyes of his host. 'Discrepancies will be found and the blame will be laid at Giles' door.'

Mr Gregory looked back at him wordlessly, wanting to challenge this news but knowing in his heart that it would be true.

'How have you come by this information?' he demanded.

'I have visited Digby Lambert,' replied Guilliam quietly.

'Ha, and you take him to be a reliable source?' Mr Gregory turned away from his guest.

'Yes, I believe I do,' said Guilliam. He knew the interview was finished. He did not understand Mr Gregory's reluctance to believe him; he felt he had failed Giles. He walked to the door, and with his hand on the knob turned back to look at the older man.

'Digby Lambert is dying. Forsaken by his friends and family. There is no reason for him to lie, he knows he goes to meet his maker very shortly. Cannot the breach be healed between you? He suffers so.'

'He should have thought of that before he set himself on this road to perdition. Begone Sir, I have nothing more to say to you on this matter.'

Guilliam went. He returned to his family home pensive and unsettled. He paced his room, leaving his valet to pack his belongings undirected. It was fortunate that the young man already knew his master's needs and was able to make a well-educated judgement on what vestments Lord Guilliam might want back at Oxford.

At last Guilliam reached a decision, and he dashed off a note to Giles warning him of what they had learned. Guilliam no longer trusted the uncle to deal fairly by Giles.

In this Guilliam was wide of the mark. Mr Gregory, aware that he had been brusque and bordering on rude to his nephew's friend, was tempted to seek him out and apologise. However, there were too many others whose confidences he would have to betray if he was to unburden himself and explain his feelings. The older man found that, much against his will and his better judgement, he wished to ease the lot of Digby Lambert. Giles he knew he could spare at any time. He had an inclination to let the boy run the gauntlet of his foes and see how he fared, knowing that he could rescue him if the need arose. Digby Lambert had no champion. Mr Gregory passed a fretful night. He tossed and turned under his bedclothes, finding even the light blankets he used in summer too heavy for comfort. At last he cast them off and stood at the window scantily clad in his nightshirt to watch the dawn steal over the horizon. The birds were singing vociferously and he wished some of their joy and enthusiasm could rub off on him. He thought of all the people around him and wondered if any of them were truly happy. He doubted it; even his light-hearted friends the Makepeaces seemed to have become weighed down by care over the last few months. He considered the alternative courses of action which presented themselves to him. He could ignore Digby Lambert's plight and do nothing for him, he could send Higginbottom to alleviate the man's physical difficulties or he could go himself.

Mr Gregory was no self-deceiver, he knew which path he preferred: Higginbottom would carry out the duty with care and attention to detail, Gregory could appease his own conscience that he had done more than he need but it would not do. Arthur Gregory, feeling drowsiness at last invade his body, climbed back into bed having convinced himself that it must be he who first visited the ailing Digby.

Higginbottom found his master unusually difficult to rouse at his accustomed time of awakening shortly after half-past seven. Fearful that something was amiss, he hovered anxiously over the bed as his master struggled to regain full possession of his faculties.

Eventually, after a liberal application of tepid water from the pitcher, Mr Gregory became more himself.

'Oh stop fussing, man,' he growled testily as Higginbottom rushed forward with a heated towel.

'But Sir, this is so unlike you,' quavered Higginbottom, desperate for reassurance that his master was all right.

Mr Gregory straightened up and drew in a deep breath. 'A restless night, that is all.' He tried to brush it aside. 'It happens to any one of us.'

Higginbottom was not convinced. 'Not to you, Sir,' he said, 'not unless something or someone unsettles you.' He eyed his master keenly. ''Twas perchance the visit from my Lord Guilliam?' he braved to ask. 'Has he news of Mr Giles?'

'You are too acute for your own good Higginbottom,' grumbled Mr Gregory. 'He did bring news of Mr Giles but 'tis no reason to stand and gawp. Where is my shirt?'

Higginbottom made haste to bring forward the shirt and held it out for his master. He then made a great show of finding the cufflinks but Mr Gregory was not deceived.

'You think if you fuss around me for long enough, I will divulge what he said to me, do you not?'

Higginbottom gave him a wounded look. He said not a word and moved away to select a cravat.

Mr Gregory sighed before conceding defeat and then gave Higginbottom a résumé of what Guilliam had revealed.

'And now you would wish me to visit Mr Digby and see him comfortable?' queried Higginbottom.

'No, no, I have decided it should be I who makes the first visit. I believe my judgement of him may have been too harsh. It was tainted by my feelings for his brother and Torrill. I will visit him tomorrow. Arrange it!'

Higginbottom attempted to accompany his master the next day, but was denied.

'If I am satisfied that his plight is genuine,' said his master, 'then you will visit him soon enough and regularly. Have patience, I must do this myself.'

Mr Gregory returned from his visit to Digby Lambert much chastened. He could see in the sallowness of the young man's skin and the glaze of his eyes that he was close to death. At first Gregory was all for bringing the young man back to his own house until he was reminded that it would bring him in closer contact with the very people he had forsworn. Eventually Higginbottom persuaded him to alleviate the young man's discomfiture with all that money could buy but leave him where he was. In the end the decision was easily made, as Digby Lambert was not well enough to travel. Higginbottom visited him subsequently and from then on daily. He learned of the young lady who too had offered services to help the patient and he divined that it had to be Felicia. He knew the ages of Guilliam's sisters and their colouring. None of them gave the hint of having red hair under their veil. It warmed Higginbottom's heart that Felicia was still so allied to Giles' interests.

Digby Lambert died two weeks after his uncle's visit and was mourned by very few. His uncle attended his funeral but not the wake. He had no aspirations to be under the same roof as either of his remaining nephews. He said all that was proper to the grieving parents but had difficulty in stomaching the hypocrisy that allowed them to be so cast down by the boy's death when they had shunned him in life. Quietly Mr Gregory paid off all the last of Digby Lambert's debts and closed the chapter on his sad and foreshortened life.

19

Studying the hasty note from Guilliam, Giles felt anger stir deep within his soul. It seemed the fates were determined to conspire against him. Not only would he have to continue to face the daily grind but he must also be looking over his shoulder in case there was someone lurking in the shadows ready to knife him in the back.

He suspected that he knew who was Torrill's man. The clerk, Littlejohn, who shared his accommodation had a habit of appearing when Giles least wished him to. If Giles was leaving the house, Littlejohn might be peering out of the window or there might be the click of a door catch. At the bank, sometimes Giles would look up and find himself meeting Littlejohn's eyes. He clearly had been looking in his direction. Giles re-read the note and felt a measure of relief that Guilliam had already informed his uncle, Mr Gregory. Gradually the relief dissipated and Giles had to acknowledge that he would gain little respect from that gentleman if he constantly had to rescue him.

Giles considered the problem deeply and determined to find a way to resolve it through his own means without recourse to help from any of his friends. This decision turned his thoughts to Felicia. Her letters still came but they lacked the spirit and the sentiment that had previously buoyed him up in the face of adversity. He knew he had hurt her with his rejection and regretted it bitterly, yet he could not backtrack; he could not unsay the words that had set them apart. He genuinely believed that he was honour bound to keep her at arm's length until she had settled it with Bertram Makepeace. In the meantime, he responded to her letters with restraint and knew a hollow feeling in his heart that he was letting her slip ever further from his grasp.

Miss Felicia Makepeace had no intention of allowing Mr Giles Thornton to escape his fate which, in her opinion, was very closely entwined with hers. To some small extent she was deliberately withholding her feelings from her letters, for she wanted Giles to feel the cold draught of her dismay and hurt although she could understand his reasoning and the make-up of his character, which forced him down this road of self-sacrifice.

After the death of Digby Lambert, Felicia turned her attention to the matter of Bertram Makepeace. He was always courteous and always marked her card for two dances at any event at which they were both present. It was not possible, however, to discuss their future as his lack of dancing prowess made conversation very difficult. Felicia also found she missed Lord Guilliam's presence. Her hand was still sought by many a dashing young man, she rarely had to sit out a dance but there was not the comfort in knowing that there was someone in the room amongst the throng, who would be looking out for her, ensuring that she was well cared for.

Exasperation was getting the better of Felicia and one evening, at the cotillion ball of one of her mother's acquaintances, she demanded that she and Bertram sit out their second dance.

Bertram, whose countenance was rather florid from the exertion of the evening, showed a marked reluctance to lead the young lady out into a very ornate orangery where fruit cups were being served.

'Oh come, Miss Makepeace, the dance is in full swing, it would seem odd to sit this one out.' His eyes pleaded with her to change her mind. Felicia would have none of it.

'No, Cousin Bertram, it is time we talked of our future. Before we know where we are, the season will be drawing to a close and nothing will have been decided. Your parents require an answer and so do mine!'

She bullied and chivvied him into a quiet spot and sat herself down amongst the fronds of a palm tree. Bertram stood a little apart from her, his hands firmly clasped behind his back and his eyes on the floor. Felicia thought he looked the picture of abject misery. Felicia made a discovery.

'You are determined not to marry me, are you not?' she asked mildly.

Bertram lifted his head abruptly and fleetingly met her eyes.

'I cannot marry you, Miss Makepeace.'

'Why not?' Felicia felt a surge of happiness fill her breast; now there was no impediment between her and Giles but she wanted to know what Bertram's reasons were.

'Because I love another, a girl from my home town.'

'Do your parents know?'

'They have known these two years or more. As have yours but they hoped that I would see the advantages of a match with you.'

Felicia quelled the anger that had followed sharply on the heels of the happiness she had felt at her release.

'I do not believe there are advantages to you,' she said. 'I have never seen them. I do not understand why your father felt obligated to mine. If my parents do not produce a son, the Yorkshire estates are yours by right; you do not need me, or Castle Leck.'

Bertram sighed. 'Forgive me, Miss Makepeace. It was not to your father that my father felt obligated but to your grandfather's memory; he, you will recall, was my father's brother. My father had taken him to task about his spending not a month before he died. The rift that resulted was never mended. My father feels it deeply.'

'And the match between you and I is to be a sop to his conscience,' Felicia interrupted him fiercely. 'No, it cannot be. It will not be. You will marry your Yorkshire lass and I will go my own way and we will be happier friends because of it.'

At last Bertram braved a smile. 'You are taking it very well, Miss Makepeace. I have put off this discussion because I feared you would rail at me if I took away your future security. You have been most sympathetic.'

'Ah, that is because I too have a sweetheart and because I know that you cannot necessarily secure my future. You must be warned Bertram, my mother is with child. There could yet be a son.'

Bertram blanched and appeared to sway; he took a deep breath. 'That was cruel Miss Makepeace,' he gasped as he struggled to regain his equilibrium, 'most unkind.'

Felicia was nettled. 'I hardly call it cruel to give you warning when my parents will not. My father does not yet know of it, I have broken my bond of silence because I fear you will rush home and declare yourself to your ladylove under false pretences. It would have been cruel to allow that.'

'She will not be mine without the estate,' he said raggedly.

Felicia stood up and placed a hand on his arm.

'Then she would be no great loss,' she said, trying to give comfort.

'Oh no you misunderstand me. Her parents' land marches with ours. They see me as an excellent prospect as heir to that land, they would not accept me on my father's meagre portion alone.'

Felicia was overcome by a great tiredness. She did not feel she could take on Bertram's trials as well. 'Then,' she said as she picked up her bag and fan to return to the ballroom, 'you must pray that my mother provides me with a little sister.'

In the carriage on the way home, Felicia could not answer Miss Cuthbert's gentle enquiries. The anger, which had been smouldering beneath the surface all night, had been fanned by thoughts of Giles' unhappiness while he thought she was promised to her cousin. She set the blame at her parents' door. They had known all along that Bertram loved another; they should not have forced her into this pantomime role. She was sorry her mother had not felt equal to this evening's entertainment for she longed to take her to task now. Instead she would have to wait until the morning. It was not to be endured.

Felicia and her chaperone entered the house to find the principal saloon ablaze with light. It appeared she had misjudged her mother; Elsie Makepeace was not in bed, she was sitting near the fire gazing unseeing into its flames. Harold Makepeace was standing across the hearth; they made a comfortable picture but Felicia was in no mood for comfort. She strode into the room, stripping off her evening gloves as she did so. The sudden movement made both heads turn towards her. Felicia was ready with her challenge.

'Why?' she demanded almost before she had their full attention, 'why did you not tell me that Bertram Makepeace has wished to marry someone else these last two years? You must have known there was no reason for him to accept me. Why did you continue this charade when you knew I was against it?'

Harold Makepeace looked thunderstruck. 'How dare you speak to your mother and father like that? It is not for you to question our judgement.' He was about to continue when he saw Miss Cuthbert hovering in the doorway. He had to break off his verbal assault to dismiss her and bid her a polite goodnight. As the door clicked behind her, Felicia made good use of the tiny pause which ensued.

'I have a right to know the reasons behind the decisions you make which involve me,' she hurled at him. 'For goodness sake, Father, what can you have been thinking? Do you really believe that my material comfort so outweighs everything else that it justifies coercing me into the arms of a man who doesn't want me? Let me tell you now, I could never be comfortable in mind allied to Bertram Makepeace. I could never love him, nor is there sufficient consolation in the knowledge that our union has appeased Uncle Bartholomew's conscience. You must know that I love another and care not for wealth or comfort.'

'Felicia please,' implored her mother, looking tired and drained. 'I beg you to moderate your language and your tone. We only wanted what was best for you.'

'But consider this, Mama,' said Felicia, coming closer to her mother and looking down into her anxious eyes. 'What if I had made the match and this baby turns out to be a boy? You would have tied me to Bertram Makepeace without any means of financial support. Without our lands he has very little.'

'Baby!' Harold Makepeace had been about to take his daughter to task when her words threw him off balance. 'What baby?' He looked wildly from one woman to another. 'What have you done, Felicia?'

'What have I done?' cried Felicia, full of righteous indignation, 'nothing but tried to be a dutiful daughter. 'Tis not me who is with child but your wife, father. Have you not guessed? Can you not see that she wants only four months before she is delivered of a child. A child which could be a boy or a girl!'

Harold Makepeace looked at his wife in speechless delight. 'A son,' he breathed. 'Oh my darling,' he squatted down and captured her hands in his, 'why did you not tell me?'

Tears were rolling down Mrs Makepeace's face. 'Because I feared just such a reaction from you, dear Sir,' she whispered. 'I knew you would anticipate a son but there is no guarantee, no guarantee at all. It could so easily be another daughter and then our troubles are doubled.'

'God would not be so cruel,' asserted Mr Makepeace. 'I believe he has granted us a reprieve. It will be a son and we will no longer fear for the future needs of our daughter.'

Felicia, seeing that he would not be shifted from this view, turned wearily on her heel and made her way to bed. Dearly as she loved her father, she knew he had inherited his optimism from his own father. Mrs Makepeace would not be able to quell its rise.

The next morning Felicia was up betimes and found her mother in the breakfast parlour. Elsie Makepeace looked ill and exhausted. She had clearly not slept the night before. Felicia was instantly contrite.

'I am so sorry, Mama. I should not have broken your trust. My only mitigation is that I was too angry to reflect until afterwards the consequences of my outburst. Forgive me?'

'There is nothing to forgive,' said Elsie Makepeace wearily. 'His reaction was always going to be as I foretold. His nature is too buoyant and the truth could not escape him much longer. It is I who should be begging your forgiveness. I knew most certainly that Bertram's affections were directed elsewhere. I should not have forced you to encourage him.'

This was so strongly in line with Felicia's own thinking that she found herself unable to respond suitably. Instead she settled herself into her seat and busied herself with the tea urn. After a pause, she found her voice.

'What now Mama? Do we stay in London or do we return home?'

Elsie Makepeace appeared to brighten a touch. 'Your father is determined that we should return home at the earliest opportunity. He wants his son,' she said the word almost acidly, 'born at Castle Leck.'

'You do not believe it to be a son, do you Mama?'

'No, no I cannot say that I do.' Her mother lifted her eyes to meet the enquiring ones of her daughter. 'You will one day know, my dear, when you have children of your own. I carry this child in the exact same way as I did you and those who have sons describe a different mode. I have a deep certainty that this child is a girl.'

'Then I shall have to look to another way to bolster our fortunes,' said Felicia brightly, determined not to allow the expression of despair that had appeared on her mother's pretty face to linger there.

Mrs Makepeace gave herself a mental shake. 'Last night you talked of loving another,' she said carefully. 'Are you being courted by another young man? Would it be prudent to remain in London 'til the season finishes?'

Felicia shook her head. 'No Mama,' she said firmly, though she marvelled at herself for doing so. Had not her sole purpose in coming to London been to facilitate meetings with Giles? 'My future will not be secured by remaining here. We must take you home to where you feel safe and at ease.'

Elsie sighed with relief. 'I would have stayed for you, Felicia,' she acknowledged, 'but I have a strong inclination to return home. I feel so tired and oppressed by the future and long to be cosseted by Nanny.' A bleak little smile came to her lips. 'She at least will have no quarrel with the baby's gender.

Felicia suddenly found she was no longer hungry. 'When do we return home, Mama?' she asked as she stood up from the table.

'Your father has a number of engagements this week and next so it will be after the end of next week. You may know that Mr Gregory has been called home on some matter of business and has asked your father to invite Giles Thornton to supper before we leave.'

Felicia found herself gripping the back of the chair to steady herself; her knees had all at once refused to support her.

'Giles Thornton?' she repeated, afraid that her mother would hear the surprise in her tone. 'I thought he worked in one of Mr Gregory's banks now.'

'Oh yes, he does indeed, but Mr Gregory has been too busy to give the young man's comfort any attention and begged your father to make up for his omission.' Mrs Makepeace's face hardened. 'You are to treat him as you do any other young man of your acquaintance, Felicia,' she said sternly. 'I will have you putting on no airs or graces because he is unfortunate enough to have to work for his living. When he visits, us he will be our guest and must be treated as such.'

Felicia was stung by her mother's words for she did not believe that she had ever treated her subordinates with anything other than courtesy and respect. She did not challenge her, however, for she did not want her mother to suspect that Giles was the object of her admiration.

20

$\mathcal{G}$iles Thornton received his invitation to dinner at the Makepeaces' London house with not unnatural surprise. He was very much aware that his uncle had not looked him out during his sojourn in London and had been most disappointed when Mr Gregory had returned to Gloucestershire leaving him with only a scratched note of apology. So Giles was touched and heartened to receive the invitation which, Mr Makepeace made no secret, had been at Mr Gregory's instigation.

He had but a week before the proposed event and after much soul searching determined that he would look his very finest on this occasion. Felicia would be shown what she had shunned in preference to an affiliation with Bertram Makepeace. This would be his one chance to shine in her presence and prompt her to make a choice.

Giles hunted through his wardrobe and found one of the fine coats his uncle had had made for him when he had visited Guilliam's home. Giles put it on with a struggle. The passing years had thickened his torso and enlarged his frame. Giles had maintained his fitness by always walking to his place of work but nothing could prevent the maturing of his physique for he was now one and twenty. He studied the seams of the coat of blue superfine and saw that some material could be gained if he could find himself a seamstress.

He sought out his landlady and made his enquiry. Mrs B had long since fallen for Giles' charm of manner and inherent consideration for others. She instantly offered to do the alterations for him. So, the night of the dinner engagement, Giles hurried back from the bank and spent as long as he dared smartening his appearance.

Mr B had shined his boots for him so the evening sun gleamed on their surface. His snowy white shirt had been carefully pressed so it lay uncreased against his chest. Giles brushed his hair until it shone like burnished gold and tied his cravat in neat and shapely folds. When Mr B arrived to help him into his coat, both men stared at Giles' image for some moments in the long mirror.

'Ye look very fine, Mr Giles,' said Mr B at last. Giles gave an embarrassed laugh.

'You would think I was away to some royal ball, not to supper with people I call my friends.'

Mrs B bustled in and crowed with delight. 'Ye do look a picture,' she said happily. 'I hope your lady-love appreciates you.'

Giles coloured. 'I never mentioned a lady, Mrs B,' he said unconvincingly.

'No, but you ain't all togged up in yer finery for some old friends of yer uncle,' she said succinctly.

Giles let it go; there was no point in denying it. He stared ruefully at his reflection, knowing as he did so that he was acting in complete contradiction to all his principles. Over the last few weeks, he had come to know that if he lost Felicia he would not be able to sustain his life of drudgery. If there was no Felicia at the end of the steep stairway he had to climb, then he would never achieve the ascent. It was melodramatic, he told himself, but experience counselled him that one day despair would overtake him if she was not there.

He pulled down the front of his waistcoat for one last adjustment and turned away from the mirror.

'Will I do?' he asked his attendants.

'Ay,' they chorused.

Giles bent forward and kissed Mrs B's cheek. 'I thank you with all my heart,' he said.

'Oh give over,' she said brusquely as she gave the cravat one last tweak. 'Ye knows we would do anything for ye, Mr Giles, so kind and helpful that ye are.' Her face clouded. 'But I warn ye, I feels that Mr Littlejohn is up to no good. He has too great an interest in ye for my comfort.'

Giles put his hand over her fluttering one and smiled at her. 'I believe you are right Mrs B,' he said, facing the truth, 'but I will tackle that anon. Tonight I wish to enjoy myself.'

Felicia had dressed with equal care but with different rules governing her decision on what to wear. She thought only to put Giles at his ease. She believed it unlikely that Giles had evening wear in his possession and so had kept her dress simple, almost drab. She instructed the maid to make no special effort with her hair and she wore a tiny necklace, a pearl pendant as her only adornment.

Mr Makepeace's reaction when he saw his daughter emerge from the bedroom was one of considerable dismay.

'Good heavens, child, what are you wearing? Go at once and put on something more suitable for guests. I will not have you slight Thornton so.' Mr Makepeace had himself changed for dinner and sported a very nice dark coat, glossy boots and a well-formed cravat.

Felicia was just about to open her mouth to protest when the doorbell rang and her father had to capitulate.

'Well, mind you behave to him with suitable consideration,' he snapped as he ushered her down the stairs.

They had just managed to install themselves in the first floor saloon when the butler announced Giles.

Mr Makepeace moved forward swiftly, shaking his hand enthusiastically and saying all the most welcoming of comments.

Felicia remained rooted to the spot in the centre of the room. In the full candlelight Giles looked magnificent; his golden hair shone and his coat enhanced the blue of his eyes. Felicia had never seen him look so handsome, so very fine. She felt her body shimmer with attraction and sensed this was a watershed. Gone was her childhood sweetheart and in its place there was a very handsome man.

Mr Makepeace drew Giles over to her and she found the control to bob him a simple curtsey.

'Miss Makepeace,' he said, raising her hand to his lips, 'this is indeed a pleasure.'

'Mr Thornton,' she whispered shakily, 'we are delighted you could visit us.'

Luckily for Felicia, Elsie Makepeace chose that moment to come into the room. Amongst her apologies for making a tardy entrance, Felicia was able to regain some of her poise. Once her mother cast her a look of deep disapproval as her gaze took in the limitations of Felicia's attire. A maelstrom of emotions assailed Felicia. She had dressed thus for all the right reasons. Giles had taken her aback by arriving arrayed like any of the society young men of her acquaintance. It cut her to the quick that Giles, who was so clearly suited to take up his place within society, should be prevented from doing so by the perversity of his uncle. The injustice of it all kept Felicia tongue-tied until the dinner gong summoned them to the table.

Throughout the meal, Giles, who was well aware of much of the news because of Felicia's letters, made easy conversation with Mr and Mrs Makepeace. He said all that was appropriate to the information that Mrs Makepeace was increasing and he listened politely to the tales of the new acquaintances they had made this season.

Sitting opposite him, Felicia could not help her gaze being drawn to his face. She feasted her eyes on every feature, determined to hold it tight in her memory for the return to Gloucestershire. Repeatedly Mr Makepeace tried to draw her into the conversation but her emotions threatened to overcome her and she could only utter monosyllabic responses.

Giles had a very clear picture of what was going on in Felicia's mind. He could see, seated opposite as he was, the admiration in her eyes where her parents could not. He knew she was seeing him as an adult at last, and even as a potential lover. She was no longer the schoolgirl whose charms he had always so strictly kept at arm's length. Now she was a woman about whom he need no longer feel guilt when he lay in bed after a long and tiring day imagining their lips meeting in a long and lingering embrace.

Several times Giles cast her a swift reassuring smile and gradually, as the puddings were taken away, she was able to make a few sensible remarks.

The evening did not go on late as Giles had to be up betimes for work at the bank. As he took his leave, Mr Makepeace drew him to one side.

'Do you have any messages I might convey to your mother? We return to Cheltenham next week.'

'But I thought you were fixed here for the season!' Giles was astonished.

'It had been the case but with my wife's condition we return early.'

'And what of Miss Felicia, I had understood ...' Giles trailed off, not knowing how to ask the question.

'Well, she only came to become better acquainted with her cousin but they have agreed that they will not suit, so there is nothing to keep her here now.' Mr Makepeace put up a hand and slapped Giles on the back, guiding him back to the ladies.

Giles, still assimilating the news, gave his thanks to Mrs Makepeace with almost mechanical civility but recovered himself enough to whisper hoarsely to Felicia: 'Meet me at the top of Birmingham Street tomorrow at noon.'

She gave him an infinitesimal nod of assent and let him go. Giles ran neatly down the steps and into the dark night.

He had planned to take a cab home but the euphoria he felt about Felicia's release, coupled with the balmy air of a June night, tempted him into walking. It was only when he had left the streets lit by the lights from the great houses of the wealthy that a certain unease began to penetrate his thoughts. He began to have a sense that he was being followed. He quickened his pace and heard the sound of a muffled voice as someone tripped on the cobbles. Twice he looked over his shoulder and saw nothing, but the third time he caught a movement in the shadows. Ahead there was a bustling tavern and he was inclined to take refuge there. He walked purposefully towards it, then, as a group of revellers made their entrance, he dived into the darkness beyond the doorway and, flattening himself against the wall of the building, waited to spy on his pursuers. Not many seconds later a trio of burly individuals came into view. In the murk of the tavern's yellowish lanterns, Giles could not make out any features and knew he would not recognise them again. Gruff voices, raised in consternation that they had momentarily lost him, sent shivers down Giles' spine. He thought again of going into the hostelry but he knew no one there and he could see no reason why anyone should take his part. The only attribute he had on his side was that he was fleet of foot and fit. He knew he could outrun the heavyweights on his tail. It seemed a craven course although discretion might indeed be the better part of valour. Giles challenged himself to find a more confrontational alternative, but there was none. No one in their right mind would take on three unknown assailants, who could easily have spent some time in the ring as prizefighters. In a blinding moment of decision, Giles burst from his cover and hared up the street and away. There was an angry shout and the men set off in pursuit. One flung a stone, which at the moment Giles turned his head to measure their progress, hit him a glancing blow on the temple. He barely felt it and ran on, increasing the distance between him and the bullies. He had not covered a great distance before he knew they were no longer following him; even so he was unwilling to slow down. His beautiful coat was already ripped under the arms by the exertion of running, he had torn at his cravat as his breath rasped in his throat but he kept his legs pounding the streets until he recognised his lodgings. Giles burst through the door to lean against it, fighting for air. Eventually he bent forward, trying to alleviate the stitch that was grinding away under his ribs, his mind still grappling with the question of whether he had been a random or specific victim.

As his breath came more easily, he climbed the stairs to his room where he locked the door and, pulling off his coat, flung himself on the bed. For all his troubles, sleep was not long in coming. The next thing he knew was it was dawn and another day had begun.

21

*N*ot minutes after the front door had closed behind their guest, Mr and Mrs Makepeace rounded on their daughter, escorting her firmly to the saloon and issuing orders to the butler that they were not to be disturbed.

'Good God, Felicia, what ails you child?' Mr Makepeace could hardly contain his frustration. 'Your mother implored you to behave courteously to young Thornton and even before he arrived, you knew my sentiments on the matter. But did you heed us?' He drew himself up to his full height. 'Did you indeed! No, instead you dressed like a serving maid and uttered barely a word to him all evening. I can only thank God that his uncle was not here to see a child of ours slight his relative so.'

Felicia looked from one to the other in wonder. They had no inkling of her true feelings. A tear escaped her eye, for she was loath to be at odds with them.

'Mama, Papa, you mistake, I assure you.' She dashed a hand across her cheek to brush away the tears. 'You cannot be more wrong about my regard for Giles Thornton. I must tell you that I love him, have done so since I was thirteen and will wait until I am thirty to marry him if needs be, but marry him I will.'

There was an aghast silence. Finally, her father cleared his throat and spoke. 'Does he know your feelings?'

Felicia steadied herself and considered her response. 'I think he may do but he would have none of me while I was promised to Bertram Makepeace. I have not had an opportunity to tell him that that is now at an end.'

Harold Makepeace made a dismissive gesture. 'He knows it for I told him this night.'

'Oh.' It explained to Felicia why Giles was prepared to meet her on the morrow.

'Felicia.' Mrs Makepeace found her voice. 'Does he return your feelings?'

'I believe so, Mama.' She met her mother's eyes. 'Yes, I think I can be reasonably confidant that he does.'

'Nothing,' said Mr Makepeace on a long out take of breath, 'would please me more than to have the connection made between our family and that of my dear friend Gregory's but there is no certainty that Giles Thornton will be named the heir.'

'My desire to marry him, Papa, is not dependent on his expectations.'

'And it is very creditable, my dear,' said her mother quickly before her father could reply, 'but Giles Thornton has very little income of his own and your inheritance, if we lose the Yorkshire estates, will be meagre. You cannot ask your papa to sanction a betrothal under those circumstances.'

Felicia moved to take a place on the settle beside her mother. 'I do not ask either of you to sanction our betrothal at this time,' she said carefully. 'There are too many uncertainties. I have no hope of it being possible for many years yet. I only ask you not to forbid it and accept that it will be my inevitable fate.'

Mr Makepeace went to the door and held it open.

'Will you leave us for a few moments Felicia,' he asked, 'your mother and I can discuss this matter more freely in your absence.'

Without a word, Felicia got up and left the room but she did not retire to her couch, for she felt sure her parents would call her back in due course. In this she was correct; not twenty minutes later a footman came to find her. She returned quickly to the saloon to find her father standing with his hand upon the mantelpiece, his foot disturbing the cooling logs in the grate. Elsie Makepeace had not moved from her place on the settle. Her eyes were weary but the lines of strain on her face, which had almost become habitual recently, had eased.

'Come my dear.' She patted the padded cushion beside her, indicating to Felicia to resume her seat there.

Felicia did as she was bid and looked from one parent to the other. Her father was the first to speak.

'Do you know if Mr Gregory is aware of your partiality?' he asked.

Felicia had wondered this many a time. 'I suspect he is,' she said after a moment, 'for certainly his valet, Higginbottom, knows and it is said that what Higginbottom knows Mr Gregory is a party to within the hour.'

Mr Makepeace considered this. 'We would do nothing that would compromise our friendship with Gregory, Felicia,' he warned her. 'If he does not like the match we will not encourage it.'

'And if he does like it?' Felicia's voice was tight and cold. She felt Mr Gregory wielded too much power over their lives already but she was not going to antagonise her parents at this stage.

'Then, as I said before, it would be the dearest wish of our hearts and we would welcome the knowledge that your future well-being is assured.'

It was the first time Harold Makepeace had even alluded to the fact that the baby might be a girl. The women exchanged glances before Felicia got up and desired her parents a dutiful goodnight.

Once in bed, she lay staring at the ceiling in the darkness trying not to let the bitterness she felt towards Mr Gregory taint the other more enjoyable sensations that she experienced every time she conjured up a picture of Giles in all his finery. However, the two things were intrinsically linked and she could not think of Giles without resenting Mr Gregory's treatment of him.

The next morning saw her exercising a degree of subterfuge. She set out with her maid on the pretext of visiting the library, then, withdrawing the maximum number of books, she sent the girl home with the heavy package. It took some little while to reach Birmingham Street but she was not late and as she hurried up its length towards the bank she saw Giles striding down in her direction. His pace quickened when he caught sight of her and before she knew it, he had pulled her into a side alley and had hold of her in a tight embrace. Their lips met for the first time. To Giles it felt even sweeter than his night-time imaginings and he accepted it gratefully as consolation indeed for all the privations he had suffered. For Felicia it confirmed all the hasty words she had said to her parents the night before.

It took a little while for them to detach themselves from each other. Both were slightly shaky with emotion and suppressed passion.

Felicia giggled self-consciously. 'My parents thought you would take offence because of my treatment of you last night,' she ventured.

Giles lifted her determined little chin with his hands so that he could look searchingly into her eyes.

'I thought you adorably confused,' he said huskily, 'and I longed to hold you in my arms as I have you now. I hoped my feelings were reciprocated.'

'Oh indeed they were and are,' breathed Felicia. She drew away from him a little. 'But we cannot remain thus. I am not even wearing my veil.'

'No one will recognise us here,' said Giles, casting an eye up and down the length of the alley.

Felicia was not reassured and was about to question it when she caught sight of the angry bruise on the side of Giles' head. She put a finger up to touch it.

'How has this occurred? Who did this?'

'It is nothing.' Giles revelled in the fact that she was so acute but he did not want to frighten her.

'Was it Nathan Torrill?' Her hazel eyes were wide with alarm.

Giles shook his head. 'I cannot say. It might have been him

who put them up to it but I did not recognise the three who followed me.'

'Three!' She covered her mouth with her hands even before the word had escaped completely. Giles took her hands and drew them away from her face, shaking them gently.

'They did not touch me, Felicia,' he said. 'I ran away like the coward I am,' he added ruefully.

'Do not speak so,' cried Felicia, 'you are no coward.'

'But I think I am. I cannot for the life of me find a way to tackle Littlejohn. I shall, no doubt, be hauled up before Mr Ponsonby in due course with no defence and no excuse.'

Felicia shivered even though the day was warm. It was the bleakness in his face that left her cold and drained.

'Surely your uncle will exonerate you again?' Her eyes implored him to confirm it but he would not.

'I believe my uncle wishes me to deal with it on my own account. Has he not returned to Gloucestershire to precipitate such an event?'

Felicia gave an angry exclamation and turned away from him.

'That man demands too much,' she hissed between gritted teeth. 'I used to view him as a friend but no longer. He is fickle and despotic.'

'Shush, you must not speak so,' countered Giles. 'He has in so many ways been kind to my family, I will not have him abused.'

'Kind to your family but it has been a long time since he was kind to you, Giles.' She wheeled around to face him again. 'Admit it. He has driven you into a corner and now baits you. That is not kindness, that is cruelty.'

'I cannot accept it as so,' Giles retorted. 'If he had not given me this employment, I would have had to fend for myself.'

Felicia almost stamped her foot. 'Oh face it, Giles. I see the truth. You are having to fend for yourself now with no certainty that he will defend you if there is another attempt to discredit you.' Angry tears began to roll down her cheeks unchecked.

Giles attempted to wipe them away with a gloved finger but

she would not let him and pushed his hand away. There was silence as a yawning chasm opened up between them. Giles saw his happiness wave him a forlorn farewell and he knew despair.

'What do you want of me, my felicity?' he asked wretchedly. 'I am yours to command.'

Felicia remained silent for what seemed like an age. Then suddenly a sob burst from her and she cast herself into his arms once more, nearly knocking him off balance.

'I want you to be happy,' she sobbed into his jacket. 'I want to be with you. I cannot bear to be separated from you. Why cannot your uncle just let it be so? Why must he test you so grievously? You have done nothing to deserve this.'

'I fear that this is his dilemma,' acknowledged Giles, holding her tightly. 'I have proved nothing, certainly not my mettle. So far I have done only what has been asked of me. I have shown no initiative, no leadership.'

'Oh come now,' she interrupted him, 'you acted entirely of your own accord when you helped Mrs Simon Gregory.'

'Maybe,' he agreed, 'but here it takes all my resolve to remain in this post at the bank, I have no further strength of mind to face down mine enemies.'

'Then you must find it, Giles,' said Felicia with vigour, 'for I can tell you as surely as we are together now that I am going to find some way of providing us with an income so that we can be together.'

Giles smiled down into her earnest little face, framed as it was by those rich-coloured curls. 'I believe you will,' he said, 'more surely than I will solve my difficulties here.'

They could not stay for much longer as Felicia had to return to eat a late luncheon with her mother and a friend and Giles had to return to his stool. Their parting tried each lover's fortitude as neither could name a day when they would see each other again. Felicia left the alley first and darted back down the street to summon a hackney cab home. Giles remained there for a few more moments, grappling with his emotions. He could only deem Felicia as his blessing and his curse, being parted from her was such agony, but the moments with her had such sweetness that he would not have traded them for having no one at all. He had to believe that if he could not, then she would find a solution to their separation.

Felicia returned home to Cheltenham in determined spirit but by the time she had completed the tiring journey she had exhausted all the avenues she could think of and succumbed to defeat. She supported her weary mother with mechanical rather than sincere words of encouragement. Mrs Makepeace had found the journey most uncomfortable and was inclined to need the constant ministrations of either Miss Cuthbert or Felicia. Everyone was glad to hear the scrape of the horses' hooves on the cobbles as they pulled into the Castle's forecourt.

Nanny rushed out to greet them and hurried Mrs Makepeace away to put her feet up on a stool and have her wrists bathed in cool water for the day was muggy and hot.

Felicia, much relieved to give over the responsibility of her mother's care to others, was tempted to walk over and see Mrs Simon at the earliest opportunity. She was forestalled by the arrival of Mr Gregory who came on a visit of congratulation.

Felicia found she could no longer meet his eye. She had entreated her father not to speak to Mr Gregory of her attachment to Giles but this did not stop her from blushing on curtseying to the older man.

'Well Harold, you old dog,' Mr Gregory had laughed heartily, 'fancy having another stab at an heir. This must make your uncle as sick as a parrot,' he declared.

If she had not blushed before, Felicia would have blushed now at such a warm sally. She retreated to the far corner of the room and let her father entertain his guest. Mr Gregory, however, was not willing to have her ignored for long. Having been given a drink, he sauntered over to where she stood looking out of the window with a commanding view of the town below and he began to ask about her sojourn in London. It seemed to her that he was expressing an unusual interest in her activities and she parried his questions as best she could.

'And how was young Giles when you saw him?' he asked finally. 'I believe your father was kind enough to invite him to dine with you all.'

Felicia's voice came out as a squeak before she could control it. 'He seemed well, Sir, but tired. He left early.'

Mr Gregory turned to his host. 'So what is this, Harold?' he demanded. 'I trust my nephew was suitably grateful to you for your hospitality. I would not have him be uncivil to you.'

'No, no,' Harold replied hastily, wondering what his daughter might have said to give Mr Gregory the wrong impression. 'He was most charming, most grateful. And I must say, Gregory, was a credit to you. He turned himself out in fine fettle and looked very much the gentleman.'

Felicia could only sigh with relief and throw a look of gratitude at her father. She realised that she would have to divest herself of the ignoble thoughts she harboured about Mr Gregory or she would find herself making matters worse for Giles. She could not expect her father to be available to come to her rescue every time.

22

*M*rs Makepeace was brought to bed at the end of October and was delivered of the inevitable daughter. Harold Makepeace stayed at home just long enough to be assured that his wife was to survive the birth before he departed for Yorkshire. He was in no mood to receive the congratulations of his relieved Yorkshire relations but he could not handle the bleak look in his wife's eyes and the pity of his neighbours. Better to be with foe than friend on this occasion; it stiffened ones lip and ensured the façade remained rigid on his face.

Only Felicia and the loyal staff truly welcomed the little girl. Elsie refused to have anything to do with the tiny child, so Nanny, very soon after the birth, was charged with finding a wet nurse. Felicia's heart wept for her little sister but no amount of entreaty would suffer her mother to acknowledge her new daughter. Eventually after a week, Felicia determined that the child should have a name. Elsie neither objected nor endorsed the decision; she remained ensconced in her bed and prey to bouts of weeping. The name Felicia and her paternal grandmother settled on was Alexa Maud. Alexa after Elsie's father and Maud after the widowed Mrs Makepeace herself.

'You should not be asked to choose a name,' said her grand-mother to Felicia. 'I feel most honoured that you would think of giving her my name.'

'Grandmama, I have to do the choosing because neither of my parents will. I informed Mama of my choice and she has passed no judgement and I have written to Father in Yorkshire. The Rector and I have agreed a christening date for four weeks hence,' Felicia sighed. 'Father has been told of this. He has that much time to proffer an opinion.'

Mrs Makepeace patted her anxious granddaughter's hand. 'On balance, my dear, I believe you are doing just what you ought. It saddens me much though, that it has to come to this.'

Felicia nodded her curly head in agreement. 'Very sad, Grandmama, that it should all be about money. I feel it deeply and wonder whether I should have made the ultimate sacrifice and entertained Bertram's suit.'

Mrs Makepeace threw her hands up in horror. 'Most certainly not, Felicia,' she protested. 'It was never meant to be. That young man has long been attached to someone else. It would not do.'

Felicia blinked in surprise. She realised for the first time that her grandmother was considerably more interested in her well being than she had previously supposed. It was information that she could store up for the future; she was too tired and too concerned about her little sister's plight to think about furthering her own ends at this time.

All this and more she wrote to Giles. There was no longer any need to conceal the exchange of letters between them. It was one small consolation amongst the misery of the current situation.

As the weeks progressed towards Christmas, Felicia hoped that her mama would quit her bed and take up her role of mother and that her father would return reconciled to the arrival of his little girl. Neither of these events took place. Thus the christening when it happened in the middle of December was low key, although Felicia was much heartened by the arrival of her Aunt Dorothea, her father's sister.

Dorothea was blessed with three sons and a daughter and a charmingly effeminate husband. How he came to have sired four such robust children was a mystery to his friends and neighbours and had there ever been a hint of Dorothea straying from her marital bed, they would happily have stigmatised them all as some other man's issue. However Dorothea had never given them even a crumb of gossip. She certainly ruled her household with a rod of iron and she enjoyed entertaining her wide circle of friends but she had never even hinted at any inadequacies in her husband nor passed an opinion on the allure of other men. Indeed it was unusual for her to leave her home and make a visit unaccompanied by her husband, so when she arrived Felicia was taken completely by surprise.

'My dear aunt,' she cried as she greeted her in the vaulted hallway having just come down the main stairway as the doorbell sounded. 'This is an unexpected pleasure. I had no notion you would be joining us.'

Dorothea embraced her niece with real fervour. 'Felicia, my child, you look so pale, so wan. It must be this dreadful business taking its toll. My mother wrote me as much and I knew I must come and see what I could do to mend matters.'

Felicia realised that she herself must be at the very depths of despair, for she felt nothing but gratitude to her aunt. Normally such sentiments would fill her with dread. She had met her aunt so irregularly that she could be forgiven for imagining that the lady had little concern for her. This now was patently not the case. Dorothea, seeing how the land lay, quickly took over the organisation of the event but she did it with sufficient tact to make Felicia feel that her efforts were being endorsed rather than superseded.

Once ensconced in one of the smaller parlours, Dorothea began to enquire how far Felicia had advanced with the arrangements.

'Godparents,' said Dorothea after Felicia had expressed her concern about the guest list. 'The child must have godparents.'

Felicia's face fell. 'I can think of none,' she said simply.

'Then we must put our heads together. It is not possible to hold a christening without godparents.' Dorothea sat for a moment and considered. It allowed Felicia time to take stock of this new force in her life. Her aunt resembled her father strongly. She had a rounded face and her body had succumbed to the portliness her father had kept at bay. Her hair was a faded brown but she dressed it up with combs and clips. She wore strong colours befitting her mature years and exuded an air of competence. Felicia felt herself relax; the arrival of her aunt was definitely having a beneficial effect on her state of mind.

'What of your father's friend, Mr Gregory? He is unmarried and would be an excellent man to have as a sponsor. I believe him to be very comfortably off.'

'No.' Too swiftly Felicia gave her reaction.

Dorothea straightened up and looked at her niece in some surprise.

'There has not been a falling out, has there?' she asked.

Felicia bit her lip and felt her eyes sting with tears. She realised it behoved her to acquaint her aunt with the facts.

'Mr Gregory has recently taken on the responsibility of his sister's family. I doubt he would wish for more,' Felicia managed.

Dorothea was not deceived. 'There is more to this young lady, you had better tell me all.'

Felicia turned her head away and looked out through the window; it was getting dark and the calls of the blackbirds could just be heard.

'I suppose I must for there is no secret. My parents know it all. I am in correspondence with Mr Gregory's half-nephew. We wish to be married but circumstance does not allow it. Giles is bonded to his uncle's bank and there looks to be no early release. I can no longer feel for Mr Gregory as I ought given that my parents hold him in such high esteem. He has set Giles so many trials. He must prove himself again and again to be worthy of Mr Gregory's patronage.' She gave a little sigh. 'Giles would be satisfied with a small allowance which would permit him to live frugally and support his mother and sisters but Mr Gregory needs must put him in situations where everyone expects him to be made heir to his fortune. And I cannot bear it for him. I cannot forgive the man for behaving thus. I could not stand at the font and be easy in my mind to see that man take on the task of guiding my little sister through her early life.' Felicia was working herself up into a state and her voice was becoming more high pitched.

Dorothea, who had some inkling of the situation from her mother's letters, came quickly to her side and took her agitated hand. 'I am sorry I asked,' she said. 'There is no need for you to agitate yourself so. We will but send him an invitation and hope for a handsome christening gift.'

Felicia collapsed against her aunt, obtaining from her the comfort she was used to receive from her mother before the advent of this pregnancy. Dorothea began to stroke the girl's hair.

'There, there, my dear,' she cooed as the tears began to slip down Felicia's face. 'We will find a way through this.'

Felicia straightened up and searched in her reticule for a hand-kerchief. 'You must think me very weak,' she sniffed. 'I am not usually prone to tears but the combination of leaving Giles in London with no prospect of seeing him and the neglect my little sister is suffering have dented my resilience.'

'Most understandable,' soothed her aunt. 'Giles I can do nothing about but your sister's situation I think we can ameliorate. We need two ladies and a man as godparents. Come, we must delve deeper into our minds and find some suitable candidates.'

There was silence while the clock ticked and the fire crackled. Eventually Felicia brightened. 'Well, there is one undisputed one,' she said enthusiastically, 'I propose you, Aunt Dorothea, what do you say to that?'

'I say thank you kind niece, I would be delighted to accept,' replied her aunt promptly. 'And,' she added on a long outlet of breath, 'I think it would be polite to invite your cousin Bertram to stand. He, after all, has had his future assured by the arrival of an Alexa rather than an Alexander.'

'I will write to him immediately,' agreed Felicia, seeing the sense in this. 'One more lady then.'

'Is there no-one you could think of?' queried Dorothea.

'Well there is but I do not know how well it would be received by either my parents or Mr Gregory.'

'We will not concern ourselves with them. Tell me of whom you are thinking.'

Felicia told her attentive aunt Mrs Simon Gregory's story and begged her to agree that Mrs Gregory would be a suitable choice.

Dorothea was cautious, concerned that her niece was becoming carried away by a moving tale. She agreed though to meet Mrs Simon Gregory and accompanied Felicia to Strawberry Cottage the very next day.

'Forgive us for arriving unannounced,' said Felicia eagerly when Mrs Simon opened the door. 'But I was wishful of making you known to my Aunt Dorothea.'

Mrs Simon looked past Felicia and saw a woman she did not recognise and of a standing she was not used to entertaining. She was about to demur and make some excuse not to admit them when Dorothea stepped forward, a kind smile on her face and her hand outstretched.

'This is indeed a pleasure, Mrs Simons. My niece speaks very highly of you and I came to thank you for your devotion to her interests.'

It was difficult to behave churlishly in the face of such an effusion of good nature and Mrs Simon found herself opening the door to the little cottage wide and ushering them in. Dorothea had an enquiring mind and had some considerable interest in matters of the still room so it was not long before the two ladies were exchanging recipes and discussing the merits of various methods of fruit preservation. Nor did it take Dorothea long to be persuaded that Mrs Simon was a suitable candidate for third godparent and she accordingly extended this invitation to her new acquaintance. The look of gratification that spread across the lady's gaunt face was recompense enough and Felicia and Dorothea took their leave knowing they had spread a little happiness.

Soon invitations had been written and preparations were under way. Despite efforts of aunt and niece it was always going to be a quiet affair. Mr Gregory sent his apologies but accompanied his reply with a set of weighty silver napkin holders so Dorothea was well satisfied. Moved by gratitude on his reprieve from poverty, Bertram made the journey down from Yorkshire carrying with him the good wishes of his family and fiancée but unaccompanied by the child's father. Dorothea urgently sent an express to her husband demanding his attendance and that of their two younger children.

'I think it would be fair to say that it passed off well despite the absence of both parents,' said Dorothea as she re-entered the Castle having first seen her own family and then Bertram depart.

Felicia nodded but could not speak. She had been much upset by her parents desertion and as equally moved by a card and tiny silver bracelet she had received from Giles. It left her choked and emotional. She knew not how to converse with her aunt in normal tones although she was so grateful to that lady for all she had done.

'You will of course be wishing me away too.' Dorothea broke through the jumble of her thoughts.

'Oh most certainly not,' Felicia found she had the words after all. 'My gratitude to you, dear aunt, is difficult to express but that does not lessen it. I know I could not have borne this occasion without you.'

'You are a good brave girl and I wish that any of the little talks I have had with your mother during my stay might have had an effect on her attitude to little Alexa but I know they have not.' She placed her foot on the base of the stairs. 'I must away soon my child but I would first visit my mother at her home and discuss this predicament. Will you accompany me there tomorrow?'

'Most certainly I will,' Felicia assured her. 'I must say though that Grandmama too has made every effort to reconcile my parents to their lot.'

'I know it to be so,' agreed her aunt. 'However, I am determined to make one last push to settle the matter before I return home.'

Thus motivated, the two ladies made their way down the steep hill into Cheltenham and waited upon Mrs Makepeace. She had attended the christening so the first part of their visit was taken up with reviewing the event. All were satisfied that it had been carried out with due ceremony while they decried the behaviour of both Harold and Elsie Makepeace.

'I absolve my son in part,' said Mrs Makepeace on a note of apology, 'because he has worked so long and hard to redress the shortfall left by my husband. It would have been only fitting and just that his efforts were rewarded with a son to inherit but Elsie is a mother. And in the main part, a most caring and attentive mother, this behaviour is so uncharacteristic and I cannot credit it.'

'From my speech with her, Mama,' said Dorothea carefully, 'I believe she feels that she has failed both Harold and Felicia. Her thoughts are morbid. She sees her death as the only resolution. Once widowed, Harold could marry again and beget an heir.'

Felicia gave a gasp of shock. She had no notion that her mother felt so gravely.

'Sadly,' mused Dorothea, 'the crux remains financial. She would have been well satisfied with a girl if it had not impacted on the loss of the Yorkshire estates. If only there could be other sources of finance.'

'Indeed,' agreed Felicia disconsolately, 'and if I had a larger dowry I could marry Giles and whistle concern about inheritance goodbye.'

Mrs Makepeace began to look thoughtful. An unaccustomed silence fell amongst them. Dorothea cast a look in her mother's direction and saw the preoccupation there.

'Of what are you thinking, Mama?' she demanded. 'I have never thought of you as devious but I see schemes in your eyes.'

Mrs Makepeace gave a little laugh and stood up to go to her

desk. She drew down its front and brought out a page of the local journal.

'Now hearken to what I say,' she said. 'I have previously advised your brother to purchase land in Cheltenham and round about for Cheltenham has become most fashionable. He will not credit me with any business acumen. He does not understand the amount of information to which I am a party at the little soirées that I attend. Recently this house has come up for sale.' She indicated the notice on the folded paper. 'It is a rambling house in vast grounds close to the town but it is much neglected and requires a great deal of work in order that it might be habitable. My thought is to purchase it and wait until the town reaches it, then sell it for building land.'

She cast her eyes around the room, to look at both daughter and granddaughter. 'What say you to making a small investment and seeing how we prosper?'

Dorothea scanned the paper. 'But Mama, they demand 700 guineas for this house, where would the money come from?'

'I have some savings,' said Felicia breathlessly, her fertile imagination captured by being able to report to Giles that she had made money enough by her own means to support them. 'Since I knew that Giles was dependent on his uncle's good nature I have saved every birthday gift and as much of my allowance as I dared. I have 160 guineas to my name.'

'And I have just short of 500 set aside for this purpose,' announced Mrs Makepeace. 'Come Dorothea, what say you? Can you not spare a hundred guineas to make this possible?'

Both Felicia and Mrs Makepeace were now on their feet and they stood before poor Dorothea, desperate for her participation.

There was a short, intense silence before she looked up at them from her seat and smiled.

'I feel sure I can find it from somewhere,' she said.

23

*M*rs Makepeace set about her task of purchasing the house with no little verve. She had already earmarked a man of business she wished to use and had him thrash out a purchase price even before Christmas was upon them. He, a canny but honest man, was able to negotiate a price considerably less than the asking price so there was capital enough to carry out repairs. In due course, the stately old house was habitable and had been rented to a young man with a large family, who was grateful to be able to accommodate them all so cheaply. The fruits of this venture resulted in a trickle of income that Mrs Makepeace guarded jealously, determined that this would not be their only purchase.

High on the hill above her, the inhabitants of Castle Leck were not faring very well. Nothing Dorothea had been able to say to Elsie had reconciled her to her lot. She remained in bed assailed by a great lassitude. Her tears continued to flow freely.

At The Chimnies they prepared for Christmas. The presence of the two little girls ensured that some attempt at festivities was made. Mr Gregory, saddened by the events at Castle Leck, sent an invitation to that family to join him on the day. Then he set about to look for a present that would make his timid sister smile.

'What can I give you, dear sister, which would truly make you happy?' he asked earnestly, his big face radiating concern that his sister seemed to be shrinking.

Mrs Thornton attempted to meet his eyes but could not; she bowed her mousy head over her hands and mumbled.

'A visit from Giles, dear Sir,' she said so quietly that it was scarcely audible to Mr Gregory. He made her repeat the request while his mind worked hard to see if it was feasible. He promised nothing but sent an express to Mr Ponsonby at the bank requesting rather than demanding a two-week leave of absence for his nephew. Some three days later he received Mr Ponsonby's response: Giles would be released from duty at the end of the day before Christmas Eve.

Mr Gregory gave nothing away and determined it would be a surprise. He set his little nieces to gathering holly and ivy and had them decorate the hallway and one large saloon. On Christmas Eve night fell very early and it was extremely dark. The overcast sky was blotting out any possible moonlight. Mr Gregory had the hall fire stoked so that it was a roaring blaze. He helped Sophia and Imogen tie bright red ribbons around the sprays of dark green and placed lighted candles amongst them, so that the great hallway looked homely and welcoming. He prayed that Giles would not be delayed; he knew the girls were ignorant of the treat he had in store for them but their excitement was contagious and an air of anticipation pervaded their surroundings.

Giles, when he was told not a day before his departure that he might return to Cheltenham for two full weeks, was at first speechless with surprise and then euphoric. He felt suddenly that he had been released from a life sentence in Newgate. He wanted to embrace his employer but settled for shaking his hand fervently. At the end of a long day's work, he packed his bags and took a chaise to Reading which was laid on by his uncle. There he spent the night to resume his journey early on Christmas Eve. His impatience to be home made every hour seem interminable but he battled with his boredom and tried to imagine the scenes at home on his arrival. He had had no chance to warn Felicia and he suspected that his uncle would not have told his mother and sisters. He wished he could arrive with an armful of booty. The meagre presents he had bought them had long since been packed and sent. He was too modest to realise that his presence would be enough for all of them.

The day with its heavy cloud layer seemed to darken soon after lunch so Giles was even denied a view from the chaise's window. He sat perched on the edge of the seat ready to leap out the moment the carriage arrived. At last the noise and bustle of Cheltenham greeted him, there was a dusting of snow and every window seemed to have a candle in it. Those souls out in the streets were jocular and heartily wishing each other the joys of the season. Some could be seen to be worse the wear for drink. Giles did not mind, it was all a treat to him. He felt the horses take the strain of the climb up to The Chimnies with a fresh surge of excitement. As soon as the vehicle drew up outside the great porch he bounded out of the coach and hammered on the door, his great cape swirling around him.

Mr Daniels, the butler, made his stately progress to the door, convinced it was wassailers calling at this time. He was determined not to give any carol singer too much licence although there were sweetmeats, pastries and sugar plums waiting for anyone brave enough to make the climb.

He opened the door wide expecting a throng and then, as he perceived who it was, his lugubrious face split into a great smile.

'Mr ...' He stopped as Giles put his finger to his lips indicating his wish for secrecy. Giles strode past him and into the jolly, welcoming hall. He saw his sisters by the fire and surged forward sweeping them into an arm apiece.

'Giles,' they screeched in excitement and delight as they fought with the folds of his cape. He let them go and allowed Daniels to remove his outer garments. He was seen to be wearing a red and green festive waistcoat under the brown of his fitted coat. Both girls jumped up and down, unable to contain their joy, Sophia forgetting her young lady's dignity to match Imogen in her enthusiasm.

'Mama,' she screeched, a thought occurring to her at last. She ran to the bottom of the stairs. 'Mama, Giles is here.'

Mr Gregory, on hand to hear the commotion, came out of his study to see Giles bound up the stairs two at a time to the half landing and enfold a shaking Mrs Thornton in a strong embrace. She held him tight, unable to believe that her dearest wish had been granted. She put a fluttering hand up to caress his golden curls.

'My boy, my dear boy,' she said.

'Welcome home, nephew,' boomed Mr Gregory's voice from below. Giles released his mother and, taking her arm, escorted her down the remainder of the stairs.

As he came up to his uncle, his gratitude overwhelmed him. He shook the older man's hand vigorously. Even Mr Gregory seemed overcome by the reunion and he had to steady himself by drawing the others to the fire.

'You must be cold and in need of refreshment. Let me summon some,' he said curtly, attempting to mask his feelings.

'Oh no, how could I be with the warmth of such a welcome,' countered Giles, putting his arm around Imogen who was now clinging to his jacket.

'Dearest Giles,' murmured his mother, grasping his other arm again. She was trembling but there was deep warmth in her eyes as she feasted on the sight of her family all together again after so long.

The girls, still unable to contain their excitement, clamoured for their brother's attention and were only diverted when genuine carol singers called at the door. The sweet voices set the seal on the evening's pleasure; the family sang along lustily to the old favourites and pressed multitudes of goodies on the performers.

'Do you go on to Castle Leck,' asked Giles as he offered the leader a dish of sugared plums, hopeful that he might convey the news to Felicia of his return.

'No Sir, we have come from there,' the heavily clad man told him, 'sad it was, never have we had a poorer welcome. Only that sweet girl and her prim governess there to listen.' He shook his head to convey his feelings. 'A bad business.'

Giles thought so too but did not comment. He deplored the attitude of Felicia's parents and suspected that it would reduce the opportunities of contact he would be able to have with her over the next two weeks. He was unwilling to ask what arrangement had been made for the next day, fearing it would make him appear dissatisfied with his present company. Fortuitously Imogen was so full of all their plans that, despite the enormity of being able to have dinner in the grand dining room with the adults, she could not be silenced.

'Tomorrow we are to have a party, Giles. The Makepeaces and the Rector's family come for an afternoon luncheon. We are to play games including hide and seek!'

Giles put up his napkin to hide his expression while he judged what best to say. At last he found a safe course. 'I had understood that Mr Makepeace was fixed in Yorkshire at this present,' he commented.

'Not for the festive season, my boy,' declared Mr Gregory. 'He returned but two days ago and has promised to provide us with his family's company.'

Giles was both heartened by this news and disquieted. He must get word to Felicia that he was at home or he feared the shock might expose her to the censure of the critical. He went to his couch that evening a prey to mixed emotions; exhilaration and euphoria that his old life had temporarily been returned to him and anxiety about Felicia.

As he readied himself for sleep there was a discreet knock on the door and Higginbottom's small form entered the room.

'Master Giles, how glad I am to welcome you home,' he said, almost choked with emotion. 'You have been much missed.'

Giles collapsed backwards to sit on the bed. 'It is good of you to say so Higginbottom. I cannot express how much I have missed you all. One becomes accustomed to the deprivations but one cannot accept them. This is like a dream, I fear if I pinch myself I will awake and I cannot contemplate two weeks hence when I must return.'

'Nor I, Sir. To see your mother so full of a great joy does my heart good. If only it could remain thus, how happy she would be.'

Giles put up his hands to halt the words. 'I pray you do not speak of it or you will reduce me to maudlin. I am committed to enjoyment of the present. I will not be turned from my purpose.' He smiled bravely, determined not to be seduced into melancholy.

Higginbottom respected his wishes and found consolation in taking up the young man's discarded raiment and beginning to brush it down with a clothes brush he had discovered on the dressing table. 'But if there is anything I might do for you Mr Giles to make your stay more comfortable or memorable, you will say, will you not?'

Giles sprang up, having suddenly been presented with the answer to his most pressing concern. 'If you would get a note to Miss Makepeace,' he said breathlessly, 'then I would be grateful.'

24

*F*elicia was just donning her outer garments when there was a knock on her bedroom door and a young maid entered.

'Mr Hayworth begs me to tell you Miss that there is a messenger from The Chimnies who would hand you a note directly. He will not permit anyone else to convey it to you.'

Felicia blanched. 'Who is it from, Bridget?' she asked faintly.

'I cannot say, miss. Mr Hayworth did not say whether he recognised the hand.'

Felicia found her fingers were suddenly wooden and she fumbled with the little buttons down her front.

Taking pity on her, Bridget came forward and began to help her. She then pulled a hasty brush through Felicia's curls and shepherded her out of the room.

Having been unable to respond quickly when first hearing the news of a letter, Felicia was suddenly assailed by a wave of energy. She pelted along the great stone passage and hurled herself down the spiral staircase to the main landing; she then ran helter-skelter down the grand staircase.

'What has occurred, Hayworth?' she demanded between gasping breaths.

Wordlessly the butler removed the folded paper from the messenger's hand and gave it to Felicia.

The wave of nausea that had begun to surge through her body, stopped in its tracks. Although her heart thumped, Felicia knew a moment of pure relief. Her name was written in Giles' hand, he at least must be safe.

'Has some accident befallen them at The Chimnies?' asked Hayworth, impatient for news.

Felicia slit the letter with the ivory paperknife that remained on the hall table for just such a purpose and read the brief note avidly. She could not have prevented it even had she thought to do so but her face broke into the broadest of smiles.

'No,' she said on a fluttering breath, 'no it is good news. Master Giles is home for Christmas.' If Mr Hayworth wondered why his young mistress should receive the news with such acclaim, he did not show it. He dismissed the Gregory servant and motioned Felicia back to the stairs.

'I believe you should be making haste, Miss Felicia,' he said almost paternally. 'Your father wishes to attend church early as he is to take the reading.'

Felicia completed her toilet in a seraphic dream. No Christmas gift could have lifted her spirits so effectively from the doldrums in which they had sunk since her aunt had left. She made no mistake this time. She re-dressed herself with the greatest care and summoned her mother's maid to fashion her hair in the latest style.

Mr Makepeace, as he waited beside the carriage in some agitation, was amazed to see his daughter turned out so well.

'You look charmingly,' he said as he helped her up the steps into the carriage. 'I am proud to call you my daughter.'

Felicia bit her lip; even in her current state of blissful anticipation, she could not help wishing her father might say the same about her little sister.

Although they were early, Felicia did not have to wait long before the Gregory party arrived. As the two principal houses in the area, both families had pews at the front of the nave, the Makepeaces' on the left of the aisle, the Gregorys' on the right.

Felicia heard the family enter and knew it to be them as she recognised the girlish voices of Sophia and Imogen. Determinedly she did not turn her head. Only when they had all filed into the pew did she cast her eyes sideways and look down the line of bodies. Giles was stationed between his two young sisters. He wore a new coat of deep burgundy that Felicia rightly assumed to be a present from his uncle. His cravat was snowy white and flamboyantly folded and his hair shone like a warm golden light. Felicia took it all in as though drinking nectar and then she caught him looking at her and she smiled as she saw a glimpse of the depth of feeling in his eyes. A warm glow permeated her soul; six months might have passed since she had last seen him but the ardour between them had not diminished. She lifted her hymn book and sang joyously.

There was no opportunity for more than a brief exchange of pleasantries after the service; it was too public a place. Felicia returned home with her father to ready herself for the visit to The Chimnies. She had a basket full of presents but had already sent to London a book she had purchased for Giles.

'I have nothing for him,' she thought desperately as she cast her eyes anxiously around her room. Then she saw it, her most treasured painting. As the summer had drawn into autumn she had taken up sketching and had painted a tiny picture of their oak tree. She snatched it up and wrapped it in the remains of some coloured paper she had bought for the task. She inscribed his name upon the label but did not put whom it was from. If he needed telling then he did not deserve the present!

She was soon ready after that and descended the stairs to be drawn up short by the sight of her mother, heavily wrapped in a number of shawls.

'Mama, how wonderful! You are out of bed.' Felicia felt her cup run over. 'Do you attend Mr Gregory?'

Elsie Makepeace showed her daughter a white face and drooping form. 'Your father insisted,' she said unsteadily. 'He would not have me snub Mr Gregory.'

'Oh I am so glad that you feel able to come,' Felicia cried. She came up to her mother and chafed her quivering hand. 'Come! Miss Cuthbert and I will escort you to the carriage.'

The short journey was soon accomplished and they found themselves being made most welcome by Mr Gregory and the Thornton family. Greetings were exchanged and gifts arrayed around the principal saloon. Mr Gregory was in ebullient mood and made every attempt to jolly Mrs Makepeace out of her miseries. She was forced to respond in part by her husband's obvious determination that she should do so. It was clear, however, that it was an effort, and her cheerless aspect would have soured the party if it had not been swamped by the tide of goodwill and jocularity that swept in with the Rector's family. The Rector, a neat man of plain habit, was blessed with an ample wife and five boisterous children.

Mrs Thornton, a normally retiring and diffident hostess, seemed to gain confidence in the presence of the uncritical Mrs Roebuck. She could soon be seen to be chatting both with her and Miss Cuthbert.

Giles, mindful of his manners, was quick to make himself known to the Roebuck children who comprised Primula, aged seventeen, bidding fair to be a replica of her mama. Prudence, a dark, gentle fifteen-year-old, Clarence, a robust fourteen-year-old with a predilection for all places dirty, Hester, aged twelve, who gravitated towards Sophia, and finally little Amy, aged eight, who latched on to Imogen and followed dog-like at her heels. Felicia watched the group, smiling as she did so. The Reverand Roebuck had only recently become the incumbent of the Birdpeak church and his children, she recognised, but did not know. She waited for Giles to introduce her. Both Primula and Prudence seemed very taken with him and Felicia felt a moment's pang. She dismissed it, secure in the knowledge that he was hers.

The repast was noisy and long. Mr Gregory wowed his guests with course upon course of exciting dishes. There were minute partridges stuffed with berries and herbs, braces of pheasants in a rich brown sauce and a great goose oozing with golden liquid.

Felicia paced herself, knowing what was to come, but the younger children ate with all speed and were soon full to bursting. Mrs Makepeace played with her food, managing only a morsel of white meat before pushing the roasted vegetables around her plate. Mr Makepeace looked pained but said nothing and she was allowed to have her way.

It was already very dark when the meal broke up. The children, having been promised a game of hide-and-seek, pestered to be allowed to rampage around the house.

With great good nature Mrs Roebuck agreed to take part, which allowed Felicia and Giles unobtrusively to step forward too. Mrs Ellis, the housekeeper, was summoned to lay down the rules as to which rooms they were to have access to and the game commenced. As the mother of a large family Mrs Roebuck had come prepared. In a small cloth bag she had collected snatches of ribbon; each participant was to put their hand in and take one. The person drawing out the red ribbon was the seeker.

Much to her dismay, Felicia was the first in receipt of the appointed ribbon. The others shrieked with delight as she put her hands over her eyes and began to count to one hundred. Very quickly the sounds of the footsteps diminished and a hush fell over the house.

At first Felicia was embarrassed to be searching through Mr Gregory's home but Mrs Ellis had made it very clear that preparations had been made and that only Mr Gregory's bedchamber and the servants' dormitories were out of bounds.

It did not take Felicia long to find the younger members of the group and dear Mrs Roebuck was not adept at concealing her well-endowed form in small places. Primula took a deal of finding but was eventually tracked down to a closet in one of the guest bedrooms, a task made more difficult by the fact that this room and several others were in total darkness. It remained that only Clarence and Giles were at large. Felicia eventually located Clarence inside a camphor wood chest whose heavy lid would not have been easily lifted from inside. He came out of it with the aroma of mothballs clinging to his clothes. Keen that the slighter girls should not attempt such a feat Felicia dropped the catch on the chest and thrust home the complicated locking mechanism, then she set out to find Giles.

When she located him in an alcove along one of the upstairs corridors, she suspected that knowing he was now the last to be found he had moved his position.

'You are teasing me,' she said when she discovered him standing stock-still mimicking a statue. He grinned, then, relaxing his pose, brushed his lips against hers before striding gaily back towards the stairs calling out that he was the victor.

Giles made rapid work of finding people in his turn but carefully avoided finding Imogen and Amy until the very last. Miss Cuthbert was then dragged from the warmth of the main saloon to aid them in their search once everyone had hidden again.

Felicia made her way along the ground-floor passage towards the servants' domain. She tried a door and entered a chilly dark parlour that had a pair of thick drapes at its window. She ducked behind them and stood immobile in the bay of the window. Not many seconds later, she heard the parlour door open quietly and someone slip through it.

'Felicia,' hissed Giles, 'where are you?'

'Behind the drape,' she responded instantly.

'Sh....' he hushed her.

Felicia inadequately suppressed a giggle and waited as he joined her behind the curtains. Carefully he pulled the two pieces of cloth together. There was no bulge to betray them on the room side, they were perfectly concealed. Once he was satisfied of this, he turned and took Felicia in his arms and kissed her lovingly. She did not resist and leaned into him enjoying his strong embrace. They stood thus for a little while but Felicia could not help but be concerned that they might be found. She rocked back on her heels and grasped at his lapel.

'We must stop,' she said in an urgent undertone. 'The children could come upon us at any moment.'

'We will hear them as they progress along the passage,' Giles replied, but he did not attempt to resume kissing her and lowered his hands so they encircled her waist. A short silence ensued, eventually broken by Felicia.

'Giles?' she said on a note of interrogation. She had to ask a question which had been niggling away in the back of her mind since she had first seen him that morning.

'Yes,' he said elongating, the word.

'Can you tell me what has come over you? You seem so care-free, so at ease. Are you a changeling?'

Giles laughed and pecked a kiss on her upturned nose.

'I am no changeling,' he said. 'Three days ago, my felicity, I was sitting in my room at Mrs B's in flat despair. The dark winter months stretched out before me interminably. I saw no relief to the monotony of the life to which I was committed. I was divorced from those I held most dear.' Here he tightened his hold upon her. 'Then I present myself at work and Mr Ponsonby announces that within two days I can be at home with you all. It has taught me a well-deserved lesson. I am resolved to heed it. This may only be a respite and I have no expectation of mine uncle making it an annual concession but it is enough to show me that nothing is as it seems. I must grasp the moment.'

'Then I will too,' said Felicia, smiling up at him and then laying her head against his chest. 'We will make the best of this time.'

'Yes,' he agreed, moving his hand so that he could lift her chin for one final kiss.

Not long after this exchange they heard footsteps in the passage and drew apart, Giles to hide behind one curtain, Felicia behind the other. No sooner were they primly stationed there than the children burst in and searched the room by the light of a candle.

'Miss Cuthbert, Miss Cuthbert,' Imogen exclaimed, 'I think there is someone behind the curtain.'

With great presence of mind Giles stepped out from his hiding place being careful not to reveal that Felicia was there also.

'You have found me,' he declared and scooped up his no-longer-so-little-sister and made his way to the door. Felicia was soon left alone to savour the encounter. Within minutes the gong was sounded for tea and though few had room for more vittles and viands, it would be accompanied by an exchange of presents, so all those who had not been found quickly made haste to answer the summons.

They were very merry around the tea table. Giles' pile of presents was significantly smaller then everyone else's as few had been able to make provision for his unexpected presence but he opened Felicia's picture and beamed a look of gratitude to her before slipping it into his breast pocket.

Once the meal was over, it was seen that it was time to break up the party. The Rector had long since departed to take the evening service and his wife felt that it now behoved her to take her family home.

Elsie Makepeace was most certainly flagging and seemed to have shrunk within herself. She leaned heavily on Miss Cuthbert's arm as they made their way through the hall to the carriage. Her thanks when expressed to Mrs Thornton were barely audible. In contrast, Felicia was able to thank Mr Gregory and his sister with real sincerity.

'You have been most kind,' she declared, 'and have made it a very special day.'

Mr Gregory was heartily appreciative of such an expression of gratitude and in his turn Mr Makepeace expressed his appreciation of his daughter's behaviour as soon as the carriage door shut behind them.

'You have behaved in every way admirably today, Felicia,' he said through the darkness. 'You have more than made up for your earlier behaviour. I think Mr Gregory was well pleased with you. It may soon be possible to discuss with him your attachment to young Giles.'

'Thank you Father,' said Felicia, hugging the memory of the day to her. She doubted her father would say anything but it was nice to hear him say that he might.

25

There were not so many opportunities for Felicia and Giles to meet during the remaining days of his stay but they did steal an afternoon to take little Alexa to visit Mrs Simon. And, if it took them longer to walk through the woods than usual then there was no one to judge the difference between the leaving of one house and the arriving at another.

Mrs Simon was delighted to see her goddaughter and overjoyed to see Giles.

'Oh my dear boy, my dearest boy,' she kept saying as she scrutinised the changes in him. 'I had heard that you were here in Gloucestershire but I never imagined you would find the time to visit me.'

'I have come to take issue with you, my good friend,' replied Giles, smiling kindly on her. 'I understand from Mr Higginbottom that you were invited to our Christmas festivities yet you refused to avail yourself of the invitation.'

Mrs Simon could not help smiling in response to him though it had been a serious decision to absent herself. She turned to Felicia.

'Had your grandmother or your aunt been there, Miss Makepeace,' she said, 'I might have come but without their protection, I feared the arrival of Mrs Torrill or Mrs Lambert.'

'How can you imagine that they might arrive?' cried Giles, interrupting her, 'they would never have been invited.'

'That has not stopped them before.'

The truth of this statement left an uncomfortable silence in the room until Felicia remembered that she had brought a basket full of gifts. It was not until they were leaving that Mrs Simon alluded to it again.

'Have a care, dear Giles,' she said. 'Ware the Torrills and the Lamberts, they have not done with you yet.'

'I know,' said Giles, grasping her thin hand, 'I will be watchful.'

Felicia could not speak of her fears for him; they were too intense. Together she and Giles walked home briskly as the winter sun was going down and the air had a bite to it. Neither wanted the baby to become chilled. Giles escorted them to the gates of the Castle and lingered on his goodbyes.

'Will you attend the assembly at the pump rooms?' he asked.

'I had not thought to as Mama still refuses to leave the Castle unless persuaded by my father. Are you going?'

'I have been invited to accompany the Rector, his wife and two eldest daughters.'

Felicia frowned. 'I will ask Miss Cuthbert to accompany me,' she said deliberately.

Giles smiled an understanding smile and flicked her rosy cheek. 'It was mere civility in response to my uncle's invitation that they asked me,' he said. 'I do not believe that there is an ulterior motive.'

Felicia nodded, though she was not much reassured and she could not help feeling a trifle aggrieved. She could not understand why the Roebucks should have invited Giles and not her. She was still gently fuming on this the next day when Miss Cuthbert came to her all of a worry.

'My dear Miss Felicia,' she fluttered, the furrows on her brow deep with anxiety, in her hand a sheaf of letters. 'I fear your mother has not been attending to her correspondence. I have just found these down the side of a chair in the morning room. I know not what to do with them.'

Felicia took the letters and sifted through them. 'There is nothing for it, Miss Cuthbert, we must attend to these.'

The two ladies returned to the morning room where there was a serviceable table on which they could lay out the letters. They began to open them.

'All bills must be put together for my father's immediate attention,' declared Felicia as she discovered the chandler's fee note. 'If we are not careful he will refuse to supply us with further candles.'

They found several bills from milliners and dressmakers in Cheltenham and a mixture of correspondence. Much to Felicia's consternation they found an invitation from Mrs Roebuck for Felicia to attend the pump rooms with them that evening.

'What must she be thinking of us?' she cried. 'Not to have replied to such a kind invitation, what am I to do?'

Miss Cuthbert was equally dismayed; she just shook her head in regret.

It was as they were sitting there searching for solutions that Miss Primula Roebuck was announced.

Felicia leapt to her feet and embraced the young lady.

'My dear Miss Roebuck,' she cried, 'we have just found your mother's kind invitation. My mother's illness has meant she has failed to attend to her correspondence. I do so beg your pardon.'

'Oh then it is as my mother divined!' replied Primula, seeming more delighted than disturbed. 'For we made enquiries at The Chimnies and Mr Thornton said that when last he had spoken to you, you knew not of the invitation. Please say you will come, Miss Makepeace.'

'I would be delighted, utterly delighted if your mother would be kind enough to overlook the transgression.'

'Think nothing to it,' Primula ordered her. 'You must come.'

She then gave Felicia only long enough to write a grateful note to Mrs Roebuck before departing on her parish errands.

That evening Felicia tricked herself out in a pale yellow underdress and topped it with a robe of primrose satin. She doubted she would see Giles again before his return to London and she wanted him to remember her at her best. If there were some other less altruistic motive then she would not admit it. Although when she met Primula and Prudence again as they good-naturedly bunched up together so that was room for her in the carriage, she felt slightly ashamed. Neither girl could be described as a beauty, Primula being too short and dumpy for the current taste and Prudence too young to have attained her full womanly figure. If Giles were to choose either of them over her then it would be because they boasted kindness and a good heart. Felicia recognised this and knew she must curb some of her own less amiable qualities of tenacity and obstinacy in order to compare favourably with them.

The evening went off very well. There was little time for Felicia to enjoy Giles' company for he was kept busy dancing with all the ladies in the party. He did, however, manage to slip out with Felicia for a few minutes into the vestibule.

'I will of course call on the morrow to say my adieus,' he said gravely as he led her to a pair of chairs against the wall, 'but you know how strongly I feel this parting from you.'

Felicia nodded, too choked to speak.

'I do not know when I will see you again Felicia,' he said. 'Me thinks my uncle will not permit my attendance here next year. I cannot expect him to make such a concession again.'

Her eyes flew to his face on a mute note of interrogation. Giles met her eyes briefly but did not argue the point.

She saw that he believed beyond doubt that he could not expect such a holiday again. She bit her lip. There was noise and bustle coming from the Pump Room.

'We must return to the dancing,' he said heavily as he rose to his feet. 'We will still have our letters,' he added as though trying to convince himself.

'Yes,' Felicia managed, 'there will still be our letters.'

The twelve days of Christmas had passed and Giles came to Castle Leck ostensibly to take his leave of Mr and Mrs Makepeace. Harold Makepeace shook his hand firmly and gave his wife's apologies and good wishes. That lady had not quitted her room since Christmas. He then considerately left Felicia and Giles alone for what he made sure they understood would be no more than two minutes.

Wordlessly they clung together. There was nothing more to be said and when the moment came for Giles to return to his horse and wave her farewell, Felicia's face was a mask. Only once his horse had disappeared from view did she turn on her heel and make haste to her bedchamber to sob her heart out on her bed.

At The Chimnies the parting was similarly lachrymose. Mrs Thornton had not borne it well. At breakfast she had said her goodbyes and had then retired to her room to enjoy her distress undisturbed. His weeping sisters, Mr Gregory and Higginbottom waved off Giles. He waved back to them for as long as they were visible and then sank back in the squabs to enjoy his misery alone, feeding on his fears and suspicions about his fellow lodger.

On reaching his lodgings, Giles strode into the building and directly to Mr Littlejohn's room. He caught the man unawares. Giles came right up to him and stood looking down at him squarely, for he was a head taller than the other man. To his surprise Littlejohn did not quiver but remained where he was, meeting stare for stare.

'What can I do for you Mr Thornton?' he enquired. 'It is customary you know to knock on entering another's room.'

'I know custom and practice, Mr Littlejohn,' Giles replied, equally polite. 'It is you who seem to have forgotten it, had you ever known it.'

'I beg your pardon?'

'As indeed you should,' averred Giles between gritted teeth. 'Your constant interest in me is offensive. I demand that you stop spying on me, taking account of my every move.'

'What can you mean, Mr Thornton?' replied Littlejohn with a slight sneer. 'I have no interest in you above any others of my acquaintance.'

Giles was finding it hard to maintain his stance. He had not expected the other man to hold his ground so well. Giles had spent the journey east determining that he would confront the clerk who seemed to be like some malevolent shadow. Now in Littlejohn's room, having burst in unannounced, he felt at a disadvantage. He tried again.

'If you are in the pay of Nathan Torrill, then tell him his schemes will fail, mine uncle will never re-establish him as the heir.'

'I do not know to what you allude.' Littlejohn had moved to the door. 'Now I ask you to leave. You will get nothing from me and you have insulted me enough.'

Giles smouldered with resentment but there was nothing he could do but comply. He went to his room feeling vulnerable and a fool. Littlejohn was clearly a cleverer enemy than he had anticipated and now he had antagonised him.

Giles did not sleep well that night. He tossed and turned, reliving the conversation over and over again but no thoughts he could muster would turn the episode favourably towards him. He returned to the bank the next day in some trepidation. To his surprise two young hopefuls had replaced one of the counting-house clerks. There was no explanation as to why Darlington had left and Giles felt unable to ask. Instead, he made friendly overtures to the new boys in a vain attempt to make them feel welcome and at ease. Littlejohn sat on his stool and divided his time between his books and watching Giles with a hint of a derisive smile.

As the weeks wore on, the presence of Littlejohn began to impede Giles more and more. Everywhere he went, he discovered the man to be there also. He could not visit the markets without seeing him at another stall. He could not saunter in the park without finding him lurking behind a tree. There was no end to his appearances and no lid to his insolence. On several occasions Mr B had been moved to suggest that they should evict the man as he was becoming such a nuisance. Giles saw all his good intentions of taking a buoyant view of the future leave him. He felt preyed upon.

One evening Mr Ponsonby had asked him to stay late to complete a task and he had seen Littlejohn leave before him. However, when he set out for his lodging house some time later, he sensed he was being shadowed.

'Begone, Littlejohn,' he yelled into the darkness, making the other few hurrying souls turn and stare at him before continuing on their journey.

There was no reply and no diminution of the feeling. Giles pressed on.

He had reached the very darkest part of the journey when the narrow streets were barely lit as the houses were shuttered. He quickened his pace for Birmingham Street was not much further ahead. He turned a corner into the penultimate walkway when he was grabbed from behind.

'Well, Thornton,' said a cruel and icy voice. 'I have you now.'

26

There was light of a sudden. A lantern was held close to his face so he could not see the person beyond as more than a silhouette. He struggled against his captors but two great men held him fast one at each arm.

'What do you want?' he demanded between rasping breaths. 'I have no money to give you.'

'It is not the coins in your pocket I am after,' came the vile voice again, 'but the money to which you aspire and have no entitlement.'

'Torrill!' Realisation came to Giles in a flash.

His captor laughed viciously. 'Take off his jacket, bind him,' he ordered and the two men holding Giles forced off his coat and began to lash separate ropes around his wrists. Giles fought against them to no avail. The men were perhaps twice his weight with limbs like tree trunks.

'There is no escape, little cousin,' hissed Torrill, confirming his identity. 'I have you now, you cannot evade me, though you have been a difficult quarry to snare. You should have been long despatched. First Norton failed me, then you outran these fools here and then I found myself paying and paying Darlington to no benefit. I should have long ago taken on the task myself.' He lifted his arm and a great whip cracked high above his head and then fell snake-like on the cobbles. 'But I have you now,' he repeated.

The noise of the whip startled Giles into struggling again but his attempt at freedom was as futile as on the previous occasion.

'Oh no,' said the voice, now full of hatred. 'You cannot escape what is coming to you. You will feel the cut of my whip across your back until you can bear it no more. Then you will crawl away and lick your wounds taking your mother and your sisters with you.'

'Never!' Giles spat the word out.

Nathan Torrill stepped forward and put the handle of the whip across Giles' throat, restricting his breathing. 'Oh yes, I think you will, Thornton. For if you don't, I will surely kill you and then who will protect your sisters from me? Eh!'

The revulsion that Giles felt at the image Torrill's words conjured up brought bile to his throat. He could no more have stopped himself from spitting in the man's face than he was able to fly away from his captors.

Torrill hit him a thumping blow across his cheek before wiping the spittle away with the back of his hand.

'That was very foolish,' he said, grasping Giles' hair and forcing his head backwards so that it hit the wall of the house behind. 'I could kill you now without a doubt. Just one more victim of footpads.' There was a pause while Torrill appeared to consider this. 'But it would leave too many loose ends. I want rid of your entire family and I cannot kill them all.' He let go of Giles and stepped back. 'Turn him,' he ordered.

His two captors twisted Giles around so that his face was thrust against the gritty wall of the building. He felt the stone graze his cheek and then his arms being drawn by the ropes so that they were outstretched, the muscles dragged almost to breaking point. Giles braced himself as best he could.

Nathan Torrill grasped the collar of Giles' shirt and tore it off his back. The button caught against his throat making him gag before it hung in tatters from the sleeves. Then Torrill raised the great whip and brought it down across Giles' back.

The pain burst through Giles like a broken dam. He felt its agony and the air rushed out of his lungs. He caught up a yelp before it could reach his lips. Another blow came and then another and then another. Giles' skin burned with the torture, he wanted to scream out his anger and his frustration, he knew he was lost; all that remained to him was his courage, he could not forfeit that as well.

There was a roaring in his ears, a bellowing which he could not divorce from the pain in his back. He braced himself for another blow. It did not come. The noise around him arranged itself into voices. The ropes holding his arms went slack. Giles' knees buckled and he sank to the ground. There was the pounding of feet on the cobbles and the sweet sound of others' speech.

'Don't be worrying about those two, Mr B, it's this one we want.' The voice was familiar but Giles could not place it. Gingerly he turned himself around. The first lamp had been consigned, broken to the floor but another swung drunkenly in Mr B's hand as he tried to shine its light on Littlejohn, who was clinging onto Nathan Torrill's whip arm.

Shaking his head to try to clear it and make sense of what had transpired, Giles struggled to his feet, leaning heavily on the wall. He drew himself up straight as best he could. Littlejohn was still tenaciously attached to Torrill's arm but he did not have the weight to contain him. After a brief contretemps, Torrill shook himself free but he did not take to his heels like his lackeys. Instead, he grasped his stick, which had been leaning against the alley wall, and drew from its depths a lethal looking sword. An oath escaped Mr B, who flung down his lantern and raised his other hand that contained a stout stick. Littlejohn valiantly attempted to stand between Torrill and Giles but he was thrust aside.

With the roar of an angry bear, Mr B launched himself at Torrill only to have his arm slashed with the fearsome weapon. Giles, overcoming his hurts out of necessity, grabbed Mr B's stick before it slipped from his grasp and parried Torrill's first thrust. In a frenzy of blows, Torrill attempted to run Giles through but the dissolute life he had led thus far made him slow of foot and short of breath. Even in his weakened state, Giles was able to dodge his dimly seen assailant, aided by the fact that the steel of the sword captured whatever light there was.

Littlejohn had caught up the lantern and lit the candle oblivious to the jagged edges of glass that now surrounded it. Watching the fight before him with an anxious eye, he used his foot to search the cobbles for the whip. Finding it at last, he picked it up and flicked it out so that it lay malevolently on the cobbles.

Giles was now panting. Every raise of his arms as he used the stick two-handed to ward off the blows of the sword tore at the lesions on his back. The force of Torrill's attack was diminishing but he could still wield the sword to good effect.

'I have the whip, Mr Giles,' cried Littlejohn urgently. 'What would you have me do?'

Giles manoeuvred himself nearer to Littlejohn and put out a hand to grasp the top of the whip. With a wry and pained smile, he remembered the lessons he had been given by Costley and Guilliam some three years before, and he whirled the great leather thong until it wrapped itself tightly around his assailant's legs. Torrill toppled and fell to the ground where Mr B promptly held him down. Littlejohn ran to Giles and supported him as he stood wavering unsteadily on his feet.

'I do not presume to understand why you have come to my rescue,' said Giles between rasping breaths, 'but I thank you from the bottom of my heart.'

Littlejohn smiled. 'All will be revealed to you, Sir, but not here, not now. Should we not retire to the lodgings?'

'Yes indeed, let us go where there is more light and greater comfort.' He turned to confront the body on the ground. 'Can you get him to the house, Mr B?' he asked.

Nothing loath and oblivious to his own injury, Mr B dragged the exhausted Torrill to his feet and slung him over his shoulder, the whip still dangling around the captive's legs.

As they entered the lodgings an anxious Mrs B greeted them. She was bobbing about trying to release the pent-up energy her fear for them had excited. When she saw the state of Giles, her hands flew to her mouth in horror.

'Oh my, oh my,' she moaned, her voice muffled.

'There's no time for 'umours,' growled Mr B, bolting the door one-handed as he struggled with his load. ''E needs you to treat them wounds. Come.' He set off up the stairs to Giles' room, Littlejohn hard on his heels, juggling Giles' discarded coat, the swordstick, the lamp and avoiding the trailing whip.

Mrs B seemed to respond to these bracing words; she recovered herself and hurried away to get water and bandages. In the bedroom, Littlejohn lit every candle he could find, then ransacked his own room for further illumination. The fight seemed to have gone out of Torrill; he sat where Mr B had placed him in an ancient open wooden armchair, his head drooping and his lank hair flopping over his face. Mr B, however, was suspicious of his docility and, before unwinding the whip from the man's legs, bound his wrists to the arms of the chair.

Giles having followed them up, collapsed on the bed, his head bowed over his chest as he tried to come to terms with what had just befallen him. Only when Mrs B appeared with a bowl of steaming water and a collection of unctions did he raise his head to look around him. Before he could say anything, there was the clatter of the knocker at the front door by way of interruption. Giles and Littlejohn exchanged glances.

'Now who could that be?' Mrs B asked the question on everyone's lips as she set the bowl on the dresser.

Littlejohn rose. 'I will investigate,' he said, indicating with his hand that he wished Mr B to guard the prisoner.

'You cannot keep me here,' hissed Torrill, breaking his silence, but he was ignored.

Afeared that the unknown callers might be friends of their adversary, Littlejohn stood at the door and called through it.

'Who is it who demands entry?' he asked imperatively.

'Lord Guilliam, a friend of Giles Thornton. Let me in I say.'

Littlejohn made haste to draw back the bolts and let him in.

'Well, my lord, may I say how pleased he will be to see you. Come, let me take your coat.'

Guilliam, who thought himself well acquainted with Giles' view on Littlejohn, was surprised into doing what he was bid.

'Where is Thornton?' he demanded when he had gathered his scattered wits.

'In his room, my lord, but I must warn you ...'. Littlejohn realised he was wasting his breath as Lord Guilliam started up the stairs in haste. Littlejohn scurried after him.

Guilliam burst into Giles' room to be confronted with the unexpectedly lurid sight of Mrs B tending to the weeping lash marks on his friend's back.

'Good God, what has occurred?' he cried, appalled by what he saw. Giles looked up at him but winced as Mrs B dabbed a gash with some evil mixture.

'You must ask Mr Torrill for chapter and verse,' said Littlejohn, following Guilliam into the room and quietly shutting the door.

Guilliam spun on his heel to confront Torrill whom he now perceived bound to the chair.

'Did you do this?' He indicated the wounds on Giles' back.

Torrill stared at him woodenly, vouchsafing nothing.

'You can't expect him to admit it, my lord,' said Littlejohn.

'But that is what he will do.' Giles had stood up shaking off Mrs B's ministrations and now he was walking purposefully, if stiffly, towards the constrained man in the chair. 'I will have your confession, Torrill, signed before witnesses,' he said grimly. 'For it can be my only insurance against further attempts on me.'

'Nonsense,' said Guilliam, 'send your man for the constable. If he has assaulted you, he should be up before the magistrate.' He turned imperatively to Littlejohn. 'Go man, fetch the constable here and now.'

'No, I say.' Giles went to his friend and placed a restraining hand on his arm. 'I will not have my uncle subjected to the indignity of having a jailbird for a nephew. He has suffered enough by Torrill's hand already.'

Torrill, with a mind to encourage the dissension between his captors, hissed his determination not to admit to anything.

Giles stood looking down at him for a long moment, his unwavering gaze laden with disgust. Eventually he spoke in a cold, unemotional voice. 'You will sign a confession, in fact you will sign three. It will list the previous attempts you spoke of. I shall keep a copy, Guilliam will have one and one will be kept in a strong box at the bank. You have no choice for you stay bound to that chair until you do.'

Guilliam cast about in exasperation but he did not counter Giles' words for he could see that his friend was determined to have his way. 'Well get on with it then,' he growled after no one moved to progress the outcome. Littlejohn jerked into action and went to the desk in search of quill and paper.

'Would you have Mr B untie him, Sir?' he asked once he had set up the table and ascertained that Mrs B had had time to bandage her husband's wound.

Giles, once again subjecting himself to the attentions of Mrs B, cogitated for a moment, shook his head, wincing as he did so.

'No, no, I believe you should take it down as dictation,' he said.

So for the next hour they hassled and threatened, cajoled and berated Torrill until they had down the full sum of his iniquities. Then, with painstaking thoroughness, Littlejohn wrote out two more copies.

If Torrill thought he could then refuse to sign, he had judged the matter wrongly. He made such an attempt but by now Giles was weary beyond tolerance and Guilliam had exhausted any patience he might normally have had. When Torrill uttered his first refusal, Guilliam advanced on him with such purposefulness that the man capitulated and scratched his signature on each of the papers proffered. Then Guilliam, Giles, Littlejohn and Mrs B signed as witnesses and Mr B made his mark.

'Go now Guilliam, go with your copy and have it safely bestowed before we release him.' Giles' words were punctuated with sighing breaths, his head was heavy and the strain around his eyes was showing as he tried to keep them alert.

Guilliam moved to remonstrate but seeing the state of his friend, he thought better of it and began to collect up his things.

'Can you be sure to hold him fast until I am away?' he asked Littlejohn.

The man nodded emphatically. 'He will cause no more trouble here my lord. Mr B and I will see to that.'

'Ay we will an' all,' growled Mr B, who had got his second wind and was of a mind to punish Torrill for what he had done to Giles.

'You should put Thornton to bed,' said Guilliam, indicating Giles who was clearly swaying with exhaustion as he sat on the bed listening to the others' conversation. Giles waved a hand in denial but it was seen that he could do no more.

'Afore you go, my lord, could you help us hustle this sinner down to the parlour, so Mr Giles can get some shut-eye?'

With little to-do the three men escorted Torrill away from his intended victim. Then Guilliam quitted the house and had Giles been awake to follow events, he would have known that his friend sent a servant an hour and a half later to give the all clear. Mr B and Littlejohn then with much relish threw Torrill out into the muddy street.

Littlejohn made his silent way back up to Giles' room and found him flat out on his stomach asleep on the bed. Afraid to lay heavy covers on the damaged back in case he disturbed him, Littlejohn stoked up the fire and kept a lonely vigil throughout the night to ensure that the fire never went out.

27

A little before six o'clock the next morning, Giles stirred and groaned as the wounds on his back protested. He rose gingerly to a sitting position and peered blearily about him. The events of the previous evening had taken on an aura of unreality, yet he could not deny it had happened because his body was reminding him with every movement. Although it was still very dark outside, the fire was giving out a warm light and in the flicker of the flames, Giles could make out Littlejohn's form slumped in the chair.

Giles carefully manoeuvred himself off the bed and took a taper to the fire; from it, he then lit a few of the stubs of candles left over from the night before.

'Littlejohn,' he whispered urgently. 'Littlejohn, awake man, 'tis nearly time to depart for work.'

Littlejohn's eyelids fluttered and then he seemed to shake off the tendrils of sleep and give Giles his full attention.

'You cannot go in, Sir,' he said in concern as he watched the painfully slow movements that were all Giles could manage.

'I must, Littlejohn, I have already been absent too long. Mr Ponsonby will soon tire of me, if he thinks me inclined to shirk because of the holiday mine uncle allowed me.'

'I much doubt it, Sir. You work so hard and are too much an asset for him to think that. He would know you would only cry off if you had no alternative. Indeed let me tell him so.' He made a hasty movement to get to his feet and took hold of the shirt Giles was attempting to put on.

'Let me do that for you, Mr Giles,' he said.

Giles paused in his contortions. 'For the first time I think I begin to understand,' he said.

'Understand what Sir?' asked Littlejohn, suddenly on his guard.

'Of course it has puzzled me, astounded me even, as to why a man I have looked on as my enemy for so long should all at once leap to my rescue and even, if my memory serves me correctly, risk his own life to save mine. However, I think I have fathomed it.'

'How so?' Littlejohn too was still now, awaiting his fate.

Giles turned to confront him. 'Methinks you are a relative of Higginbottom. I should have seen the resemblance earlier but I was so sure Torrill sent you that my eyes were blinded to it. You have carried a heavy disguise in your insolent tone and derisive smile. I was fooled. Did my uncle set you the task of protecting me?'

'No Sir,' said Littlejohn, bowing his head, as he knew this truth would pain his young charge and he could not meet his eager eyes. 'Twas all my cousin Higginbottom's scheme. Rightly he feared for your safety.' Here he fleetingly managed to meet Giles' eyes. 'He determined that there should be someone to watch over you and he asked me to do that.' He gave a short laugh. 'I had long envied him his role as a rich man's valet. To be so respected and to be so useful, that was all I craved. I accepted the role of your guardian angel with alacrity. I took up employment at the bank and moved lodgings to this place. The rest you know. I have plagued you and shadowed you knowing that I riled you but unable to do anything else. If Torrill had guessed that I championed you, he would have had Darlington do away with me long ago.' Here a gleam of triumph lit his pale eyes. 'Instead I was able to negate his attempts to stain your reputation.'

'So it was you who had him removed.'

Littlejohn nodded with a certain satisfaction. 'He was not very clever,' he said, 'but dangerous enough.'

'How can I thank you and Mr Higginbottom? What can I do to recompense you?' Giles was mortified as he realised that Littlejohn had done all this for only the same wages as he had been earning at the bank. 'I owe you so much.'

'You owe me nothing, Mr Giles,' replied Littlejohn earnestly. 'Nothing at all. Although you have had some angry words with me, I could always see that it hurt you and I watched your many little kindnesses to those less fortunate than yourself and I have been honoured to serve you and beg that you will allow me to continue to do so.'

❦ ❦ ❦

Mr Ponsonby stood in the upper bay panes of the bank and looked through the mosaic of the diamond-shaped leaded window down into the street. He took up his half-hunter watch that had been supported by his ample paunch. He flicked open the case and looked at the hands.

'Thornton is late,' he informed the dignified man who was standing quietly at the other side of a large desk from the bank manager.

'That is unlike him,' replied Mr Sherbourne. 'I have only ever known him to be punctual.'

'No matter,' said Ponsonby as he shut the watch with a snap. 'I am sure he has good reason. I shall be pleased to promote him to underfloor manager. He has worked hard and deserves to do well on his own merit.'

'Then you are pleased with him, Mr Ponsonby?' asked Sherbourne, determined to have the matter clear.

'Very pleased, save for one small thing.'

'And what might that be?'

'Tis nothing really but he has never seen eye to eye with one of the tellers. I would prefer perfect amity amongst my staff.'

Sherbourne laughed. 'Underneath your bluff and bluster Mr Ponsonby, you have a soft heart,' he said.

'Ah yes, you may be right.' Ponsonby took out his handkerchief and wiped his face. 'But I will watch with care that the young man does not single out Littlejohn unfairly for he is a good, honest man, who has been of some service to the bank recently.' He stopped abruptly and gazed raptly down the street. 'Good heavens!' he said in some surprise.

'What is it?' Sherbourne made haste to the window.

'Thornton and Littlejohn walking here together as friendly as you please. Who would have credited it!'

The two senior men watched as Giles and Littlejohn entered the bank and then Sherbourne and Ponsonby moved to a gallery that overlooked the bank floor. They saw Littlejohn remove Giles' greatcoat with the utmost care.

'Almost as though they are master and servant,' said Sherbourne sotto voce and he returned to the bank manager's office and the business of the day.

Giles spent the day trying hard to come to terms with the change in his fortunes. Ponsonby had called him in not long after his arrival and awarded him his promotion.

Giles stammered and stuttered his gratitude. He was completely unmanned, it coming so swiftly to him. He knew it meant no reduction in hours. If anything these would be longer because he would have to arrive before his underlings and leave after them but he would be able to pay Littlejohn a nominal fee for his ministrations. Not long after this, he found the means to stow one of Torrill's confessions unobtrusively in the vault. On their way home, Littlejohn and Giles arranged for a courier to take the remaining copy to Cheltenham and place it in the hands of Higginbottom, who would know just what to do with it if anything happened to Giles.

Not all that had befallen him did Giles describe to Felicia in his letters. The only person who knew all in Cheltenham was Higginbottom. When some of what Giles told her did not make sense, Felicia waylaid Higginbottom on the road down to the town and demanded from him some explanation. Reluctant as he was to betray confidences and cause the young lady concern, he saw it as some insurance that someone outside the Gregory household should have knowledge of Torrill's doings. He made a copy of the document Torrill had signed and gave the certified copy into Felicia's hands.

'Guard it, Miss,' he begged her earnestly. 'For there are but three other copies and Torrill is so determined, I can believe that he might attempt to track them down. No one knows save you and I that this copy exists.'

Felicia almost wished she had not come upon the knowledge that Giles was in real danger. Already she felt oppressed by the circumstances at Castle Leck. Her father continued to favour the Yorkshire estates with his presence and Mrs Makepeace made no attempt to shake off her melancholy. Only the baby flourished, cushioned by the love of Nanny, Miss Cuthbert and herself. When Felicia felt particularly dispirited she would bundle little Alexa up and take her to visit either Mrs Simon Gregory or her grandmother. The elder Mrs Makepeace was still indulging her talents in the property market and had generated sufficient income from their original purchase to buy a number of smaller properties connected to it. Her enthusiasm was infectious so both Felicia and her Aunt Dorothea gave her whatever cash they could spare from their pin money and housekeeping respectively. As the days lengthened and the temperature rose Mrs Makepeace liked nothing more than driving in an open-topped carriage with Felicia by her side, explaining her plans for the expansion of their empire. She talked in terms of years which inevitably countered much of Felicia's enthusiasm for where her grandmother spoke of five years hence, Felicia saw it only as the extension of the time she would be separated from Giles.

On these occasions her grandmother would chafe her hand and try her utmost to support Felicia's flagging spirits.

'There is always the possibility that we will make a fortune sooner, she assured her. My advisers tell me there is much demand for houses and that it is increasing. I would not have you despair, my dear.'

'Despair, no I will not despair, Grandmama,' Felicia responded, tight-lipped, 'but I cannot prevent myself from a feeling of oppression when I realise that I shall more than likely be four or five and twenty before we see the fruits of our toils.'

Her grandmother paused, saying cautiously, 'Now do not fly at me, my dear, but I would know that you are sure that this young man is worth the sacrifice of your youth.' She raised her hand to silence Felicia who had attempted to interpose an answer before she had finished speaking. 'I know that there are other young men who have expressed an interest in you. Would you not consider them?'

Felicia gave an emphatic shake of the head. 'You are thinking of Lord Guilliam,' she said sadly. 'I do not know how you have learned of his interest in me but I have to tell you that I can love no one but Giles. I will not swerve from my determination to marry him and only him.'

Mrs Makepeace did not again allude to the subject; from then on she spoke only as if Giles and Felicia's future union was an assured event. For this Felicia was grateful and throughout the following summer she continued to visit her grandmother regularly. Her aunt Dorothea visited during August and tried to persuade Felicia to return with her for a protracted stay. Felicia would very much have liked to accept the kind invitation; a change of scene was the one thing she most needed. She was, however, constrained by concern for her little sister. She would have wished to take the baby with her but Nanny had pointed out with rough candour that already there was some talk that the baby was not her mother's after all but her own. If Felicia were seen to travel abroad leaving her mother behind but taking the baby it would only add fuel to the gossip-mongers. Regretfully Felicia rejected her aunt's kind offer. While Alexa could very well have stayed at Castle Leck with Nanny and Miss Cuthbert, it was a point of principle for Felicia that not all her family could abandon her. Conscious though, that she must do something to turn the thoughts of the curious, Felicia began to cultivate the acquaintance of the Roebuck family, walking out with the sisters, Prudence and Primula in clement weather. This in its turn allowed Mrs Roebuck a pretext on which to visit Mrs Makepeace and do what she might to turn that sad lady's thoughts in a more cheerful direction. Throughout the summer this good lady made little headway and she was on the brink of despair when she finally hit upon discussing the gardens with her hostess. Mrs Makepeace's passion for her garden had withered and died after the birth of her second daughter and the overworked gardeners had only maintained her grand design. No new areas had been cultivated. Now with the summer enticing people out of doors, Mrs Roebuck had encouraged Mrs Makepeace out into the garden to stroll along the terraces. At first it seemed she had no interest in the borders and vistas which had once been her pride and joy, but under Mrs Roebuck's careful probing she had found the words to describe her original plans and a flicker of interest had been rekindled.

Heartened by the improvement in her mother's demeanour, Felicia began to arrange to have visitors. The Thornton girls, now sixteen and thirteen, still attending additional lessons with Miss Cuthbert, were encouraged to stay and take tea afterwards as had been the previous custom. Felicia had even made an appeal to Mrs Thornton to come and see what might be done to entice Mrs Makepeace back into her old ways. Improvement was slow and very gradual and at no time did Mrs Makepeace acknowledge the existence of her baby daughter, Alexa, but for Felicia it was tangible evidence that life might yet be carefree again.

28

As Christmas approached, neither Felicia nor Giles could bring themselves to express the hope in their letters that Mr Gregory might invite Giles again to enjoy Christmas in the bosom of his family but it was there in every line. October came and went without any clue from Mr Gregory as to what he intended to do and November was nearly at an end before he announced to his sister and her daughters that he would be taking them to London for the festive season. To Mrs Thornton it mattered not where she spent Christmas as long as she was with her children; to be close to Giles was all that mattered. Sophia, now a young lady and in some small way a party to Felicia's confidences, felt only disappointment for her friend and brother. She carried the news to Felicia with a heavy heart.

'If I could find the words to persuade my uncle, I would do it,' she said as she held out her hands to Felicia. 'I do beg your pardon for having to give you such disappointing news, I wish it were otherwise.'

'It was good of you to come,' said Felicia, maintaining her self-control with some difficulty. 'I know how uncomfortable it must be for you,' she managed with a hint of a smile, knowing that Sophia, a serious soul, took to heart the feelings of others. 'I have tried to guard against the disappointment,' Felicia assured her, not wanting the girl's own enjoyment to be spoiled by thoughts of what might have been. 'You go to London and you make it the very best of times for Giles. He will be so delighted to see you all. And if you could ensnare my friend Guilliam at the same time, I shall be well pleased with you.'

Sophia stifled a giggle. 'You should not say such things,' she said. 'How could he possibly look at me having first fallen for you.'

Felicia looked at her friend who was now an inch or two taller than her. The girl was of willowy form and her plain childhood looks had given way to a beautifully defined face. Her hair, no longer mousy, had darkened and added contrast to her clear pale skin. Her expressive grey eyes spoke of hidden depths. Felicia thought that in a year or two, Sophia would be a beautiful young woman. She was already an accomplished one, having absorbed all that her mother and Miss Cuthbert had been able to teach her.

Determined not to betray her disappointment, Felicia hugged the girl and sent her on her way. Only when she had stoically seen Sophia to the outer courtyard of the great Castle did Felicia slip away through the gardens to the woods.

It was cold and she had not taken the trouble to dress warmly as she had not intended to escape to her tree, but such was the crushing blow that Mr Gregory's decision had dealt her that she had to find refuge somewhere. At the base of the tree she looked skywards up into the bare branches. Only a few tenacious dried leaves were still clinging to the twigs above her. For a moment she considered climbing aloft but her shoes had slippery soles and she was already feeling the cold. Kissing her fingers to the tree, Felicia turned and retraced her steps to the Castle and in front of a roaring fire in one of the little parlours behind the great stairway she wrote a hard, angry letter to Giles. That she could not send it she knew the moment she started to read it, so she consigned it to the flames and began again.

What followed for her was a quiet Christmas. Her father saw fit to return from Yorkshire and her mother was sufficiently sanguine to accompany him and Felicia to church. The Rector had invited the family to luncheon with them but Mr Makepeace had declined, knowing that the Roebucks were also having the

Rector's brother's large family and the Rectory would struggle to house them all. Felicia spent the better part of the day in the nursery with her little sister, who now, at more than a year old, was toddling around the room on leading strings. Felicia's grandmother had joined her there in the afternoon, only withdrawing when the tea bell had sounded. For Felicia the bittersweet memory of the year before could not fail to obtrude. Her thoughts were in London with the Thornton family and even the delight of the first real snow of the winter could not lift her spirits.

With the advent of spring and all the beautiful bulbs, Mrs Makepeace seemed to be restored to her normal self again and, except for the absence of any mention of Alexa, she behaved to Felicia and the servants much as she was used to. Even Mr Makepeace could perceive a change and he began to reside more of the month at Castle Leck than had been his recent practice. Felicia hoped daily that her mother might ask to see the child. In fact so great was the change in her that Felicia was moved to ask whether she might bring Alexa to the great saloon after tea one day. Mrs Makepeace simply ignored the question. Felicia did not pursue it that day but asked again on the following day. For a week Felicia subscribed to the course of action without any encouragement, so nearly she gave up, then she noticed her mother's eyes flicker to her face and she knew that her mother was taking account of the question. Two weeks later she was even given an answer.

'We will see, my love,' said Elsie Makepeace, 'perhaps some day.'

Felicia was so overjoyed with even this hint of a thaw that she had to visit her grandmother to share the good news. She took Alexa with her the following morning for Mrs Makepeace had not seen the baby since Christmas, as the hill had been slippery and impassable for much of the months of January and February. It was now the end of March and although the snow had gone and the daffodils were promising their golden glory, there was still a nip in the air. Felicia wrapped rugs around Alexa and Nanny to keep them warm and hoped her grandmother's house was well heated. They spent a happy hour together indulging Alexa and allowing her to show off her prowess at walking. She was a pretty baby with soft strawberry-blonde hair that already curled all over her head. She was beginning to utter a string of words and was fascinated by her grandmother's King Charles spaniel that spent most of its indolent life sitting on a silken cushion near the fire.

Felicia quitted her grandmother's home with some reluctance. It was so nice to be free and easy with the child without having to guard what was said and where she was taken. Having extracted Alexa from her grandmother's arms, she bundled Nanny and the child into the carriage and commanded the coachman to make haste. The clouds were gathering and Felicia feared there was to be a torrent.

The storm hit them as they wended their way up the steep incline to the Castle. Great lashings of rain hit the carriage and drenched the poor coachman and the groom who was sitting beside him. The wind roared and a great gust made the vehicle sway. Felicia had to grab the straps to stop herself falling forward. Nanny gave a shriek and clutched little Alexa to her. Looking out of the window Felicia could not imagine how the coachman was seeing his way for the cloud had descended and closed in around them. There was suddenly a ghastly lurch as the carriage wheel hit something hard and the ladies were thrown from their seats. Alexa's head hit the door-stay and she fell limp to the floor.

By some miracle the carriage had righted itself and in the gloom Felicia scrambled back on to the swabs to be met by a wail from Nanny.

'Oh my baby, my baby,' she sobbed as she scooped up the child from the floor of the carriage.

Felicia pressed forward to look into the pale face of the child. 'Oh Nanny, what has she done, is she alive?' Felicia could see no movement of the child's chest. Nanny, her first panic giving way to the need for action, put her cheek near to the child's mouth.

She nodded emphatically. 'The Lord be praised, the child is

still alive. She must be concussed, Miss, 'twas a fearful bang she received.'

The coach had come to a halt and the coachman came to the door.

'I am very sorry Miss but we hit a milestone. The wheel is damaged and will not hold if we go further. I must send Shaw on to fetch some help.'

'Well let him be quick, I beg you,' cried Felicia, her face ashen with anxiety. 'My little sister is hurt and we need to fetch the doctor to her.'

The man was appalled and sent the young groom off on the lead horse with instructions to make haste ringing in his ears. The cloud continued low and it gave an eerie deadened feeling to the air. Felicia felt she had lost all sense of time as she watched Nanny cradling the motionless child in her arms. Several times she begged the older woman to check Alexa's pulse just to be reassured that the child was still alive.

'Why does she not wake and why does Shaw take so long?' she demanded as her patience began to wear thin.

Nanny shook her head, unable to give an answer, but the coachman who had been standing by the door of the carriage protecting his passengers from foes unseen said gruffly, 'It is still a fair distance to the Castle, Miss, and 'tis a vast place in which to find help.'

Felicia bit her lip, knowing this to be true. Above them on the road there was suddenly a flurry of movement and the sound of more than one horse descending the steep incline at speed. Before she knew it, people surrounded the carriage. The coachman was pushed unceremoniously out of the way and the door was forced open. Mrs Makepeace's anxious face was before her.

'Alexa, my little girl,' she wept, snatching the inanimate bundle from Nanny's arms, 'my baby girl. What have I done, God forgive me.'

'Oh, hush there Ma'am. It is nought but a bump on the head, she will come round soon enough.' The words of reassurance tripped from Nanny's tongue even as she knew it was a bad bump as the child remained unconscious.

Mrs Makepeace peered into her child's face, swathed as it now was in the blanket. 'She is so pale,' she mumbled anxiously, 'oh where can the doctor be?' She turned to her husband who was hovering behind her. 'Harold, where is the doctor? He must come immediately. It is a matter of great urgency.'

'Come, Mama,' said Felicia, extracting herself from the carriage, 'do not upset yourself so, he will be here directly, I am sure of it.' And indeed she was seen to be correct; through what now, thankfully had subsided to drizzle, came the upright figure of the doctor driving his gig with some care down the treacherous hill.

Doctor Rickerby soon made his presence felt; he was a man of severe aspect with bushy eyebrows but under his gruff and dour exterior he had a heart of gold. He might curse and swear at a family who had called him out in the middle of the night or dragged him out up miles of potholed track in driving rain or drifting snow, but he always made the journey and never made a distinction between those who could reward him and those who could not. Thus he was a man who commanded considerable respect in the district.

As he drew the gig up beside the damaged carriage, the men who had been inspecting the broken wheel stood back to let him through.

'Let me see the child then,' he said testily and received the small body of Alexa into his capable arms.

Felicia attempted to draw her mother apart from the throng but she would not leave her child.

The doctor, who had made a cursory inspection of Alexa's head, announced with some force that he could not do a full examination until he had the child safe in her bed away from the elements. Abandoning the carriage to the coachman and his subordinates, the Makepeaces and Nanny trailed back to the Castle. Dr Rickerby drove his gig with Mrs Makepeace holding the child in her arms next to him. Nanny, a reluctant rider, had elected to walk beside the gig whose progress was slow as the doctor wished to prevent too much jolting. Despite the lessening of the rain all parties, except the doctor, who had provided himself with a rainproof cape, were soaked to the skin by the time the Castle's environs were reached.

There were many anxious people crowded around the great doorway when they finally reached it, allowing Mr Makepeace to command that someone take care of the horses in the absence of the coachman. Two of the under-grooms rushed to do as he bid.

Relieving Mrs Makepeace of her burden, Mr Makepeace swept through the great hallway and up the grand staircase, striding through the corridors to the nursery turret, his footsteps ringing as they went. Felicia had to run to keep up with him.

'Have a care, Papa,' she gasped, 'please wait for Nanny and the doctor, they will know what is best to do.'

He slowed his steps and allowed the doctor, who had taken a moment to put off his wet overclothes and pick up his bag, to catch up. In the nursery Mr Makepeace laid Alexa on the bed and withdrew to the door; he did not let his wife enter.

'Come,' he said, 'you must change out of your damp clothes or we will have you with a chill on our hands.' She looked at him with eyes blank of emotion; she was already too anxious to heed him. She tried to push past him but he barked a command and it penetrated the mists of her agitation and panic; she allowed herself to be led away by a solicitous Miss Cuthbert.

Having seen her sister safely disposed in the cot bed, Felicia went to change too, knowing Nanny would not leave the child until she had returned to take over.

Although she dressed rapidly, Felicia was still bested by her mother on her return to the nursery.

The doctor had made his examination and the child now lay motionless in the bed dressed in a pale nightdress and swathed in the cotton sheets. She was still unconscious but, even in the gloomy light from the window supplemented by several branches of candles, it could be seen that her colour was returning. Felicia shooed Nanny out of the room to get changed and then went back to take the child's hand.

'How is she, Doctor?' she asked the man who was just repacking his leather bag.

'Only time will tell, Miss Makepeace,' he said clearing his throat. 'I can discover no limbs broken and no obvious damage to her vital organs.

Felicia bent nearer to the child and kissed her soft cheek. Alexa's eyes fluttered and she began to move her head upon the pillow. She let out a pained whimper then opened her eyes fully.

'Feefee,' she murmured and struggled to get her arms above the restraining covers. She began to cry in earnest. The doctor returned to the bed but it could be seen that he was viewing her revival as a positive step. Mrs Makepeace went to embrace her child, Nanny though was before her and little Alexa stretched out her arms to the older woman.

'Nana, Nana,' she cried.

29

*I*t took some little while to reconcile Mrs Makepeace to the fact that her tiny daughter wanted only Nanny or Felicia to care for her during her recovery. It was not for two days that Alexa would allow herself to be left unattended by either one or other of them. She was not feverish although it was clear that her head ached and she was a little sick.

Felicia was embarrassed by her sister's rejection of her mother and feared that it would prevent Mrs Makepeace from pursuing her expressed wish to figure in her daughter's life. It took the sage counsel of Mrs Roebuck to point out that the child could not be expected to take to a stranger upon first sight. Mrs Makepeace would have to introduce herself to the child through a slow and gentle process. Much, then, to Felicia's relief, her mother followed the Rector's wife's advice and visited the nursery with ever-increasing frequency. She had not made Felicia a repository for her guilt, feeling her too young to listen to such remorse. Mrs Roebuck, instead, she honoured with her confidences. On one occasion sobbing out her guilt on that good lady's ample shoulder.

'My folly and conceit knew no bounds,' she scarified herself. 'I was so regretful that I had borne no son, that I abandoned my daughter. What punishment is harsh enough for such a sin?'

Mrs Roebuck assured her that she had done penance enough. The knowledge that she might have lost her daughter brought into sharp relief all the less noble sentiments. It was not too late to retrace her steps and establish herself with affection in her daughter's eyes.

Once her head had stopped pounding, Alexa revelled in her new-found companion for she discovered that her mother would allow her far more licence than either her beloved Nanny or adored Felicia. Mrs Makepeace was rueful in acceptance that she spoilt the child and did not compound the error by preventing Nanny and Felicia from maintaining their own level of discipline. She just allowed herself at last to enjoy the pleasures of watching a diminutive person take on the world.

Felicia, thankful that rectitude had been re-established within her family, furthered her friendship with Prudence and Primula and sought out the company of Sophia and Imogen more and more often.

Sophia seemed not only to have grown in beauty but also in spirit. Having attained her seventeenth birthday, Felicia found her preparing for her come out.

'My uncle proposes to allow me to have a season,' she told Felicia with shining eyes when Felicia was guided to her in her mother's sewing parlour. The spring sun was streaming in through the windows of the corner room giving excellent light for all manner of needlework and crafts.

'When do you leave?' asked Felicia, trying to keep the hollow ring from her voice. There had been no mention of the Makepeaces' removing to London.

'Four days hence,' said Sophia, getting up from her knees where she had been sorting out a box full of threads. 'My uncle will escort me. I go to stay with his cousin, Lady Stonehatch. She has undertaken to present me and bring me out.'

'My, my,' cried Felicia, 'this is indeed a surprise. I had no notion your uncle was so well connected.'

Sophia pulled a face at her friend. 'Sometimes you are not so aptly named,' she said with a little constraint, 'that was a very unfelicitous thing to say.'

Felicia immediately begged her pardon. 'I meant no disrespect to either you or your uncle,' she said hurriedly. 'It is only that I have been racking my brain to find a way to bring you and Lord Guilliam together and now it is all being arranged for me.' She grasped Sophia's now free hands. 'I wish I could come with you,' she said impulsively, 'I long to see Giles again and if we were together there it would be so much easier.'

'Would you like me to enquire of my uncle whether you might join us?' asked Sophia, her face betraying the dismay she felt at having to ask such a favour of her revered relation.

'No, no of course not,' cried Felicia. 'I know it would be too much to ask. You go,' she smiled, 'but you must write to me weekly and tell me how you go on.'

'Of course I will' said Sophia, giving her a quick hug in relief.

Sophia was as good as her word and wrote regularly and where she could, she would give news of Giles. She was dimly aware that Felicia and Giles corresponded, so she gave details of aspects she felt he would not describe himself. She spoke of his maturity and good looks, of the increasing quality of his clothes and the little treats he was able to bestow on her now that his income would stretch to such things. Sophia was no fool and she knew that in order to buy her evening gloves or other frills and furbelows she could not ask her uncle to purchase, Giles had to go without himself, but she was trying to give Felicia hope that in the not too distant future, Giles would be able to support a wife. Felicia was not deceived either; now twenty she saw herself dwindling into an old maid and cursed Mr Gregory that he should still be holding out on Giles. She continued to scrimp and save herself, determined to help her grandmother make their fortune. She had just handed over a whole month's allowance when her father called her into his office and announced that Lady Stonehatch was holding a party in honour of Sophia's come out and that the Makepeaces' had been invited to attend.

'Your mother has no desire to be away from Alexa above a week,' he told her ponderously, 'so I have accepted the invitation to stay at Stonehatch House on that understanding. It will mean two long journeys not seven days apart but your mother is now well and I have never feared for your constitution so I would have you make your preparations. Miss Cuthbert remains here to help Nanny.'

With feelings reminiscent of the Christmas two years before, Felicia made her preparations with a glad heart. She dashed off a letter to Giles, sure in the knowledge that Sophia would have already conveyed the information to him. Then, with the help of Miss Cuthbert, she reviewed her entire wardrobe to see which dresses could be refurbished to reflect the ever-changing fashions. It took both women several long evenings while the candles burnt low and guttered in their sockets to alter the dresses so that the most critical amongst the ton could not recognise them from her first season.

'I do not credit there is anyone who will remember me, setting aside what dresses I was wearing,' complained Felicia when she had stabbed her finger for a second time trying to draw a needle though three layers of material.

'Oh come, come, Miss Felicia. If I remember aright you were much sought after. Especially when Lord Guilliam showed a tendency to flirt with you,' said Miss Cuthbert, her neat head bent over a pile of flounces she was reducing in fullness.

Felicia gave a chuckle. 'I do not think Lord Guilliam saw himself as flirting,' she said, 'he was in earnest.' She sobered. 'I only wish I had been able to return his regard.' Then she brightened. 'However, I have high hopes for Sophia and he. I have every confidence that they will suit each other.'

Miss Cuthbert lifted her eyes from her work at last. 'It would be unkind to encourage Miss Sophia to look to him as a suitor, Miss Felicia,' she said gravely. 'Miss Sophia cannot hope to aspire to his station in life.'

'Do you think not?' Felicia cut a thread with a decisive snip. 'Now that I know she has the Stonehatch connection, I am sure the disparity is not as great as you perceive.'

'There is also the lack of a fortune,' counselled Miss Cuthbert. 'Mr Gregory cannot be expected to dower her.'

'Oh fiddle to that,' responded Felicia briskly. 'Lord Guilliam has enough money not to need to ally himself with a rich woman.'

Miss Cuthbert need not have worried, for it was soon revealed on Felicia's arrival in London that relations between Sophia and Lord Guilliam were going on prosperously. Almost before the Makepeaces' had settled into the opulent and rather gothic guest rooms of Stonehatch House than Lady Stonehatch was whispering the good news to any of the family who came into her orbit.

Lady Stonehatch had been an ambitious woman in her youth and had pursued her lord with a vengeance until she had ensnared him. Forty years on she had retained little of the plump prettiness that had finally captivated Lord Stonehatch and much powder and a huge turban concealed any remnants. She had also been unfortunate enough to suffer from the bright red face of matron's mask while dutifully providing his lordship with a string of children. Lady Stonehatch, now more than plump, wore strong colours to disguise the limitations of her face and figure and indulged herself in much matchmaking and gossip. Afraid to rely too much on the good lady's word, Felicia waited until she was private with Sophia before challenging her on the subject.

'So is it true?' she demanded, her hazel eyes wide with eager anticipation.

A pretty blush stained Sophia's cheeks and she nodded. 'Is it not too good to be true? Am I not the luckiest girl in all London. Lord Guilliam waits only until after the ball to ask my uncle leave to pay his addresses.'

'And what of his parents? Do they approve of you?'

'I cannot answer you specifically. All I know is that he has made his sentiments known to them and they have given the betrothal their sanction.'

Felicia moved forward and embraced her friend. 'I could not be more glad except if it were myself and Giles announcing our engagement,' she said gaily, hiding her regret that the likelihood of her own betrothal continued to be small. However, she would not let herself repine while in London and in the knowledge that she would see Giles on the morrow at the come out ball.

Lady Stonehatch, whose last daughter had flown the nest some four years before, had made enthusiastic preparations for the event. The musicians were so numerous that chef was grumbling that he had to prepare almost as many refreshments for them as the guests. Great swathes of satin swirled around the pillars in the large hallway and lines of tiny lanterns hung decorating the double stairway. The magnificent chandeliers were adorned with hundreds of candles, making the whole area ablaze with light.

'You have done my niece proud,' said Mr Gregory warmly to his cousin as he greeted her on his arrival, attended by his half-sister. Felicia had to agree. She found once again that her feelings towards Mr Gregory were ambivalent. One moment she was resenting his control over Giles; the next acknowledging his generosity to Sophia, Imogen and their mother. She stood slightly away from the main entrance in an alcove pondering the matter as she waited for Giles. She wanted the earliest knowledge of his arrival and a few moments of preparation before their eyes met for she feared if she was caught unawares she would cast herself into his arms with abandon.

Giles did not arrive in the first flush of guests and, when he did, he came accompanied by Lord Guilliam. From her vantage point Felicia had to admire the pair. Both tall, both handsome, one dark, one fair. To see them there it would be impossible to judge who had all the worldly goods and who had nothing. Felicia wished it were possible for Giles to have half of what Guilliam had for then their future would be assured. She knew though even with the two families joined in marriage that Giles would not accept any largesse from his friend.

Once she had sated her first appetite for the sight of him, Felicia slipped back into the ballroom. It would not do to be seen greeting the young men in the hallway.

The band was playing and the first dance had begun. Most of the high-ranking ladies who wished to dance were already with their partners. Felicia made her way to the Gregory party in the hope that Giles would see her there and ask her to dance.

The dance had finished before Guilliam and Giles reached them. Both men had eyes only for their respective loves.

'May I have the pleasure,' asked Giles as he took Felicia's hand and bowed over it.

'Indeed you may,' she said with a long sigh. The dance sets were already forming and they had to hurry to take their places. Felicia thought she could never stop feasting her eyes on him. Conversation was difficult because of the dance but Felicia in any event would have found it impossible. Her heart was too full.

'This was an unexpected delight,' she heard him say but all she could do was nod. He seemed to understand her feelings and did not attempt to speak to her again until they were wending their way through the throng to Mrs Makepeace's side. Before they had managed to exchange but two sentences, Lady Stonehatch was upon them, whisking Giles and Guilliam away to dance with other unpartnered ladies. By the time supper was announced Felicia had danced with some six young men of differing ability and seen Giles only at the other end of a long dance set.

'Why must the lady be such a good hostess,' hissed Felicia into Sophia's sympathetic ear. 'I have not exchanged two words together with Giles yet.'

'Nor I with Guilliam.'

It seemed the men were equally frustrated and, ignoring all representations from their hostess, arrived determined to escort Sophia and Felicia to supper. The ladies aided them in their efforts and the foursome had soon secured a corner table in the marbled dining hall. Sophia was inclined to be overawed by the wealth on display around her.

'I have not penetrated this part of the house in all my stay here,' she said, round-eyed. 'I hope you have no such monstrous edifice amongst your properties, my Lord Guilliam?'

'If I have, they will be pulled down if they are not to your taste!' he replied, not quite able to hide a smile.

Giles looked from one to the other.

'You do realise,' he said teasingly, 'that it is in fact my consent you require to wed my sister, not mine uncle's.'

Guilliam flung up his hands in mock horror. 'Then we are undone,' he cried, 'for I know that you will never accede to it.'

Felicia choked on her lemonade. 'Oh Giles you must consent,' she giggled, 'for then there can be a wedding and we can both attend. I might have the good fortune to see you twice in one year.'

He made a funning rejoinder but the mirth had died on Felicia's lips; looking across the small table over Giles' shoulder she could see a dark-haired, dissolute man whom she vaguely recognised, watching them with a predatory eye. She nudged Guilliam who was sitting beside her.

'Who is that man?' she asked in an under-voice.

Guilliam looked up and then away. 'Good God, how did he come to be here? Do not let him know that his presence unsettles you.'

'It is N-Nathan T-Torrill, isn't it?' Felicia could barely utter the man's name.

'Yes, yes it is.'

Giles, who had been laughing with his sister, became sober all at once. 'It is no surprise that he is here,' he said. 'You can be sure Lady Stonehatch knows nothing of his history.

'Of whom do you speak?' asked Sophia in a voice sharpened by the anxiety she could suddenly feel around her.

'No one of import,' said Giles, rising to his feet. 'Come Sophia,' he said, 'I have been neglecting Mama, take me to her will you.'

Sophia rose as she was bid and Felicia was left with Guilliam to bear her company. 'I am glad to have seen him,' she said resolutely, 'for an image of him like some great malevolent bat has resided in my minds' eye for many a year now, a legacy from childhood, I hardly know what to think. Does he still pose a real danger to Giles?'

'You will forgive me, I know, for speaking plainly,' said Guilliam after tossing back a glass of red wine, 'but I believe he has not wholly given up his claim to the Gregory fortune. I know Giles believes he has forestalled any further attempts but I cannot be so sanguine. I still think him a very dangerous man.'

For Felicia the rest of the evening was spoiled. She had seen the stormy look in Giles' eyes as he had left the table and knew that he did not want the matter discussed in front of his sister. She wanted to apologise but there was no subsequent moment when she could be private with him. They stood up together for a second dance without managing more than a few common-place sentences. Felicia finally sought her couch in considerable disquiet and spent what was left of the night tossing and turning in fitful sleep.

She woke the next morning very little refreshed and wished she could send out a letter to Giles. However, she knew none of the servants and although she had her father's permission to exchange letters with Giles, she was aware it would be much frowned upon in a household such as this.

It was only on the penultimate day of their stay that she was able to see Giles again. Lady Stonehatch had invited him and Lord Guilliam to dinner to allow him to bid his friends from home farewell. Sophia had the luxury of hugging her big brother in greeting. Felicia could only look on enviously although she was able to find solace in the fact that Giles was seated beside her at dinner.

Even before she made the attempt, he dismissed her apology as unnecessary and expressed his regret to her that he had acted so hastily on the night of the ball.

'I would have Sophia kept in ignorance of Torrill's intentions. She, like my mother, has a tendency to be over-anxious. I would have her enjoy this year of her come out and once she is my Lady Guilliam, she will be safe.'

'I too would have it so,' replied Felicia hastily. 'It was but the shock of seeing him there. It will not happen again.'

Under cover of the table Giles squeezed her hand; there was little chance of more private talk. It was all very unsatisfactory. Felicia found she was able to have more conversation with Lord Guilliam than with Giles.

'I wish you happy,' she said to Guilliam at their parting. 'You at least will not have to wait too long for your Thornton.'

Lord Guilliam gave a rueful laugh. 'Even I have to wait for longer than I would wish. Mr Gregory agrees the marriage but requires us to wait until Sophia attains her eighteenth birthday. It will not be until spring comes around again that we can wed though a formal announcement will be made in the papers next week.'

Felicia gave an exclamation of annoyance and bowed her curly head. 'That man takes too much upon himself,' she said in a hard angry voice. 'Almost I am decided to run away with Giles and live in some hovel with him. I cannot endure this protracted wait for his uncle's convenience.'

'What, and forswear your Castle?' countered Lord Guilliam. 'Miss Makepeace without her Castle would not do. I see you clearly as Rapunzel in her turret, her golden tresses cascading down the walls of the Castle.'

'You mistake my lord,' she said, unamused, 'I am more like the sleeping beauty awaiting her prince for a hundred years.'

30

*C*heltenham glided through the summer, disturbed only by the increased building work on the southern outskirts. The elder Mrs Makepeace watched and smiled her satisfaction at its progress. Felicia, on the other hand, idled her time away collecting fruit and herbs for Mrs Simon Gregory. She carried basket after basket to Strawberry Cottage and sometimes applied herself to making jams and potions. She felt her letters had become dreary and longed for some excitement to enliven her days. Inevitably, when the excitement did come in early September, she wished it never had.

The days were still warm and mostly sunny but Felicia had caught a head cold and had stayed at home one morning to coddle herself. If was not long before lunch-time that a distracted Sophia was ushered into the morning room where Felicia had been reading.

'My dear, what is the matter?' cried Felicia thickly, before even the door had closed behind the servant.

'Oh Felicia it's most dreadful, my mother is prostrate with anxiety. Uncle Arthur received an express just this morning to say that Mrs Torrill and Mrs Lambert intend to make him a visit after this very weekend.'

'No! Surely not! Can he not refuse to receive them?' Felicia's complexion, that had fluctuated during Sophia's jumbled speech, had now darkened into anger.

'He will not.' Sophia was weeping in her alarm and despair.

'He says that though he will never again receive the nephews, he must act in fairness to his sisters. He believes he cannot house my mother permanently yet refuse them a visit.'

'I do not see why not!' cried Felicia hotly. 'They come only to make trouble.'

'Indeed they do,' sobbed Sophia, casting herself into the chair by the fire and pulling out her handkerchief. 'They will probe and jibe at my mother and make her acutely uncomfortable in her own home.' Sophia gave another gusty sob. 'Oh I cannot bear it. I cannot. My poor, poor mama.'

Felicia pulled up a chair beside her and tried to comfort her with little success. Eventually she came to concede that Sophia needed to cry herself out. They huddled together, desperate for some reassurance that the visit would not be the ordeal they both feared.

The following Monday brought the arrival of the two gorgons. Felicia heard the news from the Castle servants, who were in constant dialogue with those at The Chimnies. She tried to coax her mother into making a visit of ceremony, ostensibly to welcome the ladies but more to support the Thorntons. Mrs Makepeace was reluctant and would do nothing until her husband returned from Yorkshire the next day. He then accompanied his wife and daughter to The Chimnies on the morrow. Already after only three days of their occupation the effects could be felt. Mrs Thornton had shrunk back into her shell and sat virtually cowering in her corner. Sophia was being admonished and supervised to serve the refreshments. Felicia's eyes began to flash and her head went up.

'Do you make a long stay, Mrs Torrill?' she asked boldly when receiving a cup of tea from Sophia's shaking hand distracted her mother.

Mrs Torrill looked down her beak of a nose to suppress the pretension of such a pert young lady but Felicia was unabashed and stared her out.

'I believe we remain here six weeks if my brother allows,' she said, giving Mr Gregory a sycophantic grimace to acknowledge his rights. Mr Gregory, standing in front of the fire with his hands clasped behind his back, nodded graciously. Mrs Torrill could take it as acquiescence if she so chose. Felicia saw it as a reluctance to commit himself.

'Then you will be staying for harvest festival,' said Felicia brightly. 'It is now a tradition that Mrs Thornton arranges a magnificent harvest supper each year. Is it not, Mrs Thornton?' said Felicia, determined to draw the sweet lady into the forefront.

'Oh yes of course, if my brother wishes for it to continue,' fluttered Mrs Thornton.

'Of course you do, do you not, Mr Gregory?' Felicia prompted, wanting a public affirmation of Mrs Thornton's role.

'It would be much missed and there would be much consternation amongst the servants if it were not to go ahead,' said Mr Makepcace, adding his might. 'You're not thinking of cancelling are you, Gregory?' he challenged.

'No, nothing of the sort,' said Mr Gregory hurriedly, 'only my sister Torrill here had expressed a wish to hold a cotillion ball instead.'

There was suddenly silence. What separate conversations had been carried on now stopped in their tracks. Mr Gregory was left to make the decision: a choice between one sister or the other. Felicia had had no notion that she had hit upon a running sore. She had just unerringly anticipated that an event where Mrs Thornton took all the honours would likely be a bone of contention.

Mrs Makepeace, studying the maelstrom of emotion manifest on the company's faces said brightly: 'Entertaining, as a Cotillion ball would be, it would be most unfair to disappoint the staff and the parish at this late stage. I know my friend, Mrs Roebuck, has already started on her preparations.' Here she turned to Mrs Lambert. 'The Rector's wife, you know, she and her daughter weave the most wonderful decorations out of sheaves of corn and strands of ivy.'

Mrs Torrill looked furious, Mr Gregory looked relieved and Mrs Thornton looked terrified. Felicia wondered whether between them, she and her family had made things worse.

The next day Mr Higginbottom drove Imogen over to the Castle in the gig so that she might have her Italian lesson. The young girl was much agitated and Mr Higginbottom made an excuse to visit the servants' hall so that he might chance to meet Felicia. His enquiries of the butler and the housekeeper gave him no clue as to where she was, so he left disappointed, having only driven Imogen over on a pretext so that he could confer with Felicia.

Luck, however, had not completely deserted the little man and he was fortunate enough to see her coming around the base of one of the turrets just as he went to clamber into the vehicle. She came running up to the gig.

'Mr Higginbottom, how glad I am to see you!' she exclaimed. Then, coming around the side of the horse which protected her from prying eyes in the Castle, she questioned him conspiratorially on what was occurring at The Chimneys.

'Miss Imogen will be able to enlighten you further, Miss Felicia, but I believe Mrs Torrill and Mrs Lambert are behaving charmingly to the Thorntons when Mr Gregory is there and threatening and taunting them when he is not,' he sighed. 'I know one thing for certain though: that lovely room where Mrs and the Miss Thorntons do all their sewing has been appropriated by the sisters, Mrs Thornton is no longer allowed admittance.'

'But how can they do that?' cried Felicia, appalled. 'What does Mr Gregory say to such doings?'

'I believe that he remains in ignorance of it.'

'You surprise me,' replied Felicia tartly, 'I had understood that you kept no secrets from him.'

Higginbottom had the grace to look sheepish. 'And you have cause,' he admitted, 'but my fear on this occasion is that it would benefit no one for me to add my mite. Mrs Thornton abhors being the centre of any commotion and Mr Gregory finds it very difficult to decide how to handle any dispute between his sisters. He fears to be accused of favouritism.'

'What does Sophia say?'

'Miss Sophia has had to retire to her bed, she has caught a severe cold and is feverish.'

'Oh dear, I fear that must be set at my door,' said Felicia guiltily. 'Poor Sophia, I will write at once to her.' So saying, Felicia bade Higginbottom farewell and went to attend Imogen and Miss Cuthbert.

As she came to leave, Imogen held back from going down to the hallway to await Higginbottom's return and grasped Felicia's arm.

'Is there nowhere I can be private with you?' she said beseech-ingly. 'I must tell you how awful it is at The Chimnies now that Mrs Torrill and Mrs Lambert are come to stay.

Felicia's heart sank but she took her young friend into her bedroom and allowed Imogen to unburden herself of all the slights and criticisms the two women had uttered during this first part of their stay.

'Mrs Lambert even spoke to Mama of the inheritance,' whis-pered Imogen, her blue eyes full of dismay. 'She says that we are not to imagine that The Chimnies will continue to be our home if anything were to happen to Uncle Arthur. They are determined to have us out on the streets if they may and they talk,' here she broke off to collect herself, 'they talk as though it is almost certain that Uncle will predecease them.' She gave a gasp and a shudder of alarm. 'I am so scared for him and us, Felicia, and I do not know what to do.'

Neither did Felicia. After some thought she decided to write all that had been told to her to Giles. She knew it would pain him but equally she knew he would be angry if he had not been told. Also, secretly, deep in her heart Felicia could not help wishing that it would make him discard his position at the bank and come home to find some small cottage where they could be safe together.

Each day was full of little alarms and uncertainties. Mrs Makepeace had invited the whole family from The Chimnies to dine at Castle Leck. She neither liked the sisters, Torrill and Lambert, nor aspired to any kind of intimacy with them but she knew that any extraordinary civility extended to them would please her husband and Mr Gregory.

When the allotted evening arrived, Mrs Makepeace was dismayed to discover that only Mr Gregory, Mrs Torrill and Mrs Lambert were to attend.

'I prevailed on my poor sister Thornton to remain at home,' said Mrs Torrill in great condescension. 'I believe her to be succumbing to the cold her daughter, Sophia, is suffering with. It would have been imprudent for her to subject herself to the night air.'

Felicia felt a hand clutch at her heart. What were these tyrannical women plotting and how could she combat it.

There was a scratch of a note the next day from Mrs Thornton, expressing her regret that she had been unable to attend the dinner. Mrs Makepeace handed the missive to Felicia.

'What make you of this?' she asked.

Felicia was surprised. 'Do you feel uncomfortable with what is going on at The Chimnies, Mama?' she asked.

Mrs Makepeace looked at her daughter's face keenly. 'I have become increasingly aware that you do not trust these ladies and so I have been scrutinising their behaviour,' she said with surprising candour. She stood up from her seat and walked to the narrow slit window. 'What I have seen disturbs me. Mrs Thornton is clearly besieged,' she shook her head distractedly, 'but there is no substance to it. I cannot find a specific cause for my concern.'

'Mama?' asked Felicia, making a decision. 'Are you aware of what Nathan Torrill and the Lambert brothers did to effect the breach between themselves and Mr Gregory?'

Mrs Makepeace shook her head. 'Your father knows the detail. He did not discuss it with me.'

'I see.'

'Are you aware of what happened?'

'Yes, yes I'm afraid I am.' Felicia could not lie to her mother. 'And I know what further iniquities they have perpetrated. They had been grievously cruel to Giles. Once,' she broke off to compose herself, 'once Torrill took a horsewhip to his back. There are no bounds to what they are prepared to do to benefit from Mr Gregory's money. I have a real fear for both Mr Gregory and the Thornton family.'

Mrs Makepeace saw suddenly the burden her daughter had been carrying all her teenage years.

'I have been so very blind, have I not?' she said quietly. 'First I failed your little sister and now I see that I have been failing you. I have let you plough your own furrow for too long without my guidance and support. We will meet this challenge together.'

While it was a great relief to know that her mother too was keeping a weather eye on developments, Felicia could not be convinced that there was anything effective either of them could do. They planned between them to visit The Chimnies regularly on all manner of pretexts. The sisters suffered it for a while but then had Daniels, the butler, deny them on more and more occasions.

'I would see Miss Sophia, Daniels, please,' said Felicia brightly one day when she had been denied access as Mrs Torrill and Mrs Lambert were not at home to visitors.

'I'm afraid Miss Sophia is not receiving visitors today,' said the butler in some discomfort.

Felicia eyed him speculatively from under her poke bonnet. 'Forgive me, Daniels,' she said with a smile to remove the sting from her words, 'but I do not believe you. I am sure Miss Sophia will see me if she knows I am here.'

'That's as maybe, Miss, but I cannot admit you.'

'On whose orders?'

'Mrs Torrill, Miss.'

'Then take my card to Mr Gregory if you please. I am sure he will welcome me.'

'I'm afraid Mr Gregory is unwell and confined to his room. I am sorry miss I really cannot allow you in.'

Felicia admitted defeat and trudged wearily home, even more disturbed than she had been previously. She decided it was time for her mother to have words with her father on the subject. However, taking a short cut through the woods all thoughts of a calm recital of events so far left her head. Lurking a little way off was a cloaked man, who in the late afternoon gloom looked very like Nathan Torrill.

Felicia lifted her skirts and took to her heels.

31

rs Makepeace was greatly disturbed to see her distraught daughter come hurtling through the grand hallway and cast herself into her arms.

'He is here,' she gasped, 'he is here. They are gathering like vultures and Mr Gregory is ill. They would not let me in, they would not let me in.'

Mrs Makepeace held her daughter away from her and gave her a gentle shake. 'Come now Felicia, calm yourself. I will take you to your father. We will see what can be done.'

'No, no, not yet.' Felicia put her shaking hands to her dishevelled hair. 'I cannot see him like this. I cannot think clearly. I cannot reason with him.'

'I will do that my love, we must go to him directly. There is no time to lose.'

The anxiety the ladies felt was not matched by the master of the house. Much to the ladies' disappointment, Mr Makepeace was reluctant to intercede. He listened politely to their concerns but would do nothing.

'I do not perceive what you expect me to do,' he said rather peevishly. 'I cannot demand entrance to The Chimnies when the man could be genuinely ill and his sisters only protecting him from intrusion.'

Mrs Makepeace was furious with her husband but she had not lived with him for more than twenty years without knowing that she could not shift him once he had made up his mind. What saddened her was that neither could she acquit him of cowardice.

Over the next few days the ladies' concern crescendoed. Word kept coming from The Chimnies via the servants that Mr Gregory's condition was worsening and that his sisters refused to call the doctor. Mrs Makepeace, fired up by the look of grave anxiety on her daughter's sweet face, had continued to visit using Mr Gregory's illness as an excuse. She carried jellies and fruit and all manner of remedies for someone of ailing health, but she was only allowed to hand them over to the harassed butler. Of Sophie, Imogen and Mrs Thornton there was no sign.

'What can have happened to them,' wailed Felicia when her mother returned unsuccessfully for the umpteenth time. 'They would not dare to harm Sophia surely, not now she is betrothed to Lord Guilliam.' The next day crawled by with both women unable to settle to anything. It was only as evening fell that Felicia received a note via one of the footmen. It was a request from Higginbottom for him to speak with her.

'Where is Mr Higginbottom?' she asked the servant.

'He awaits your answer in the butler's parlour, Miss.'

Felicia fled down the hallway and spiral stairs to the nether regions of the Castle.

'What has occurred, Mr Higginbottom?' she demanded as she burst into the little room. She was brought up short by the sight of him. He appeared shrunken. He had great hollows around his eyes and his skin had the grey hue of anxiety. 'Tell me,' she said bracing herself, 'tell me what horrors have been perpetrated.'

'I fear for Mr Gregory's life, Miss Felicia,' said Higginbottom desperately. 'He is virtually delirious with fever yet his sisters will not allow the doctor to attend him. They say they know what he needs and do not wish to incur the expense of the doctor. Pshaw, to be using money as an excuse at such a time, I cannot credit it.'

'But what of the Thorntons. What has become of them?'

Higginbottom shook his head in despair. 'Mrs Thornton has been so frightened by them that she keeps to her room and insists that Imogen remains with her. I fear she will fall victim to a state of nervous collapse. Only Miss Sophia has been brave enough to tackle them and she is merely pushed aside and ignored.'

'Oh my poor Sophia. What can be done Mr Higginbottom? What can be done? For you know that my mother and I have done our best to breach their defences.'

'I know it and am very grateful but what is needed is someone who commands the respect of the servants, and whose lead they will follow.'

'Yes, yes, I see that,' she looked eagerly at him. 'They would follow Giles, would they not?'

'Oh indeed yes, I know they would.'

'Then I will send him an express, but tell me this, Higginbottom: has Nathan Torrill been in evidence?'

Higginbottom's brows snapped together. 'It is possible,' he said as though a realisation of the significance of some previous event was occurring to him. 'Yes indeed it is very possible. Please warn Mr Giles that it is so.'

Felicia assured him that she would and went immediately to her mother for the money to defray the cost of sending an express. Mrs Makepeace looked at her askance but did not challenge her on her lack of finances. Both women were too concerned that it would still take a minimum of two days for Giles to reach The Chimnies and Mr Gregory might not last that long.

At The Chimnies, Mr Gregory's condition continued to decline and his utterings were increasingly incoherent. Quick to capitalise on his vulnerability, Nathan Torrill had quitted his guesthouse in Charlton Kings and had moved into The Chimnies. He brought with him a document that looked suspiciously like a will. On the evening Higginbottom was absent, visiting at Castle Leck, Torrill entered the sickroom and attempted to make his uncle sign the document. Dimly Mr Gregory was aware that someone was coercing him into doing something he did not want to do. He fought with what little strength he had to resist the strong arm that was guiding his hand and the signature that resulted was little more than a spidery scrawl. Then, bullying two of the maids, Torrill made them sign as witnesses. Weeping, both girls knew not how to refuse

On his return Higginbottom was appalled, yet even he did not know whether he would have been able to withstand the determined Torrill. The man had a sinister tone of character that moulded others to his will. Higginbottom feared now that having got the semblance of a signature, he would put a period to Mr Gregory's existence but it seemed the man was content to let the illness run its course as it certainly looked as though it would do the business for him.

The express, sent immediately the decision had been made, arrived with Giles late the following evening. He read the contents and knew he must act. He gathered his belongings, sent a note around to Guilliam and visited Mr Ponsonby in his own home to inform him of what must be done. Ponsonby did not stand in his way and Giles, choosing to set off at first light on horseback, requested Littlejohn to follow as best he could. In fact, Littlejohn fared better than he had expected for Lord Guilliam, on receiving the note, had prepared to set out that morning himself travelling in his curricle and four. He took Littlejohn up beside him.

Changing horses as frequently as he could fund, Giles clattered into the stable yard at The Chimnies a little after nine that evening. He was bone weary and saddle-sore but the reception he received from the grooms and stable boys was enough to recharge his energies and persuade him that his frantic ride had been justified. Each face, as it registered his presence, lit up and many cheered as they gathered together around him. He raised an arm to silence them.

'Not a word to those in the house, I beg,' he said to them all. 'We must make plans. Firstly,' he turned to the head groom, 'does my uncle still live?'

'He does, Sir, as far as we can make out,' replied the man, 'though it 'ud be hard to be sure given as we 'ave been banned from the house. Bread and cheese in the barns is all we've been given this last week.'

'Then send one of your lads for Doctor Rickerby. We will be in need of his services and my uncle will require careful nursing. Another lad must go to Mrs Simon's cottage, if you please.'

No sooner was the order given than the lads were despatched.

'Now don't think me craven,' said Giles to his followers, 'but I must discover the circumstances within. I will send word if I need some heavyweights to rid the house of its unwanted guests.'

'We'll be here, Sir, an' we'll be ready,' was the chorused response he received.

Quickly Giles made his way to the back door and slipped in quietly. There was an uneasy hush about the place. The kitchen was ill lit and empty save for the scullery maid who was returning the pots she had washed for the morrow's use, dinner having been served many hours earlier.

'Good evening, Penny,' said Giles.

'Goodness me, Mr Giles,' she squeaked, 'you gave me such a fright.'

'Sh,' he put his fingers to his lips, 'tell me where are Mr Higginbottom and Daniels?'

'They are in the butler's parlour, Sir, with Mrs Ellis. Deeply anxious for the master they are.'

'Well they need be anxious no more for the doctor is on his way. Not a word now that you have seen me.'

Knocking briefly on the parlour door, Giles slipped into the room to startle its occupants.

'Oh la, thank the Lord,' cried Mrs Ellis as she saw him. 'Now we are saved.'

Higginbottom stood up from his chair and straightened his back, his small frame seeming to swell with pride.

'Tell me then,' said Giles without preamble, 'where are Torrill and his mother and aunt? The sooner we can rout them the sooner we can have my uncle restored to health.'

Higginbottom indicated to Daniels. 'Daniels has the surest knowledge of their whereabouts,' he said.

Mr Daniels, for all his concern about his master, rather revelled in the excitement now that someone had appeared to take the lead. Puffing out his chest like a robin redbreast, he began to speak in throbbing tones.

'Mr Torrill has retired to the library, Mr Giles. He has taken it for his own since Mr Gregory fell ill, as the ladies have taken over the morning room from Mrs Thornton.' He drew a deep breath. 'Mrs Lambert has retired early to her bedchamber while Mrs Torrill sits with the master. All the female servants, save Mrs Lambert's and Mrs Torrill's dressers, have been sent to bed and only Patrick and Cyril, the footmen, remain abroad to snuff the candles when Mr Torrill retires. We here,' he drew an arm wide to include all the occupants of the small room 'have not retired for fear that there might be a crisis in the master's health. Mr Higginbottom has not been allowed admittance to his room these last twenty-four hours.'

There was silence as he finished. Giles grasped the back of one of the chairs and applied his mind to how best to approach the situation. Eventually he spoke.

'I will not creep into the house like some felon when it is essentially my home. I will come in the front door. Be sure you are there to admit me, Daniels, then the doctor and Mrs Simon as they arrive. Right,' he squared his shoulders, 'let us do this thing.'

Minutes later there was a great clanging of the front doorbell and Daniels, already at the baize door, walked with great dignity across the hall to open it.

'Good evening, Mr Giles,' he said as he held it open for him. 'This is indeed a pleasure to see you home again.'

Giles gave a brief conspiratorial smile and stepped fully into the house.

'Get out.' Nathan Torrill had come to the doorway of the library on hearing the doorbell. He could be seen to be rather the worse for wear. His dark hair was dishevelled and his cravat dangled loosely around his neck. His coat-tails were severely crushed and his pantaloons were stained where he had spilt some red wine. 'Get out,' he yelled again. 'You have no business here. This is not your house.'

'It may not be my house,' said Giles, allowing Daniels to remove his overcoat and hat, 'but while my uncle breathes it is still my home.' He put his riding whip down on the hallway table. 'Thank you,' he said politely to the butler as though nothing was amiss.

'Ha, you may think so,' said Torrill, starting forward, 'but I now own this house, Uncle is as good as dead.' He waved a scroll of parchment in Giles' face. 'I have his signature here. You are nothing, nothing, seize him, seize him,' he ordered the two footmen who had appeared in the hallway in response to the commotion. 'Seize him and cast him out of doors.'

Neither man moved. 'You will find,' said Giles, stepping forward and nipping the scroll from Torrill's hand, 'that the matter stands at exactly the reverse.' Before Torrill could protest, he had torn the document into pieces and cast it on to the fire.

'You–,' Torrill lunged at him, hands outstretched for his throat. 'You will suffer for this.'

Patrick and Cyril weighed in and dragged the seething Torrill off Giles. He struggled like a fiend for a few moments, then, sensing he could not escape their clutches, gave up and directed a stream of venom at Giles.

For a moment it looked as though Giles planned to ignore him. Then suddenly he began to strip off his riding jacket, neck-cloth and boots.

'I have borne enough,' he said in a hard angry voice. 'We will finish this now once and for all. Release him. This is ultimately between him and me.'

The men did as they were told and Torrill wasted no time before closing with Giles, his murderous hands seeking Giles' throat once more.

Above them on the landing, Mrs Lambert had come out of her room clothed in her nightdress and dressing gown. She wore a cap upon her brittle hair and her face devoid of make-up looked harsh and lined. She was about to shout down to call a halt to the brawl when she thought better of it and stood at the top of the stairs watching the swaying lurching bodies of the two men as they fought for the upper hand. A few moments later, Sophia appeared from her room. She put a hand to her mouth in horror but ignored her aunt as she was ordered back to her room. Then, grasping the banisters for support she too watched intently the events unfold below them.

Giles, innately honourable, was at a disadvantage because of his resolve to keep to the rules of engagement. Torrill had no such constraint. When Giles dislodged the man's hands from his throat, Torrill scrabbled for anything in his reach. He tugged at Giles' ears and hair, he ground his shod foot down on Giles' feet and he constantly fought to land Giles a blow below the belt.

Despite his long ride and draining weariness, Giles' determination drove him on to parry every punch and dislodge every hold. Both men's breathing was rasping in their throats and their movements were becoming heavier and less accurate, but both fought on as if to the death. Torrill, constantly searching for a way to slay Giles, took up the brass-ended bellows from the grate and swung them round with a mighty force. Giles threw himself backwards only in time to prevent them hitting him a heavy blow but the end came off and struck him on the cheekbone. He made a quick recovery but saw that Torrill would soon be in reach of the great metal poker that stood by the fire. With a mighty leap he assailed Torrill and brought him to the floor but he could not keep his own balance and landed four-square on the man. Torrill heaved him off and scrambled to his feet while Giles struggled to follow suit. Both men were now panting heavily. Torrill, still nearest the fire, grabbed the poker and attempted to strike his adversary with it. Giles dodged behind one of the two armchairs that were arrayed round the hall fireplace. The poker landed on the back of the chair. Giles grabbed it and twisted it with all his strength, determined to remove it from Torrill's hands. Double-handed, Torrill clung on as Giles turned it further down the side of the chair towards the floor.

While Giles had removed his boots before the fight, Torrill had been so determined to come to grips with his cousin that he had not readied himself for the fray. He still wore his top boots with their slippery leather soles. With all the shuffling and shifting to keep hold of the poker, Torrill's feet suddenly slipped on the polished wooden floor of the hallway. Torrill toppled and landed heavily on his shoulder, emitting a great moan of pain. With a deft flick Giles removed the poker from the man's hand and gave it over to Patrick, the footman. Then he stood and looked down at Torrill, who was now clutching his upper left arm in great discomfort.

The doorbell sounded strongly.

'That will be the doctor,' said Giles with some satisfaction, 'what excellent timing.'

32

Giles moved to the doorway to welcome the doctor as soon as Daniels had opened the door.

'Thank you for coming so promptly,' said Giles, shaking his hand. 'My uncle is in grave need of you.'

'So I am given to understand, Mr Thornton. I had heard rumour and had planned to visit him myself tomorrow if I had not already received your summons.'

'Then if you would be kind enough to follow me.'

The doctor indicated his willingness to do so once he had put off his great cloak. As he stepped further into the hall, he saw Torrill on the floor, moaning in pain. He made a move to go to him.

'My uncle first, if you please,' said Giles. 'We will attend to my cousin when you have finished with my uncle.' The doctor looked disapproving but made his way to the stairs. He was no fool and the hallway with its drunken furniture and bevy of wide-eyed servants told its own tale, not to mention the graze and rapidly darkening bruise on Giles' cheekbone.

Upstairs Mrs Lambert had cried out when she saw Torrill lose the upper hand. She had made to come down the stairs but had been prevented by an unexpectedly cool and self-possessed Sophia. Mrs Ellis had appeared from up the back stairs and Penny, the scullery maid, accompanied her.

'Please escort Aunt Lambert to her room, Mrs Ellis,' said Sophia, 'and please lock the door until Mr Giles has decided what is to be done with her.'

Mrs Lambert, seeing that there was nothing to be gained and her dignity to be lost if she remonstrated, gave up in defeat and walked like one condemned to her room.

Sophia gave a defiant little sniff and flicked her hair, which had been plaited ready for bed, over her shoulder. Then she smiled a welcoming smile as the doctor and Giles progressed up the stairs.

Once they were on the landing, Higginbottom fell into step behind them. He too had used the back stairs bringing Mrs Gregory with him. She now waited in the small ante-room to Mr Gregory's bedroom to be told what was needed of her.

Ushering the doctor in, Giles went forward and took one of her hands, which just showed itself from under a huge shawl.

'Thank you,' he said gratefully, 'thank you so much for coming.' He turned back to the doctor. 'I'm sure you know my aunt-in-law, Mrs Simon Gregory.'

The doctor nodded without showing any real surprise at Mrs Simons' sudden change of name. 'So that's the story is it,' he said in his matter-of-fact way, 'so you have come to nurse your brother-in-law, Mrs Si... Gregory,' he said. 'Come let us see what is to be done.'

They went together into the great chamber that was Mr Gregory's bedroom. Their entrance was greeted by the sonorous noise of Mr Gregory's breathing. Mrs Torrill started up as she saw them.

'What is this?' she demanded, having been cushioned by the double doors and therefore completely oblivious to the noise and fracas that had unfolded downstairs. 'I did not summon any doctor,' she said angrily as she registered Rickerby's calling.

'No Aunt you did not, but I did,' said Giles, coming into the lamplight so that she could see him better. 'You will oblige me by going with Higginbottom to your room.'

'I will do no such thing, you have no authority here. None whatsoever. I command you to leave immediately.'

Giles gave a hollow chuckle as he watched Rickerby brush past her and begin to tend to his patient.

'I think you will find you are wrong, you would be well advised, Aunt, to accept that you are no longer able to command anything in this house.' He turned as a noise behind him alerted him to the fact that others had entered the room. Sophia and Mrs Ellis had come to escort Mrs Torrill. Mrs Ellis jangled her keys menacingly and Mrs Torrill, seeing that she was so outnumbered, finally accepted the situation and made to leave. She cast a look of utter loathing at Giles and then saw who was now ministering to Mr Gregory.

'You cannot have her here,' she yelled, scandalised. 'You cannot bring that woman into this house. She has no right.'

'She has every right to be here,' responded Giles without a moment's hesitation. 'It is a right you have denied her for years but that is about to change. Mrs Gregory will be residing here as her rightful home from now on. Now if you please, I would ask you to go to your room.' Lacking any alternative, Mrs Torrill angrily acceded to his wishes.

Having ensured that the doctor had all he needed, Giles left the sick-room just as the smell of Mrs Gregory's balsam and elderflower pastilles began to burn. He discovered his sister on the landing; they embraced each other briefly but with feeling.

'Will you come to our mother, she is in so much distress. I believe she has suffered an emotional collapse,' said Sophia urgently.

Giles shook his head. 'I must deal with Torrill before he gathers his senses enough to escape. I am sorry for it but Mama must manage for herself for a little longer.'

Sophia nodded and made to follow her brother down the stairs. There was another loud and imperative clanging of the doorbell. Daniels, who was now in his element, made haste to open it. There, waiting impatiently to be admitted, was Guilliam with Littlejohn behind him.

'Am I glad to see you,' cried Giles, his voice full of joy, but before he could move to welcome his friend, Sophia had run forward and cast herself into her fiancé's arms.

Guilliam swept her up and carried her over the threshold as though she was a featherweight, then set her on her feet keeping one arm around her.

'So what stirring events have you allowed to happen without me?' he demanded as his eyes took in the room and Torrill now sitting on the floor resting his damaged frame against the chair.

'I think we have recovered the situation,' said Giles, shaking Guilliam's free hand. His face clouded, 'but my uncle is gravely ill. If you are able to take charge down here, I will return to the sickroom and get a more accurate account of him.

'Surely, surely, you go. I will ensure this jackanapes causes no more disruption here or elsewhere.'

Giles, when he returned to the bedchamber found the doctor looking deeply concerned.

'He has a high fever and congestion of the lungs,' he told Giles. 'I cannot determine whether I can save him at this stage. You will see that the fever has greatly weakened him and the lack of sustenance over many days has taken its toll. He will need very careful nursing.' He shot a look at Mrs Gregory under his brow, 'but you have chosen wisely in your nurse. She knows just what to do.'

'And I shall stay with him, Sir,' said Giles. 'I beg you show me too what needs to be done.'

'I will leave you a draught which must be administered to him every two hours, but first he must be made more comfortable in dry sheets and clean covers.'

Between them and with linen provided by Mrs Ellis who had been in the ante-room holding herself in readiness for any such task, they rolled Mr Gregory one way and the other until the soiled sheets had been removed. Mrs Gregory sponged him clean and with the help of Higginbottom had him into a new night-shirt. By the time they had finished Higginbottom was close to tears.

'They would not let me near him,' he stammered. 'My poor master, to see him reduced to this. I cannot....' He broke off as his feelings overcame him. Giles gripped his shoulder.

'You did the best you could, Higginbottom,' he said comfortingly. 'No man could ask for a more loyal servant.'

'But had I been more purposeful, more tenacious in my determination to serve him.'

'I doubt it would have served the purpose. Torrill would have had you evicted from the house and then you would not have been on hand to report to Miss Makepeace. Do not berate yourself. We could all wish that the situation was otherwise but we must do our best now that it is as we see.'

The doctor, having satisfied himself at last that he had done all he could, promised to return on the morrow and made his way down the corridor to where Guilliam awaited him with his next patient. Giles was glad to hand the doctor over and after a hasty visit to his mother, returned to his uncle's room.

All was quiet now, Mrs Gregory had turned the lamps down low and had banked the fire.

'You should sleep,' she said looking at Giles' drooping shoulders and heavy eyes.

'I cannot for fear that he might die while I slumber,' he said thickly.

Mrs Gregory drew up a chair so that it was close to the bed. 'Then I will call for some chocolate and a round of bread and preserves for you and you can eat it while you hold vigil.'

Giles made his way to the chair but once seated put up his hand to grasp her wrist. 'I have not thanked you sufficiently for coming. I know that I must have frightened you by sending a servant and asking you to come under the same roof as that man. I cannot believe that you should have had such courage.'

Mrs Gregory patted his hand with her free one. 'You have always given me courage, Giles,' she said simply. 'And I am glad to be able to repay some of Mr Gregory's kindness' to me over the years.'

They fell silent then, one each side of the bed. Presently a servant appeared with the vittles for Giles which he forced himself to eat to please Mrs Gregory. All the while their proceedings were accompanied by the laboured breathing of their patient. Sometimes he flung his arm about and muttered deeply troubled but unintelligible sentences. Giles, though every part of his body begged for sleep, could not let his mind rest. The loss of his uncle would be too tragic to contemplate and if all he could give was his vigilance, that was what he would do.

As the long night slowly dragged by, Mrs Gregory dozed in the chair. A light sleeper, she had no fear that she would not wake if there was a crisis. Giles meanwhile knew that if he closed his eyes then he would not wake come thunderstorm or tempest. He fought the determination of his eyelids to shut and tried to rub away the deep ache that had invaded his muscles and joints. Nothing could avail him though, so at the darkest hour before dawn when he saw Mrs Gregory rise to tend to his uncle for perhaps the tenth time, he lost the battle and succumbed to sleep.

He had been slumbering fitfully for about an hour when Guilliam strode into the room with a perfunctory knock. He was dressed for departure. Mrs Gregory tried to remonstrate with him, determined that he should not awaken Giles but Guilliam would not be deterred.

'Wake up, man,' he said, vigorously shaking Giles' shoulder.

'Sh, sh.' If she could not prevent him from waking Giles, she could try to stop him disturbing Mr Gregory.

Giles gave a startled grunt and came quickly to his senses. His first thought was for his uncle and his eyes flew to the bed. Mr Gregory continued to breathe noisily, he was clearly alive.

'What is it?' Giles demanded of his friend. Then he saw Guilliam's attire. 'You are leaving?'

'Yes and I am taking your erstwhile relations with me.'

Giles was moved to protest but Guilliam forestalled him. 'I think I know what you would wish to be done. The ladies I will return to their homes but Torrill I will put on a packet boat to France. He must take what refuge he can there. For whatever you say Giles, these events will leak out! Although the signed confession failed to deter him, this scandal will finally ruin him.'

Giles nodded sadly. 'I accept what you say and I am grateful.' He held out his hand and shook his friend's warmly. 'But what of his cousin, Lambert? I have seen and heard nothing of him through this week?'

'It would appear that he wanted no part in this nasty little plot. The death of his brother had affected him profoundly and no amount of coercing would shift him.

'Not even his mother's involvement overbore his better judgement. You might look for some sort of reconciliation with him if your uncle survives.'

Again Giles nodded although he could not trust himself to speak.

Mrs Gregory looked on helplessly, too overcome with the implications of Guilliam's words to utter a farewell. Giles recovered himself enough to see his friend to the door.

'Do you have sufficient men and carriages to escort them securely?' he asked after a moment's thought.

'Oh yes, I have commandeered your uncle's travelling coach and I take his groom and two stable boys so that the carriage will be returned to you. I have said my adieus to Sophia, she knows I must do this. I will send word when I have completed my task.' He quitted the room then with a swish of his driving coat.

As he left, Higginbottom and Littlejohn appeared with jugs of warm water and Giles stood back while Mrs Gregory directed them to sponge Mr Gregory down. After a few moments a thought occurred to Giles and he went to the dressing table and searched for pen and paper. Soon he had dashed off a brief note to Felicia, expressing his gratitude and anxiety in equal measure.

The doctor arrived a few minutes after nine. There was little further he could do beyond praising Mrs Gregory's methods and giving what little reassurance there was on the situation. Mr Gregory's fever continued dangerously high and there was precious little any of them could do but attempt to relieve its effects.

The day outside was dull and low cloud hung around the May and Robinswood hills. Mrs Gregory, Giles and the two valets were not given the opportunity to view it for Mr Gregory began to cast himself around the bed in the most alarming manner. It was all any of them could do to keep him from falling to the floor. Only as darkness fell did he become calmer and it was deemed safe for any of their number to rest. Giles insisted that Mrs Gregory took some hours away from the sickroom and rang for Mrs Ellis to allocate her a bedchamber. Her normally pale face was as porcelain with fatigue and her straight hair had long since escaped the loose chignon in which she had placed it at the start of the day. Mrs Ellis took one look at her and gently steered her to a bedchamber.

Once she had retired, Giles set about restoring the room to order. He knew he would have to keep moving or he too would succumb to exhaustion.

'Did my note reach Miss Makepeace, Higginbottom?' he asked, forcing his voice to work.

'Yes Sir, I had Patrick place it in her hands, and in her hands alone.'

'Thank you.' After that he lapsed once again into silence and settled into the winged armchair next to the bed, his hand lightly grasping that of his uncle.

Leaving Littlejohn to help watch in case anything was needed by patient or carer, Higginbottom went down to the kitchens to fetch some broth and bread for Giles. When he returned he bullied Giles into taking the proffered food.

33

I
t was close to noon some four days later that Mr Gregory
finally regained possession of his senses. He came fretfully
into consciousness and began by attempting to fight off any
hands that held him. It seemed he knew himself to have been
under some kind of threat and was resisting it with whatever
energy he could muster.

'Calm yourself Uncle,' Giles beseeched him, 'there is nothing
to alarm you now. You are safe.' He signalled to Mrs Gregory to
come over to the bed. 'Please,' he said to her, 'add your voice to
mine.'

'It is indeed true, Arthur,' she said, taking both of the ill man's
hands in a firm grasp. 'You are quite safe. Giles has rid this house
of those who would harm you. All you need do now is get well.'

'Giles! Giles here?'

'Yes Uncle, at your side. There is nothing to fear now, it is as
Mrs Gregory says. The Torrills and the Lamberts are gone. Save
your energy for your recuperation.'

It could be seen that he had heard and understood their
words. His eyes closed and he drifted off into a settled sleep, not
to wake until early evening. Giles had remained at his side all that
time.

'This is a lengthy vigil, Mr Giles,' Littlejohn had remarked
when he had brought Giles a plate of cold meat. 'Can I not take
over from you just for an hour, so that you might rest?'

'No, no I thank you. I would be here when he wakes again.'

Mr Gregory must have been awake for some little time before he gave his nurses notice of it for he seemed to have assimilated that his sister-in-law was his nurse and that the doctor had been attending both to him and his half-sister. His first thoughts were for Clara Thornton, although he did not know just how ill she had become.

'She improves, Uncle, thank you,' said Giles cautiously. 'Sophia and Imogen attend her and believe that with just a little more help from the composer Dr Rickerby gave her, she will be well again.'

'I should have seen what they were doing to her. I should have seen,' burst from him. 'Oh Giles forgive me, by the time I realised they were persecuting her, I was too ill to prevent it.'

'It is of no moment now, Uncle. She knows the danger has gone and will not return. She will recover given time.' Giles received a glass of lemonade from Mrs Gregory and, raising his uncle's head, guided the glass to his lips. Mr Gregory drank eagerly, then sank back on to the pillows with a sigh. The illness had aged him and his face was haggard and grey. Giles wished there was something he could do to ease the man's mind but he could not erase the memory of what had occurred and what Mr Gregory's nearest relations had attempted.

'I begged too for the doctor to be called,' said Mr Gregory suddenly, 'but my sister Torrill would have none of it. I cannot credit it. She sat as you are doing now, Giles, and watched my suffering and refused steadfastly to aid my recovery.'

'My dear Arthur, please.' Mrs Gregory had come away from the medicine table she had set up by the window. 'Please do not dwell upon it, she is gone now and need never enter your life again. Come, banish the three of them from your mind.'

Mr Gregory acknowledged what an extraordinary event it was to have Mrs Gregory in his house.

'My dear Emily,' he said taking her hand and drawing it to his lips. 'To think you have overcome your abhorrence of the multitude to come and nurse me. I do not deserve this.'

Both Giles and Mrs Gregory cried out spontaneously to refute his words.

'No,' he said, with almost a hint of a smile at the emphatic expressions on their faces. 'You must follow me in this thinking. I have been three parts a fool. I should never have subjected you, Giles, to all these years of graft. It would have turned a lesser man against me. I have virtually held you to ransom, housing your mother and sisters while I insisted you worked for their keep.'

'Oh Uncle no,' countered Giles. 'I was glad to do my bit. I never expected you to frank my whole family, I can assure you of that.'

Mr Gregory nodded. 'I know that my dear boy, yet some perverse demon in me determined to uncover the limit of your gratitude. But,' he attempted to struggle forward making both his nurses rush to assist him and to put more pillows behind his head and back so that he might be supported, 'had I been content with the knowledge I had.' Here his glance flickered to his sister-in-law. 'If I had trusted the judgement of those with a discerning taste, you would have been here in residence and this last week would have been prevented.' He gave a gusty sigh that rattled in his chest.

'Please Uncle do not torture yourself so. All is well now. No harm has been done that cannot be undone. You will recover and my mother will recover. Nothing more is of the least importance. And although Torrill believed he had your signature on that will of his, it was most nearly illegible and any solicitor worth his calling would not have approved it. Your final wishes would have been acceded to whatever they had been.'

To Giles' surprise his uncle gave a throaty chuckle which brought on a fit of coughing. It took some little while for him to recover himself despite the ministrations of Mrs Gregory. It seemed, however, that Mr Gregory was not prepared to let the matter drop and no sooner had his breathing eased than he continued to speak.

'An old fool I may have been Giles,' he said with some satisfaction, 'but I was not such a fool that I had not taken steps to combat any attempts to wrest your inheritance from you.'

Giles blinked, baffled.

'You are mystified, my boy, and well you might be given the way I have used you.' He sighed and sipped the lemonade Mrs Gregory had prepared for him. 'I do not recall exactly when but it was after some attempt had been prosecuted to destroy your reputation in my eyes, I made over this house to you and set up a trust, administered by Ponsonby and Sherbourne, into which I put a majority share of the banking business. You are the sole beneficiary and you become master of it on your five-and-twentieth birthday unless I die before then. Torrill, had he succeeded in having his will ratified, would still have been a wealthy man but he could not have taken from you what was already yours!'

Giles' mouth fell open with astonishment. He struggled to assimilate the meaning of what his uncle had just told him. The older man went on speaking.

'Before that I settled money on your family, each to receive an income of £500 per annum. Now do you see how cruel I have been, how manipulative?'

Giles shook his head and sprang to his feet, his mind seething with conjecture, his heart a maelstrom of emotions.

'This cannot be,' he cried, both delighted and appalled. 'I cannot accept such generosity. Indeed I cannot. I have done nothing to deserve it!'

'Oh come now Giles,' said Mrs Gregory, her voice quiet and calm in contrast to his, 'no-one deserves it better than you. Arthur has done only what is right and proper for him to do.'

Giles came back to the bed and slipped to his knees beside it; he grasped his uncle's hand and kissed it. 'How can I thank you. This is beyond anything. I never dreamed you might settle on me.'

'Then you are the only one not to think so,' said his uncle, smiling at him fondly. 'For there is a certain young lady who resides not far from here who had made it plain on several occasions that she thinks my treatment of you too harsh. And even Higginbottom, my most trusted servant, would have had you named as the heir long since.'

Giles got unsteadily to his feet. 'Miss Makepeace has been my strength since the days when I came here as a grieving boy, lost without my adored father. Miss Makepeace rescued me from despair, Sir. Whatever you deemed to be her faults, I cannot accept them.'

'Oh I make no criticism of her, my boy. None whatsoever. Her parents are, after all, my dearest friends. Nothing would make me happier than to know that our two estates will be joined. You most surely have my blessing.'

Before Giles could answer Mrs Gregory cut in. 'It is to be remembered Arthur that it was Miss Makepeace who sent the express to Giles to come to your rescue. You too owe her your life.'

Mr Gregory was much moved by such news and would have written there and then to thank Felicia but neither Giles nor Mrs Gregory would allow it. He had become somewhat flushed and when they took his temperature it was seen to be on the rise. Fortuitously the doctor called on the way back from a lying-in and was happy to reassure the anxious family that it was not surprising that his temperature should rise in the evening. So, eventually Giles was persuaded to seek his couch and allow Higginbottom and Littlejohn to divide the nursing overnight between them.

Giles longed to tell Felicia the news and would have sat down to write her a letter if a glance at the clock had not told him that it was well after ten o'clock in the evening and therefore too late for delivery that night. He resolved to wake early and visit her on the morrow.

34

*H*aving received the initial note from Giles, the Makepeace family had been left to glean what information they could from news passed on by the servants. They heard an elaborate and colourful description of Giles' fight with Nathan Torrill, Mrs Thornton's emotional collapse was gone into in vivid detail, with much speculation about her probable recovery, and Mr Gregory was reported to be as near death as it was possible to be. There were stories of Giles' devotion as he sat by the bedside and tales of how Lord Guilliam had rounded up the Torrills and Mrs Lambert and carried them off to jail.

Between them, Felicia and her mother believed only part of what they heard but each fresh wave of revelation left Felicia jumpy and brittle. She longed to see Giles but respected her mother's decree that solicitous enquiries at the house should only be made by her father, and Giles should be left to concentrate on his uncle's needs. It seemed to her the longest four days of her life. While she never wearied of discussing the matter, Elsie Makepeace's mind began to wander on occasions to other topics that needed her consideration. It occurred to her as she mulled over the events of the previous weeks that she rarely saw her daughter spend money on anything but the absolute necessities. They had quite recently shopped in Cheltenham together and only now did it seem irregular that Felicia had bought nothing except a small length of ribbon to trim one of her bonnets. She had in fact made quite a show of looking for material and some such but nothing had pleased her enough to make the purchase. At the time Mrs Makepeace had thought little of it besides feeling it was tiresome that there was nothing Felicia liked. Now, in the light of the fact that Felicia had not enough money to pay for the express, which, though expensive was well within the means of a young lady with a generous allowance, Mrs Makepeace began to speculate on what Felicia had done with her money.

The matter began to take over her thoughts and so one evening, after she had readied herself for bed, she awaited her husband's arrival to gain his views on the matter.

'You are still making over an allowance to Felicia, are you not?' she demanded before even the poor gentleman had closed the door with a click.

'Of course, why should I not?'

'No reason, merely that she seems to have no funds and I have no notion as to what she has been spending it on.'

'Well ask her then,' grunted Mr Makepeace, implying exasperation that he should be bothered with such a trifling issue.

Mrs Makepeace knew better than that. He had understood her perfectly. Their finances had not yet reached such a state that he needed to deprive his daughter of her pin money.

The following afternoon when the family was taking tea in the drawing room, Mrs Makepeace asked her daughter outright what had become of her money.

At first Felicia, taken aback, pretended to misunderstand her but a curt word from her father, who was standing with his hands clasped behind his back in front of the fire, told her that she needed to embrace the truth.

'I have given it to Grandmama,' she said, her head held high in defiance.

'Grandmama!' cried her parents in unified disbelief. 'What can have possessed you to do that?'

Felicia hung her head, not wishing to disclose her grandmother's secret to those who did not value her business acumen.

'Come on girl,' said her father impatiently, 'I want no die-away airs. Tell us this moment what prompted you to give all your allowance to your grandmother.'

'It was not just me,' Felicia blurted out, 'my Aunt Dorothea has done the same.'

'Good God,' exclaimed Mr Makepeace, 'what coil has she found herself in that she needs borrow from her daughter and her granddaughter.'

'It was not a loan,' Felicia assured him earnestly, 'it was an investment.'

Neither parent could have been more astonished.

'Investment, investment in what pray?' asked her mother, flabbergasted.

'In land and property.'

'Oh dear, oh dear,' railed Mr Makepeace, 'I told her not to get involved in such risky speculation.'

At that very propitious moment the butler, Hayworth, opened the great double doors and announced Mrs Makepeace Senior.

'What risky speculation might that be?' she asked as she stripped off her gloves and made to sit down on the nearest settle. Felicia ran to her for support.

'I have had to tell them, Grandmama,' she said contritely. 'I would not have done had they not discovered I had no money.'

Mrs Makepeace patted her agitated granddaughter's hand soothingly.

'There, there dear,' she said calmly, 'there is nothing to concern yourself about. I was coming to tell them myself anyway.'

This revelation surprised even Felicia.

'Good heavens, why?' she asked, baffled.

'Because,' said Mrs Makepeace, eyeing her son with a gleam of mischief and a certain air of satisfaction, 'as I foretold, the land we bought is becoming much sought after. I have just closed a deal with a local building syndicate to sell a parcel of land that was part of the first property we purchased. We have agreed a price of some eight thousand pounds.' She swivelled to face her granddaughter. 'Your investment, my sweet, has just increased manifold. You will soon be a very rich woman.'

If Mr and Mrs Makepeace had been astonished and appalled before, they were now aghast. Neither could believe that the quiet unassuming widow had a head for finance. Mrs Makepeace allowed herself the luxury of giving her son a homily on listening to his elders and betters.

'You would have been much better following my lead,' she said in conclusion, 'and putting the money you spend on the journeys north into the property on the outskirts of this increasingly fashionable resort. It would then have been you enjoying the fruits of this deal rather than your mother, sister and daughter.'

'I cannot believe it,' said Felicia, still unable to take in the fact that she was in a fair way to amassing a fortune, 'so I can keep the Castle?'

'Yes my dear, if the price of property continues to increase as this first one has done. And, more importantly, you will be able to marry your young man without fear of destitution.'

It took some little time for the Makepeaces to come to terms with the change in the family's fortunes. Felicia asked her grandmother over and over again for the assurance that it was not a dream. When it finally dawned on her that Giles could give up the bank and make a home for them both with her share of the proceeds she rushed upstairs to write to him immediately.

Seated, however, at her dressing table she could find no satisfactory words to describe the events or her feelings. She consigned her many attempts to the cheerful little fire and decided she must speak to Giles in person. The gong was already sounding for dinner so she knew she was too late to visit The Chimneys. Her visit would have to be in the morning.

Felicia, who then only fell asleep in the early hours of the next morning, such had been her excitement, slept later than she had meant to. It was therefore not until close to noon that she put on her bonnet and pelisse and set out to walk to The Chimneys. The air was clear and crisp and Felicia felt the deep joy of spring both in her step and in her surroundings.

At the great house she banged on the door with some verve, forgetting in her desperation to have communication with Giles that there might still be a need to preserve quietness.

Daniels opened the door to her with some circumspection but welcomed her warmly enough.

'Have you heard the news then, Miss Makepeace?' he said, unable to keep the throb of drama out of his voice.

'No, no indeed. What news is this? How is Mr Gregory?'

'He regained his senses last night,' said Daniels in a thrilled voice. 'He is on the mend.'

'Oh,' cried Felicia in delight as she stepped into the hallway. 'Oh I could not be more pleased. What a relief for you all and for the Thorntons.'

'Yes, oh yes to be sure,' said Daniels, carried away with his need to broadcast the news. 'And would you believe it? He had already made Mr Giles the principle heir. There was never any danger of the house being wrested from them.'

Felicia felt as though she had been punched in the solar plexus; she gave a gasp and bent forward, her pulse racing.

'Are you all right?' asked Daniels, suddenly assailed by guilt that his tittle-tattle had brought on such a reaction. For a moment Felicia could not answer him but eventually she tottered to a chair and grasped the back of it for support.

'I will be fine. A moment that's all I pray you. It is just such a surprise. Such a great surprise.'

'Yes, yes, I am sure it is. We after all have had the morning to accustom ourselves to the news. Shall I fetch Miss Sophia to you, Miss?'

'No, I thank you, I will not take her from her mother's side at this time. Would you perhaps inform Mr Thornton that I am wishful of seeing him.'

Mr Daniels' expression changed. Realising that he had already overstepped the mark, he took steps to ameliorate his lapse and looked at her in some disapproval. 'I beg your pardon, Miss, perhaps I did not hear you aright,' he said. 'Mrs Thornton,' he stressed the title, 'is not currently receiving visitors.

Rather thrown by his sudden change of attitude, a flush crept up Felicia's face; she straightened and repeated her request. 'I would see Mr Thornton, please. I would have him know that I am here.'

'I am sorry Miss Makepeace, but Mr Thornton is not receiving visitors today. If you wish to leave your card, I will present it to him later.'

The words acted upon Felicia as though someone had thrown a glass of cold water in her face. After all the weeks of being refused admittance on the instructions of the Mrs Torrill and Mrs Lambert, she had expected that all would have changed and that she would be free to enter the house as she had been wont to do before their arrival. Now she understood herself as being dismissed as a troublesome caller. She could not believe that Daniels would be taking this line on his own volition or initiative, it had to have been a decree from Giles. Though there was a pit in her stomach and nausea rising in her throat, she marshalled her dignity, declined Daniels offer and quitted the house in the best order she could.

35

To Felicia the centre had been taken from her world. Giles had denied her; Giles had not wanted to see her. She walked away from the solid form of The Chimnies not knowing how she was putting one foot in front of the other, her mind a sea of conjecture. She could not imagine what might have happened to turn Giles from her. For seven long years she believed she had been at the kernel of his thoughts. Now she realised she could not even be sure of that. Gradually the numbness she had felt at her initial rejection gave way to a dull ache in her heart and then it began to swell to a searing agony of mind. As the distance between her and The Chimnies increased the tears began to trickle down her face until suddenly she was engulfed by a wave of sobbing which she could not control. The only reason she could find to explain Giles' attitude was if his uncle had made the inheritance conditional on him denying his love for her. Felicia knew she would never, could never stand in the way of a better life for him but she wished she could have heard it from his lips rather than through the supercilious dismissal by the butler.

The crying ravaged her face and her delicate colouring became swamped by a blotchy redness leaving her unable to present herself at home in such a state. There could be no facing her parents yet, she was not yet equal to explaining to them her dashed hopes. Felicia broke into a lurching run and found herself in the woods.

She did not consciously make for the old oak tree but it was not long before she was standing beneath its arching boughs. She looked up into its branches and remembered a younger Felicia who had thought nothing of climbing into its heart. She blew her nose defiantly on the already sodden handkerchief, then placed a resolute foot on the first of the great branches. It was not as easy as she had remembered. She overlooked the fact that previously she would have cared nothing for a scratched leg or a torn dress. Now these considerations weighed with her unconsciously. When she eventually attained the great bowl, she sank against a wide limb and looked out through the branches down the escarpment and across to the Malverns. She tried to find solace in the fact that this view would now always be hers. There would be no losing the Castle thanks to her grandmother's skill but it was a hollow victory without Giles to share it. Although the deep sobs were held at bay Felicia could not prevent the tears continuing to leak from her eyes. She stayed there for what seemed like hours, knowing that she was missing her lunch, knowing that at some time before darkness fell she would have to find the courage to return to Castle Leck.

Felicia had been there for perhaps an hour and a half when she heard the sounds of someone drawing closer through the woods. Her body, already stiff from inaction, went rigid and she found herself almost holding her breath. The footsteps grew noisier as the walker approached. Twigs cracked under their feet and last year's dead leaves rustled as they were disturbed. Then all at once there was silence. Felicia shrank back harder on to her branch knowing the person was now standing directly below the tree. There was the scraping of boots on the trunk. Felicia let out her breath in a long sigh as Giles' head appeared over the rim of the bowl and he swung himself nimbly upwards.

To Felicia, who had not seen him for months, the frisson of attraction had not lessened. She felt her heart surge with love before it was snared by the knowledge that he no longer wanted her. She looked at him, drinking in the sight of him in case it was to be her last. Despite the long days and nights of anxiety and the fading bruise on his cheek he was still the most handsome man she had ever encountered. His golden hair glowed its warm light and his blue eyes sparkled as they looked at her. Felicia saw it as a cruel coincidence, and so missed the significance, that he was dressed only in a white shirt and smart breeches as he had been at their very first meeting.

His eyes, which had been smiling on his arrival, now took in the state of Felicia's countenance and her very obvious distress. Concern spread across his face; he moved towards her.

'What has happened?' he asked imperatively. 'Why are you crying?' He put out his arms to grasp her to him but she warded him off. He stepped back in considerable surprise.

'Felicia, please, tell me what has happened, what has befallen you?'

'What has befallen me!' she cried out, angry now. 'How can you ask that when it was you who denied me? You who have rejected me after all these years.'

'What are you saying? When have I done these things? What are you talking about?'

'This morning! This very morning!' She was shaking with rage that he could prolong her agony. 'You had the butler deny me. You would not see me.'

'This morning, Felicia,' he said, determinedly coming towards her again as the explanation of her distress became clear to him. 'This morning I was asleep. I had meant to rise early to come to you and tell you that all was well. To tell you that you had been right all along, that my uncle had made me the heir and that he has given us his blessing. But such has been the toll of this last week, I did not wake and Higginbottom and Littlejohn would have no one disturb me. How can you think that I would have served you such a trick?'

Felicia looked up into his face searchingly. 'Is this indeed true: that we have your uncle's blessing? I made sure he would be against our alliance and refuse you the inheritance if you married me.'

'Well you were wrong,' he said emphatically, drawing her firmly to him and then wiping away her tears with a gentle finger. 'You were wrong to think that. Surely you must know that I would choose to live in a hovel with you rather than in The Chimnies alone, if that was the stark choice.'

Joy burst through Felicia's soul vanquishing all earlier emotions.

'But you would not have had to live in a hovel,' she said gleefully. 'For I am on the road to making a fortune in property speculation. I have been in partnership with my grandmama and aunt and we are making money. Now what do you say to that?'

'I say that you are, as always, my felicity,' he replied, and kissed her.

THE END